M000311376

In A Pirate's Debt

by

Elva Cobb Martin

SMITTEN
HISTORICAL ROMANCE
LIGHTHOUSE PUBLISHING of the CAROLINAS

IN A PIRATE'S DEBT BY ELVA COBB MARTIN
Published by Smitten Historical Romance
An imprint of Lighthouse Publishing of the Carolinas
2333 Barton Oaks Dr., Raleigh, NC, 27614

ISBN: 978-1-946016-18-8
Copyright © 2017 by Elva Cobb Martin
Cover design by Elaina Lee
Interior design by Karthick Srinivasan

Available in print from your local bookstore, online, or from the publisher at:
lpcbooks.com

For more information on this book and the author, visit:
http://www.elvamartin.com or http://carolinaromancewithelvamartin.blogspot.com

All rights reserved. Non-commercial interests may reproduce portions of this book without the express written permission of Lighthouse Publishing of the Carolinas, provided the text does not exceed 500 words. When reproducing text from this book, include the following credit line: "*In a Pirate's Debt* by Elva Cobb Martin, published by Lighthouse Publishing of the Carolinas. Used by permission."

Commercial interests: No part of this publication may be reproduced in any form, stored in a retrieval system, or transmitted in any form by any means—electronic, photocopy, recording, or otherwise—without prior written permission of the publisher, except as provided by the United States of America copyright law.

This is a work of fiction. Names, characters, and incidents are all products of the author's imagination or are used for fictional purposes. Any mentioned brand names, places, and trademarks remain the property of their respective owners, bear no association with the author or the publisher, and are used for fictional purposes only.

Scripture quotations are taken from the King James Version (KJV).

Brought to you by the creative team at Lighthouse Publishing of the Carolinas: Eddie Jones, Kathryn Davis, Pegg Thomas, Shonda Savage, Brian Cross, Judah Raine, and Lucie Winborne

Library of Congress Cataloging-in-Publication Data
Martin, Elva Cobb.
In a Pirate's Debt / Elva Cobb Martin 1st ed.

Printed in the United States of America

Praise for *In A Pirate's Debt*

Looking for adventure, romance, pirates? Go no further. *In a Pirate's Debt* is one of the most adventurous books I've read in quite some time. It starts off with a bang and then continues to explode with one exciting scene after another. From the Caribbean to Charleston to the Atlantic and then back again, there are storms, battles, intrigue, and plenty of romance. Throw in some great characters and a nasty villain, and this is a book that will keep you entertained until the end. In addition, *In a Pirate's Debt* is a refreshingly clean read with a strong Christian message that will remain with you long after you turn the last page.

~ **MaryLu Tyndall**
Author of *She Walks in Power*

Elva Cobb Martin has written a real page turner in her novel, *In a Pirate's Debt*. From the opening line, paragraph, page, and chapter she captures your imagination and carries you into her story. Most of the time, you would not find yourself pulling for a pirate, but in this case, her main character, Lucas, the infamous Captain Bloodstone, evolves into a hero in every sense of the word. You'll be glad you read this story.

~ **Mark L. Hopkins**
Syndicated columnist, author of *Journey to Gettysburg*

This action-packed story is set in a time when pirates ruled the sea and money ruled the land, a time when the brutal seemed to easily bypass the laws of God and man. In Elva Cobb Martin's tale, the schemes of one wicked man who preys on the weak and defenseless is eventually overthrown by the power of love.

~ **Martha Jacks Batten, PhD**

Dedication

I dedicate this book to my grandson, Samuel Timothy Martin, who loves pirates—the good ones—who sailed the seas in the seventeenth and eighteenth centuries. They were known as privateers and buccaneers, like our fictional hero Captain Bloodstone.

They that go down to the sea in ships, that do business in great waters; these see the works of the Lord, and his wonders in the deep (Psalm 107:23-24 KJV).

Acknowledgments

I want to give a hearty thanks to Dwayne, my husband and computer helper when glitches threatened to highjack my sanity. And for understanding the fast meals and allowing me to sit at the computer hour after hour without interruption. Thank you, dear husband and friend.

I thank Foothills Writers' Guild of Anderson, South Carolina, the talented group who first encouraged me to become a writer. I want to thank Yvonne Lehman for her friendship, for the many conferences she has directed that helped me, and the critiques and advice she and her writers' group freely gave.

I want to express my appreciation to all my writer friends in the South Carolina chapter of American Christian Fiction Writers, especially Edie Melson, Fran Strickland, Kelsey Messner, Angela Major, and Misty Beller. You have helped and encouraged me in so many ways. Thank you. I thank all the readers and reviewers who have given of their time to read and write a review. I truly appreciate each of you.

I thank Lighthouse Publishers of the Carolinas—Eddie Jones, Yvonne Lehman, and Kathryn Davis—for deciding my book was worthy of publication. And thank you, Kathryn, for your great editing that has made this novel so much better.

Most of all, I thank my heavenly Father and Lord and Savior Jesus Christ and the Holy Spirit, who have been with me in this effort, inspiring me to write, helping me strive for excellence, and keeping me on task. *Being confident of this very thing, that He who has begun a good work in you will complete it until the day of Jesus Christ* (Philippians 1:6, NKJV).

CHAPTER 1

Jamaica, 1720

Marry Sir Roger Poole? Never! Travay Allston rushed up the staircase and into her bedroom. She eased the door shut and sank against it, hoping the men downstairs had not heard her flight. She wrapped her arms around her middle to prevent loud sobs from escaping. Tears ran down her cheeks onto her dinner gown. How could her stepfather, Karston Reed, gamble away the plantation *and her hand in marriage* in a game of cards? Lighting a small candle, she sprang into action. How much time did she have?

Travay snatched the men's clothing she'd stashed under a floorboard after her mother's untimely death. Somehow she had known the day would come when she would have to leave secretly. She quickly donned breeches, shirt, and knee boots. The oversized top required a belt, and she contrived one from a scrap of cloth. She flattened her curls tighter to her head with extra pins and struggled to stuff the mass under a cap. Her fingers brushed against her mother's locket. *Oh, Mama, I miss you!*

From the back of a drawer, she retrieved a leather coin purse filled with her savings from seventeen birthdays and stuffed it into her pocket.

Swallowing the huge lump in her throat, Travay swung her mother's dark cloak over her shoulders. Her reflection in the candlelit mirror caught her attention. A slender young man stared back at her with troubled blue eyes and a stray auburn ringlet springing from under a sailor's cap.

Travay tucked in the curl and lifted her chin. Somehow she would make it to Kingston. She would secure passage on a ship to

Charles Town to her aunt, her only living relative. She pushed a small knife into the top of her boot like she'd seen her stepfather's overseer do, and darted from the room.

Could she make it to Kingston parish and to her mother's old minister friend before her stepfather and Sir Roger discovered she was missing?

A gusty wind with the threat of rain whipped across her hot face as she hastened down the servants' steps at the back of the house. The moon sailed in and out of clouds like a ghostly galleon, and she sought the shadows while running across the lawn to the barn. The slaves would be in their cabins at this late hour, including Ruby Grace, her personal maid. A sob escaped Travay's lips. The young African girl, Travay's only friend, might bear the brunt of this night's decision. Her stepfather would assume the slave knew of her mistress's plan to run away, and he would order the girl beaten.

A horse's soft nicker met Travay as she entered the shadowy stable. She slipped the bridle over Arundel's head, tossed the saddle onto the silky black back, and tightened the cinch. Opening the stable door, she led the filly out and mounted. At the touch of Travay's knee and the sound of her whisper, the horse paced across the stable yard toward the main entrance.

A high-pitched neigh trumpeted across the front lawn as they neared the house. Travay stiffened. The two men inside could not miss hearing Sir Roger's stallion, which was tied at the steps. Arundel tossed her head, and Travay urged her to a gallop.

Twisting in the saddle as they passed the front of the plantation house, Travay saw a lantern move across the front window toward the staircase. Her stepfather and Sir Roger would be calling up to her. How long would it take them to realize she had run away?

She leaned forward and urged the surefooted Arundel down the ribbon of road and onward, past wind-blown acres of sugarcane that weaved and stretched toward her like sentinels guarding her escape. A crack of lightning split the sky, followed by a deafening boom of thunder. Travay trembled but did not slacken the pace.

Before they reached the crossroads, hoofbeats pounded behind them. Travay bit the side of her lip and tasted blood. It could only be Roger Poole on the mount he'd ridden to Allston Hall, reputedly the fastest horse on the island.

She turned Arundel left at the crossroads, hoping she could make it past the field worker huts and onto the open road toward Kingston before Sir Roger caught up with her. Surely the minister and his wife would shelter her until she could secure passage to Charles Town. The moon disappeared behind turbulent clouds, enveloping her and Arundel in the safety of darkness. "Thank you, God—if you're up there," she whispered.

Half a mile down the road, the salty scent of the wind jerked Travay's head up. She clenched her teeth. How could she have taken the fork to the ocean instead of the road to Kingston? Confusion fogged her brain as her pursuer grew closer.

Arundel came to a bone-jolting halt at the edge of the cliff overlooking the Caribbean. The filly snorted and reared. Travay gripped the reins and moved the horse as far back as possible into a shadowy grove. What should she do? Sir Roger would soon be upon them. Gripped with indecision, she leaned across Arundel's hot neck and patted her, trying to calm the animal, while a cold sweat dotted her own brow.

Roger Poole reined in and headed for the thicket. The moon sailed from behind a cloud and revealed his sickening smirk. "I know you're in there, Travay. Come out, my dear."

His lustful laugh, the odor of stale tobacco, and his heavy perfume carried on the wind. Shivers of revulsion drew Travay's stomach into a knot, as had all the man's advances since her mother's death. Arundel pawed the soft earth.

"I'll never marry you, Sir Roger. I don't care what my stepfather promised. Why don't you leave me alone?" She ground the words out between her teeth.

"You want to have a little rendezvous now, right here at Lovers'

Leap? Then you'd marry me for sure, dear girl. Yes?" His voice was hoarse with rum and anticipation.

Travay froze and clutched the reins tighter. Would he dare? And in this deserted area of the coast, who would hear even her loudest scream? The saliva dried in her mouth. Then a memory, an old story, swept across her chaotic mind. Was the legend true about the girl who jumped from the cliff into the bay below and lived to tell about it?

Sir Roger dismounted and tied the stallion's reins to a small tree. Now his threatening form blocked her escape up the road. He stood with his fists propped on his hips. "Why do you think I came to Jamaica? I watched you growing up in Charles Town and knew one day I'd make you mine, whether I won your hand gambling or by some other method."

The moon cast an evil glow on his handsome, falcon-sharp features. Approaching his mid-thirties, he was still as strong and wiry as younger men—and attractive to most women, if the servants' tales were true. Tonight his silk cloak swirled around him in the wind like the ebony wings of a bird of prey. His arrogant voice did not move her, but the way he accented the words *by some other method* chilled her.

Travay tried to swallow, but her throat was bone dry. Taking a deep breath that ended with a sob, she turned Arundel and coaxed her out of the copse. She leaned close to the horse's wet neck and whispered, "Forgive me, my sweet friend. Jump high and wide. If we die tonight, we die together." *Please God, don't let us get caught on the rocks.*

Arundel blew air through her nose, arched her neck, and sidestepped toward the figure blocking their way up the road.

"That's my girl." Sir Roger sauntered closer and reached for the bridle.

With a gut-wrenching cry, Travay wheeled her mount around toward the sea and swung her riding crop down on the powerful rump. Arundel reared with a high-pitched squeal and shot forward.

Behind her, curses exploded from Sir Roger's mouth.

Travay screamed as she and Arundel hurtled over the cliff's edge. The mare's body slammed into the water. Travay's forehead collided with the horse's neck as the sea sucked them both into its shadowy depths, shutting out sight, sound, and breath.

※ ❦ ※

Captain Lucas "Bloodstone" Barrett rowed up the bay at twilight with Sydney, his cabin boy, to fish for sea trout. When they reached the cove close to a cliff's rock wall, Lucas brought up his oar and set the anchor. He removed his leather baldric, which held his rapier and pistols, and launched a hook into the deep water. The boy cast his line on the other side of the boat.

For several days, Barrett had kept his brigantine hidden in an inlet on the backside of the island until the careening of the ship's hull could be completed. His raucous, sweating, and bare-chested crew had labored in the southern sun all day. Scraping the barnacles that had attached to the underside of the ship and patching places that had begun to rot had taken three days. Tonight, in celebration that the difficult, dangerous job was done, he knew his men would drink themselves into a rum stupor. They would pick quarrels and fight amidst the cursing and vulgarities Bloodstone no longer enjoyed.

As pirates went, they were as tough as any. And he had to command their respect at all times, or he'd find a mutiny on his hands. Fishing, when he got a chance, provided a little diversion from their offensive behaviors.

"Sydney, you be sure and watch that line. These waters used to be full of sea trout. I am expecting to take a catch back to the ship."

"Sure, Cap'n. I got me eyeballs peeled for the lit'lest quiver in this here string." The thirteen-year-old leaned over the side of the yawl.

Lucas's line jerked and grew taut, then slackened as the fish slipped away. He bit back a word he'd been trying to eliminate from his vocabulary since meeting Reverend Wentworth.

A terrible scream from the rock cliff above riveted his attention upward. A horse and rider flew over the longboat and plunged into the bay a stone's throw away from Lucas' boat. Waves rocked and scraped their small craft against the rock wall.

"Blimey!" Sydney dropped his short pole. "Cap'n, you see that?"

Lucas dropped his fishing line and searched the churning water where the two had disappeared. Iron bands tightened across his chest. "Yes. May God have mercy on them."

"I trove it was just a boy in that saddle! What we gonna do?"

Pebbles slid down the rock embankment above them. Lucas motioned for Sydney to be quiet. A man's angry voice above them loaded the evening air with curses. Next, the sound of galloping hooves confirmed someone leaving the top of the cliff.

The captain peeled off his shirt, stuck a knife between his teeth, and dove into the bay. The moon sailed from behind a cloud and revealed the dark forms of the horse and rider plunging about in the deep water below the surface. Lucas swam down toward them, praying he would be in time. He reached the limp form of the rider, whose long hair floated up into his face. He brushed the strands from his vision and loosened the boot caught in a stirrup. The horse, struggling to rise, had its reins caught between two rocks. Lucas hacked them loose, then pulled the rider to the surface. The horse surfaced beyond them and swam toward the opposite shore, emerged, shook, and trotted away.

Lucas swam back to the boat with the rider in tow. He pushed the cold body with its deathly pale face into the boat and then climbed in himself. He slung the person and his dripping mane of hair over his lap and pounded on the undersized back. As the soft curve of a bosom pressed onto his knees, Lucas' hand stopped in midair.

The person coughed and spewed vomit on Lucas' boots. "Stop

it, you're killing me." The irate, feminine voice left no doubt about gender.

The captain glanced at Sydney.

The boy's mouth dropped open. "Swounds! Cap'n Bloodstone, it's a milady."

The girl issued another sharp command. "Let me up!" She kicked and squirmed.

"Yes, ma'am." Lucas placed his hands about the small waist, hidden among layers of a soaked shirt, and lifted her from his lap.

He set her on the rower's bench and held her steady a moment. She pushed his hands away, bent forward, and retched again. He moved his feet just in time.

❧ ❦

Travay wiped her mouth and clawed dripping strands of hair from her face. She peered through the mist at her rescuers, a man and a boy. Both wore bandanas tied around their heads and bright sashes around their waists. The man's wet, bare chest and muscular arms glistened in the moonlight. Something about his untamed look and scent of sea and spice caused her heart to hammer against her ribs. Captain Bloodstone—that was what the boy had called him.

Above them, a rock dislodged and tumbled down the cliff. Travay looked up. Fear struck her heart. She jumped back into the captain's lap.

"If you are worried about your pursuer, ma'am, he is gone."

His deep, confident voice sounded like that of a gentleman, and the strong arms he placed around Travay comforted her but did nothing to clear the confusion in her mind. *What pursuer?*

The captain's heart beat against Travay's shoulder, and the welcome warmth from his body enveloped her, reminding her of when she sat on her father's lap as a child. She twisted to glance at his face. He smiled, and she could not help admiring his square jaw, slim mustache, and white teeth. His breath feathered her cheek, but a mischievous glint emanated from bright eyes. Who was he really? And fie! What was she doing jumping onto his lap?

Travay pushed away from him and crawled back onto the rower's bench. Shivers shook her whole body, and dizziness flowed over her in waves. She touched a bump on her forehead and clasped her arms. She tried to focus on her rescuers and to recall what had happened to bring her into their longboat. The young man's gold hoop earrings twinkled as the boat rocked with the tide. A gleaming silver sword and a carved leather baldric lay on the floor of the boat. She glanced across the bay. The moon sailed from behind a cloud and illuminated a sleek brigantine bobbing with the tide. A black flag waved from its masthead.

Pirates. Murdering, thieving pirates.

Darkness crept over Travay, and she slumped forward.

CHAPTER 2

Lucas caught the girl before she slid to the longboat floor. "Sydney, we've got to get back to the *Blue Heron*. We are going to need Mama Penn's help." He cradled the cold, wet form in his arms. "And I'm going to need whatever is still dry in the boat to wrap her in."

"Yessir." The boy ripped off his shirt and watched the captain swathe it and his own shirt around the girl. Then Sydney grabbed an oar and rowed toward the brigantine. He glanced over at Lucas, who used one arm to row and held the girl with the other.

"Cap'n, is you praying over that girl?" The cabin boy still grappled with the change Lucas had made a few months earlier when he converted to Christianity.

"Yes, I am. She may be going into shock."

On board the *Blue Heron*, Lucas carried the girl to his own quarters, shouting as he strode across the deck, "Send Mama Penn to my cabin!"

The crew of half-drunken pirates leered at the limp, sodden figure with long, shining hair swinging in the moonlight and a delicately molded face pale as death. They murmured among themselves.

One shouted, "Another woman? Women is bad luck on a ship." Several ayes followed.

Lucas didn't even glance at them. "Get back to your posts, men. We'll be clearing out of here at first light."

Dwayne Thorpe, first lieutenant and best friend of the captain, came to stare from his cabin doorway. He folded his thick arms and raised an eyebrow. "You, uh, need any help, Captain? Is this what you went fishing for?"

A grin started at the corners of Lucas' mouth. "No, just get Mama Penn, fast."

❧ ❧

Travay fought her way toward consciousness through a black tunnel and brittle coldness. Gentle hands removed her soggy clothing.

"Now, Seema, you git yo hands off them purty underthings. Ye hear me, girl?"

A smack echoed in Travay's ears. She moaned.

"The crew out there is arguing about this girl, Mama Penn. They are saying we should hold her for ransom, but I saw the way the captain looked at her. It would be better to throw this wisp of a thing back overboard and be done with a lot of trouble."

"Hush yo mouth, girl. This here little lady deserves as much help as you did when the captain rescued you from that slave block. And we best be finding out why she jumped off that cliff. Sydney say it clear took his breath away, an' Cap'n Bloodstone's, too. She got grit and courage, that's fo sure."

The younger woman snorted. "This girl is nothing more than one of the spoiled, uppity rich folks we will spend our lives fetching and toting for. Grit and courage has nothing to do with it. Can I have that pearl knife you found in her boot?"

"No, you can't have it. I'se giving it to the Cap'n. Now git on out of here."

The dark tunnel claimed Travay again.

The next morning, light flowed through the porthole above the bed and played across Travay's eyelids. The scent of the sea tickled her nose. The ship rolled and tossed her in the cot. She sat up, gasping and clawing the air as if coming up from underwater. "Arundel—poor dear Arundel!"

A black woman beside her bunk bed leaned forward. She gently pressed Travay back onto the bed and stroked her hair, which was

❧ 10 ❧

spread across the pillow. "Hush now, little lady, ye be fine soon." The plump woman's soft dark eyes were friendly.

"But … Arundel!" Tears pooled in Travay's eyes as she looked into the kind face.

"Arundel be your horse, young ma'am?"

"Yes, yes. Do you know what happened to her?"

"Mama Penn doesn't, but I do," a deep voice intoned from the door.

The woman stood. "Oh, Cap'n Bloodstone. The lady, she has come back alive. I was getting ready to come tell you."

Travay's attention riveted to the man who entered the cabin. Sunshine and a spicy scent came in with him. The one who'd rescued her from the bay. Even with a day's beard shadowing his firm jaw, he was a most handsome man. His three-cornered hat sat back on his head, and his thick black hair flowed to his shoulders in braids. A billowy-sleeved white shirt clung to his lean torso and a crimson sash overlaid with leather crossed over one shoulder, buckling around his waist. Two pistols protruded from the baldric, and a sword swung at his side.

Their glances met. Travay had seen such clear green eyes only once before. He smiled. She lowered her eyes as heat rose in her cheeks.

"Your horse surfaced and swam to the shore. She's probably home by now and causing quite a stir, I warrant." The room vibrated with his presence. Again his words and voice made her think more of a gentleman than a pirate.

"Oh, I am so glad Arundel did not perish! Where am I?" Travay started to sit up, then gasped and clutched the blanket. Where was her clothing?

The man chuckled. "You are on the *Blue Heron*, and I am Captain Bloodstone." He swept off his hat and bowed. "And who do we have the honor of serving as our fair guest?"

Travay stiffened and blinked at the man and the slave staring at her. "I—I don't know." Her voice rose an octave.

Mama Penn's brown eyes darted to the captain's.

He met the woman's stare and winked. A mocking smile spread over his face. "But you remembered the name of your horse."

He doesn't believe me. A shudder traveled up Travay's spine. "I—I don't know how I remember that and nothing more."

"Well, don't worry. I am sure your memory will soon return. Meanwhile, you are our guest. But I must warn you, don't venture out of this cabin unescorted. My crew is not to be trusted around lovely ladies." He gestured toward her breeches and shirt, which had been hung across a line to dry. "Even in men's clothing."

Travay stretched the blanket to her chin. With her other hand, she gingerly touched the knot on her forehead. Was she safe from the captain?

The man stepped to the door, then turned back. "Our ship's doctor did take a look at that bump. He said it will be fine in a few days." He cleared his throat. "I'll send some clothing for you, milady." He gestured to Mama Penn. "Bolt this door. You and Seema will admit no one but me, Thorpe, or Sydney."

"Yessir." Mama Penn moved to the door, keeping her back to Travay. "Cap'n, I found this in her boot." Travay glimpsed what the woman handed the captain—a small knife.

The captain glanced back at Travay, smiled, and left.

At the sound of the bolt sliding back into place, Travay relaxed, but the blank spaces in her mind caused iron fingers to grip her throat. Who was she and what had caused her and her horse to end up in the Caribbean bay? Who was this handsome man who had rescued her? His voice and words were those of a gentleman, but his clothing and braids were surely those of a pirate. Why did the thought of him cause a tingling in the pit of her stomach? She turned her face to the wall and gave in to the drowsiness pressing against her bruised limbs and heavy eyelids.

At sunrise the next morning, Captain Bloodstone strode across the deck of the *Blue Heron*. He loved everything about the brigantine, from its long, sleek hull and square-rigged masts, to the way all 200 tons of it skimmed across the sea in pursuit of larger, heavier ships. Now that the hull had been scraped clean of barnacles and all repairs had been made, they would be able to make top speed with a good wind. For now, the ship lay at anchor in the bay, waves lapping her sides.

He greeted his crew, busy at pre-sailing tasks. They raced each other to set up the shrouds and stays and to check all the rigging. Everything would soon be in trim. As he passed, the men stopped and turned questioning looks on him.

First mate Byron Pitt sauntered out in front of the captain and said in *falsetto*, "I'm sorry my dear, brave Captain, but my memory seems to have drowned in the bay. Why didn't you save it, too?"

Sinbad, the ship's huge black Muslim carpenter, and a loyal crew member and friend of the captain, rose from the block of wood he was shaping near the lower deck entrance. His dark eyes under his red fez hat turned in the direction of Pitt and the captain.

Bloodstone ignored Pitt, but the nearby crew members guffawed, especially the almost toothless boatswain Knox, Pitt's friend. The first mate's jesting always carried a barb. Bloodstone did not trust Pitt after the past weeks at sea with him. He knew the man was itching to discredit him, even kill him, and take over the ship. He planned to get rid of Pitt as soon as they arrived in Charles Town if he didn't have to battle him before that. And he didn't want to fight him, not now. Once, he wouldn't have hesitated. Actually, the younger man reminded him of himself a few years back, before he met Reverend Wentworth and his life changed.

Lucas also knew the crew's thoughts. What was to be done about the rescued woman? Would they stick to the plan to sail to Charles Town? The men had prize money burning in their pockets, and several had family waiting in Charles Town. "Get back to work, lads," he shouted. "That means you, mate. We sail within the hour." Bloodstone nodded to Sinbad and bounded up the quarterdeck steps.

Was his lovely traveler telling the truth about a loss of memory? Not likely. After all, she asked about her horse. She was probably a runaway of some kind, which meant he needed to get the ship out of the cove and onto the high seas before her pursuers showed up on the banks with the king's men—the very kind of trouble he didn't need.

He took out the small, pearl-handled knife and tested the edge against his thumb. Sharp steel. The young woman's face passed through his mind. How lovely she was, even with freckles across her nose and a bump on her forehead. He could not forget how she looked with her thick auburn hair fanned out across his pillow. A rare beauty. He had seen a splatter of freckles like that somewhere before, but where? And who or what had driven her off that cliff? One thing was sure: she was no runaway servant. Her speech and her entire demeanor spoke of quality, even nobility.

The angry words of the man who had pursued her flowed back over Lucas. He was up to no good. Lucas knew it in his gut. Maybe the girl needed to disappear for a time like he himself had done years earlier. Only by God's grace had he survived those days. He shook his head to banish them from his mind.

The least he could do for the young lady was give her a chance to get her memory back or, if she were lying, decide to trust him with the truth. He would proceed with the original plan that had started in Charles Town months earlier. Their work was finished in the Caribbean for a season. Meanwhile, he'd need to get busy thinking how he could keep the girl protected from his lusty crew until he could find out where she belonged. He forced the image of her and her full, lush lips from his mind.

Lieutenant Thorpe walked up the steps to the quarterdeck and leaned on the railing beside Lucas. He pulled a tinderbox and a pipe from his pocket. "Where are we headed, Cap'n?"

"To Charles Town as planned."

"What about our guest?" Thorpe struck the flint and lit his pipe.

Bloodstone shot him a quick look and tried to stop his eyelid from twitching, which it did when he had something he didn't want to discuss. "I don't know what to do with her. We need to give her time to get her memory back or decide to be honest. We can't just drop her off at Kingston. Someone or something made her jump off that cliff." He pushed his hat back and gazed out to sea.

Thorpe cocked his chin and suppressed a smile. "Right, right. I'm sure her memory will soon return. And who knows what dreadful thing caused her to lose it in the first place. That is if the lovely lady truly has lost it." He puffed on his pipe. "Of course, I am sure you will enjoy giving her some time to decide what she wants to tell us." Thorpe stepped off the quarterdeck, whistling on his way to check on the crew and readiness to sail.

Lucas turned a dark scowl after his best friend. Why would he enjoy having a third—not-to-mention nameless—woman on board who may or may not have lost her memory? God forbid. At that moment, her striking face pushed its way into his mind. He shook the vision away and leaned across the quarterdeck rail. Everyone appeared ready on deck, awaiting his command. He yelled, "Weigh anchor! Man the sails! Northwest to Charles Town!"

Action erupted below.

Sailors scurried across the deck, shouting, cursing, and laughing. The squeaks of the anchor being rolled up from the sea's bottom, the stretching and flapping of sails, and the screeching of strained rigging filled the morning air—all sounds Lucas loved and breathed.

Back on the beach, the flock of seagulls that had kept the ship and the rowdy crew company the past week rose into the air, squawking as if in death throes.

Was it some kind of omen? Lucas shook his head. Reverend Wentworth would tell him to put no stock in omens.

The clamor on the deck above awakened Travay from her napping. Was Captain Bloodstone giving them orders to sail? Clutching the blanket around her, she sat up and stretched to look out the porthole. Blue waters and a bright sky filled her view. The tide slapped against the sides of the vessel, and she heard sails snapping in the brisk breeze that sailed through the opening. Travay took a deep breath laced with the scent of the sea. The fog in her mind sent a shiver up her spine. What had happened to her? And who was Captain Bloodstone? Just remembering the way the man's presence had filled the room and his strange magnetism caused warmth to rise in her cheeks.

"He's a good man, the Cap'n."

Travay twisted around and stared at Mama Penn, who sat near the bed. Had she spoken her previous thoughts out loud, or did the woman read minds? She pulled the blanket tighter around her shoulders. "Yes, I am sure he is. Is he not a pirate?" She couldn't keep the contempt from her voice. But anxiety over the blank in her mind almost choked her. How did she and Arundel end up in the ocean, being rescued by this strange captain and ship?

"He's not really a pirate. I think he's a merchant, of sorts, and he's a good—"

"Don't bother to defend him. Mama Penn is your name, I believe?"

"Yes'm."

"I know all I want to know about pirates. And I hope and pray every one of them will one day swing from a hangman's noose." What did she know about pirates that made a statement like that come out of her mouth?

Mama Penn's eyes widened. "Oh no, miss, not the Cap'n." Then she thought a minute. "Maybe that Knox. I don't trust him no mor'n I'd trust a crow not to peck out your eyes if he had a chance."

Travay smiled and relaxed her viselike grip on the blanket. "Who removed my clothing?"

"I did, with Seema's help. Your things was all wet and torn, and the Cap'n sent them dresses in for you to try on." Mama Penn pointed to clothing laid across a chair. "And I've brought you a bucket o' water to wash with and here's a bar of lilac soap I found with the stuff the Cap'n sent."

"Wear dresses and use soap he's stolen from God knows where or from whom, even if he calls them spoils of war?" Travay shivered with disgust. But she gritted her teeth, rose, and let Mama Penn help her bathe and don a green satin dress over a matching petticoat. She found small slippers and stockings and pulled those on as well. Her hair felt like a matted mess, but soon the competent hands of her helper had pulled out the tangles and seaweed and brushed it till it fell in shimmering auburn waves down her back.

Travay stood and fingered the fine soft fabric of her billowing skirt, and her new lilac scent relaxed her. The ship rose on a wave and then dropped down the trough on the other side. She grabbed the edge of the bunk to keep from losing her balance. "Where is this ship heading? We are surely sailing."

"Cap'n sez we gwine to Charles Town."

Travay's thoughts fluttered around like butterflies. *Charles Town?* For some reason, the fact they were sailing there made her heart lighter. What did she know about Charles Town? And what did she know about pirates that made her hate the word? She gently touched the knot on her forehead and trembled. Where did the knot come from? The questions and the haze that still hung over her brought on weakness, and her head began to ache. She lay down on the cot.

She must have dozed, for a knock awakened Travay. She sat up and smoothed her gown.

Mama Penn went to the door. "Who is it?"

"It's me, Sydney, with the leddy's food."

The woman opened the door, and the lad entered with a tray.

The cabin boy's brown eyes widened as they fell on Travay. "Blimey, ma'am. Blimey!"

"Give me that tray before you drop it, Sydney." Mama Penn took the tray and set it on the table. "Ain't you never seen a lady before? Now shut your gaping mouth and git back out that door. And don't go telling no tales to the others."

"Wait." Travay stood and crossed to the young man, her skirts rustling. "You helped pull me from the water, didn't you?"

The boy's chin lifted. "Yes'm, me and Cap'n Bloodstone, milady."

Travay laid a gentle hand on his thin shoulder. "Thank you."

The boy's face lit up in shades of red. He ducked his head to hide a smile before scurrying out of the cabin.

Travay sat at the table and found herself famished. It was only ship fare of hard bread Mama Penn called tack and a thick soup of vegetables, but it tasted good.

Later, when the black woman left to return the tray to the galley, Travay glanced about the cabin. Two cots lined one wall and a bookcase the other. Several history books lined the shelf, and an open Bible lay on the table in the middle of the room, along with a chart and compass. Whose cabin was this? The captain's? She pulled out several books to peruse.

Mama Penn returned and tidied up, gently folding Travay's clothing, now dry.

When darkness gathered, Travay undressed to her petticoat and lay down across the bunk. Mama Penn blew out the small lamp and walked to her cot in the corner. Suddenly she turned and headed toward the door. As she reached to push the heavy bar down, the door flew open and knocked her backward.

Travay gasped. A burly, bare-chested man filled the doorway, gawking at her. A grin creased his leathery, bearded face, exposing rotting stubs of teeth. The smell of rum and his unwashed body pervaded the room and turned Travay's stomach.

"Well, blow me down if the little fellow ain't a real lady after all." His hardened appearance and slurred words filled Travay with revulsion. Shivers tripped up her back as his bloodshot eyes traveled over her. She grabbed a blanket to cover herself. The man licked thick, scarred lips and grinned. She braced against the wall, ready to jump up and run. But where? He blocked the door with his bulky, unkempt person.

Mama Penn recovered from her fall and moved in front of Travay's berth. "Git out of here, Knox. Cap'n said nobody's to come in here but him or Mister Thorpe."

"Who cares what the Cap'n said. I just want to git a better look at what's sailing on this here ship with us." He pushed Mama Penn against the wall like she was a piece of fluff and staggered into the room.

CHAPTER 3

Captain Bloodstone entered his borrowed cabin and prepared for bed. He shed his weapons and baldric, then his shirt. As he sat down at the table, he remembered the Bible he liked to read before retiring. It was in his captain's quarters, now occupied by the women, but it was too late to get it. He leaned back in his chair and yawned. Suddenly he heard heavy, running steps outside his door.

"Cap'n Bloodstone, Cap'n Bloodstone!"

He recognized Mama Penn's voice, although it was two times louder than usual, almost a shriek.

He grabbed his baldric, placed it around his bare chest with a sword and pistol, and opened the door.

"It's that devil Knox. He's pushed his way into yo cabin." Mama Penn's eyes bulged.

"I'll kill him if he's hurt our guest." Bloodstone strode ahead of the woman to his former compartment. Dwayne Thorpe, who had been standing at the entrance to his own cabin, fell into step behind him.

The door to the captain's cabin hung open. Knox stood holding Travay's wrist in an iron grip as she sat pressed against the wall, screaming.

Bloodstone's icy voice cut the tense air like a sword. "Unhand her, Knox, you slimy squid."

Knox dropped his hands and cocked his head as if it took a moment for the words to sink in.

Travay moved as far away from him as possible.

The pirate wiped his mouth with the back of a hairy hand. "Just wanted to have a look-see at our little passenger, Cap'n. No harm done. I swar it. You can ask the lady."

"Lock him in the hold, Mr. Thorpe."

The lieutenant stepped forward. Knox swung a blow toward him, missed, and fell across the table. Fast as lightning, Thorpe pulled a rope from his pocket, tied the man's hands behind his back, then jerked him to his feet. He gave the rum-dazed captive a few well-placed punches to encourage him toward the door, and they both exited.

❧ ☙

Travay sank into a chair and drew her blanket across her shoulders. She expelled a huge breath, and her eyes locked on the source of relief—Captain Bloodstone, who seemed bigger than life. He made the room seem smaller. He stood so near she could smell his musky scent and feel the heat emanating from his body. Dark hair curled across his chest. She looked away.

"Are you all right, milady?" His husky voice sent tremors up her spine. He leaned down and gently tilted her face to the light. His breath exploded. "That swine!" With his thumb, he wiped a trickle of blood from the corner of her mouth.

At his touch, a wave of weakness surged through Travay. She pulled her chin aside. "I'm fine. I just bit my lip when he …"

Captain Bloodstone's eyes glittered, and his voice turned hard. "Knox may spend the rest of this voyage in the hold."

Then his glance swept over her, and she pulled the coverlet closer.

He turned to the older woman. "Mama Penn, I am going to post a man outside this door." He then turned back to Travay, and his voice softened. "Believe me, I'm sorry I didn't do it before. I should've known at least Knox would try something."

She took a deep breath. "Thank you for coming so fast." She suspected the intruder had nothing to do with the continued pounding of her heart.

Captain Bloodstone strode over to the table, picked up the Bible, chart, and maps, and headed out the door.

That's when Travay saw the captain's back. She barely suppressed a cry. Scars crisscrossed the tanned shoulders. What had the man done to receive such a beating? Was he a criminal who had received the crippling thirty-nine lashes?

Before Mama Penn could pull the heavy bar in place, Seema slipped in and plopped down on a corner cot. The young woman gave Travay a sullen glance before turning her face to the wall. Mama Penn sank onto her own cot.

Travay climbed into her bunk and tried to erase the memory of Captain Bloodstone's scarred back. And even with three people now inside, the room seemed empty after he left. She pushed that thought from her mind. Tomorrow she needed to get up on deck for fresh air. Maybe it would help her regain her strength and memory. But would she be safe even with Knox in the hold?

꽃 ꌞ

Back in his borrowed cabin, Bloodstone fought a battle to get Travay's lovely oval face out of his mind and blot out the memory of her generously curved lips he'd been foolish enough to lean close enough to kiss. And before she pulled the blanket back around her … He took a deep breath and focused on the Bible opened on his lap. Was this the kind of temptation Reverend Wentworth was talking about earlier? He'd told Lucas that because of his past womanizing, women would continue to be a battleground for some time. Hopefully, the battles wouldn't be this hard forever. If so, what hope did he have to live this thing called the Christian life?

No hope, a dark voice whispered in the room, and a strange heaviness settled about him.

He shook his head and began reading from the book of Ephesians. *For we do not wrestle against flesh and blood, but against principalities, against powers, against the rulers of the darkness of this age, against spiritual hosts of wickedness in the heavenly places.*

He finished reading chapter six, prayed, and closed the Bible. Ethan Wentworth's calm, confident words came to him, the ones he'd spoken when Lucas had made his decision to become a Christian: "You'll make it, Lucas, I am praying for you. Don't forget it."

It sure did seem as if he were in a fleshly battle. Whoever the young woman was, he knew she spelled trouble, including tempting him to give in to desires he once pursued. But those days were behind him, and he was determined they would stay there.

The heaviness left the room, and he dropped onto his cot and slept.

❦ ❦

The next evening, Travay presented her request when Captain Bloodstone came to the cabin.

"I would love so much to be able to walk on deck in the morning."

She looked into his face and once again was shocked at the green tint of his eyes. It came to her why he was called Bloodstone. That was the name of a gemstone she'd seen somewhere that was a rich green with distinctive fiery sparks—like the way she'd seen his eyes flash when the captain faced Knox. Her heart lifted—surely her memory was returning.

The captain stood just a step inside the door. "I'll see to it. But don't go anywhere, milady, until I send Thorpe to escort you." He smiled and glanced at Mama Penn, then back at Travay. "By the way, we need to get a name for you. Have you any suggestions?"

Travay searched her mind for her name. A cobweb hovered over her thinking. She stood and walked across the cabin to look out the porthole. Her voice was shakier than she would have liked. "I am sorry, but I still can't remember." She tried to squelch the cold knot in her stomach. How could she forget her own name, her family, where she lived?

"Your memory will most surely come back soon, milady. Meanwhile, you're welcome to be our guest, of course." He ducked his head, but not before she saw a patronizing grin play across his thin lips.

Did the man think she was lying? Her temper flared. What would it feel like to slap his handsome, arrogant face?

Up early the next morning, Travay quickly finished her breakfast of hardtack and tea. Mama Penn helped her lace her stays and don a hoop, petticoat, and a silky yellow gown found in the trunk the captain had deposited in the cabin.

The woman pulled Travay's hair up in curls and pinned them tightly. "You hear that flappin', snappin' sound? That's them trade winds coming strong against our sails, so these here pins are to keep your hair in place."

Travay smiled. She didn't care if her hair blew any which way as long as she could just get out of the cabin and stretch her legs.

When she had finished dressing, Travay listened for the steps of her promised escort in the corridor. She stood and began to pace the floor. Would Captain Bloodstone keep his word and allow her on deck? How she longed to stroll in the sunlight and take deep breaths of those trade winds Mama Penn talked about.

A knock sounded at the door, and she swished across the room and stood in front of it. "Yes?"

"It's me, Lieutenant Thorpe, to escort you on deck, milady."

Travay unbarred the door. She recognized the square jaw, dark eyes, and bushy brows of the man who had helped overcome Knox. This morning he was dressed in a clean striped shirt and dark pants stuffed into boots, his straight brown hair tied in a queue.

Thorpe flashed an appreciative look over her and gave a small bow. A grin started at the corners of his mouth as he extended his arm. "Well, the crew will probably go berserk, milady, but I'll be by your side to protect you."

"Well, thank you, Lieutenant." Travay touched his arm and preceded him up the narrow passage and the steps, her skirts rustling with every movement. On deck, she refused to return the stares of swarthy pirates who stopped to ogle her. One, however, a handsome blond-headed pirate, bowed low to her. He had the dress and cocky air of an English gentleman. But that was impossible, wasn't it? She honored him with a quick glance but turned her face when he smiled.

Once on the outer deck, she took deep, satisfying breaths of cool air. They walked under the canopy of a clear blue sky. The sun stood high above, and a crisp breeze filled the sails and pulled tendrils of her hair loose. She stopped, leaned across the railing, and looked out at the white-capping turquoise waves and occasional jumping fish. Her heart lightened.

She glanced at the tall man beside her, seeing for the first time the gray mixed in the hair at the temples. "Mr. Thorpe, have you ever had a memory lapse?"

He turned clear brown eyes toward hers. "No, ma'am, I can't say as I have, but I've known others who have."

Hope rose in Travay's breast. "Did it last long?"

"No, ma'am. It all came back after something triggered it."

Just then a shout came from the lookout. "A sail! A sail!"

From nowhere, Captain Bloodstone bounced up to the quarterdeck. Travay's heart bumped against her ribs at the sight of him dressed in a billowing white shirt and fitted black trousers that disappeared into black boots. A red sash about his chest and waist held a sword and brace of pistols. He shouted to the lookout, "Where?

"To westward."

Bloodstone pulled his spyglass from his waistband and leaned on the railing toward the west.

Beside Travay, Thorpe sucked in a deep breath.

"Ma'am. I best be escorting you back to the cabin. I need to get with the captain." His words ran together.

"Oh, but we've just gotten on deck." Travay frowned and scanned the ocean. From where she stood, she couldn't see another ship. She had spoken louder than she intended. Captain Bloodstone turned from his glass and looked at her. Their eyes met, and a tremor shot through her.

"Get below deck, milady. Now." His commanding voice and stiff face squelched any argument.

Thorpe took her elbow, and she returned to the cabin with him, howbeit none too happy. This was a pirate ship. Would the *Blue Heron* attack whatever vessel was out there?

❧ ❧

Bloodstone studied the approaching craft across the distant waves. He knew it was loaded by the way it sat low in the water. Then he saw the oars moving in fast synchronized order. When he confirmed the flag on its masthead, the twist in his gut pained him as it had for seven long years. A hated Spanish galleon with galley slaves, and soon within reach of his guns. The water sheeted off the enemy vessel's hull in scrolls of blue-white spume as it made a path through glassy waters eastward, probably toward Spain with a load of silver ore.

Thorpe strode up beside him. "Seen her colors yet?"

"Take a look." Bloodstone handed the glass to Thorpe.

"The Red Cross of Burgundy, Cap'n." Eagerness warmed the lieutenant's voice.

"Yep, that's exactly what it is. You know how I'd love to go after them." Lucas' insides churned, and he pushed away the flicker of hope that arose with each new sighting. He could find out something about his parents, who had been captured by a Spanish vessel years earlier. He lowered the lens and frowned. "But we've taken three women aboard since our last battle, and it would be much too dangerous for them."

"Yeah, I guess you're right, Cap'n. God forbid the Spanish dogs got hold of them, or even some of our own crew." Thorpe looked around at a commotion below. "But do you think the sea dogs are gonna be happy if we sail away?"

In less than three minutes, a swarm of pirates stood before the captain and Thorpe.

Mate Byron Pitt came to the front, a smile on his tanned face and one broad hand resting on the hilt of his sword. A wild and devil-may-care attitude made the rest of the crew look up to him. He swung a blond lock back from his face and confronted Lucas. "Why aren't we hearing your orders to give chase, Captain? We think it's a Spanish treasure ship out there." The mate's suave voice rolled over the deck, loud enough for all to hear.

Ayes erupted from the crew members gathered behind Pitt.

"We have three women aboard. I'd like to see them to safety before we attack any more ships." Bloodstone directed his answer to the mate.

Grunts of disapproval filled the air.

Bloodstone looked into the faces of his men and knew their mouths were already watering over the prospect of treasure. He quickly assessed the ones he knew would stand with him—Kirk, the cook, Edwin Bruce, the surgeon, Sinbad, his always loyal African boatswain, and Thorpe. Five against the rest of the crew, most of whom were loyal to him except when greed got a grip on them—greediness Pitt could fan into a fire.

"We have articles, Captain, that give us a say in these decisions. I say we hide the women below deck and go after that treasure floating out there." Pitt's hand closed over the hilt of his sword. More ayes sounded from other crew members who inched forward, their attention latched on Bloodstone's face.

Sinbad moved in close beside the captain, his shiny bare shoulders towering over Pitt and the sailors behind him. He held a crescent-shaped cutlass, the hilt enclosed in a fist the size of a small haunch of beef, which was attached to an arm as thick as a pillar. Lucas shook his head without turning to look at his carpenter.

Several of the crew stepped back, but not Pitt. He spat on the deck in front of Bloodstone.

Lucas' jaw stiffened, and he whipped out his sword.

A loud blast shattered the tense silence as a cannon shot landed less than a hundred yards to the left of the *Blue Heron*—a warning to show colors. All attention shifted to the fast-approaching ship. Lucas sheathed his sword, the choice now out of his hands.

"Make clear and ready for engagement!" he shouted.

Amid whoops and jostling, crew members scrambled to their assigned tasks. They stowed hammocks and sea chests at the bulwarks to help stop shot and splinters. Men quartered at the guns knocked gun ports loose from the caulking that kept out seawater, and they rigged the train tackles. The gunner checked the charges in each gun to make sure they were dry and laid out loading materials and ammunition. Men appointed as musketeers brought up small chests of muskets, pistols, and cutlasses. Aloft, the newly appointed boatswain had his small sailing crew adjust the sails to "fighting sail" so the vessel could be managed with only a few men.

"Post colors!" Lucas trumpeted through the melee.

"Which one, Cap'n?" a pirate yelled from the deck.

"The Spanish, of course." They would let the other ship think they were friendly until they drew close enough to make every shot of their cannons count.

The blood surged through Lucas' veins. The hope he always carried in his heart about his missing parents blossomed like a rose in a winter garden. This time the expectation seemed to have more substance. Even if disappointed again, he would rejoice that every conquered, plundered Spanish ship meant less treasure in their coffers for war and their despicable Inquisition. Surely Reverend Wentworth would agree. And he would free the poor galley slaves manning their oars. The scars on his own back from two years as a galley slave tightened.

He turned to his ship's boy, who had hurried up beside him.

"Go warn the women to stay in the cabin, Sydney."

"Yessir! But can I come back and help fight?"

"No, sir, I need you to stay with them."

The boy's shoulders slumped, and his face fell.

Bloodstone stood to attention and gave the young sailor a serious salute. "You will be their only guard."

Sydney straightened, returned the salute, and hurried below deck.

Lucas turned to Thorpe. "Have the master gunner ready. I'll give the order as soon as we get close. Right after we post our true colors."

His lieutenant spun on his heels and hurried below.

In a few minutes, Lucas shouted, "Hoist the Jolly Roger!" What a shock would take place on the deck of the enemy ship, now too near to escape damage and capture. The black flag, rather than his English flag, raised such fear these days that many ships just heaved to and surrendered without firing a single shot. Lucas prayed that would be the case today.

CHAPTER 4

T he hope of a bloodless capture turned with the Spanish ship. When the cumbersome galleon veered about to do battle, Lucas cursed the captain under his breath. As they came about, the Spaniards fired several rounds toward the *Blue Heron*. One hit home. Lucas and the crew near him barely escaped part of the mizzenmast crashing to the deck.

A splinter of wood pierced Lucas' left arm. He ignored the burning pain and shouted, "Guns away! Open up and show all our teeth. Don't aim at the galley slave ports. Fire when I give the signal!"

The Spanish ship sat deep in the water and right in the brigantine's beam, clearly in the sights of all twelve guns that comprised Lucas' larboard battery. Gunners stood with wicks soaked in saltpeter and spirits of wine, the fuses glowing red hot. Others stood ready with wadding, shot, and powder, ready to reload the moment the cannon was fired.

"Fire!" Lucas roared across the deck. The wicks were lowered to the touchholes, igniting the charge of powder in the cannon breeches. A moment later, the guns exploded almost simultaneously.

The deck shuddered underfoot from the heavy collision of the carriages jumping back in recoil. Choking smoke clouded back over the deck, engulfing the crew as they hauled the guns in for the reload.

About six hundred feet away, wood splintered from smashed rails and bulkheads on the galleon. Men screamed as falling shrouds and blasted spars created bedlam on the shattered deck. One cannon, blown from its carriage, hung over the smashed remains of the gun port with its snout pointed toward the water. Smoke billowed from several places on the deck.

❧   ❧

When the enemy's round blasted into the *Blue Heron,* Travay jumped and smothered a scream. Were they going to die?

Mama Penn sat in a corner, her arms wrapped around herself and her eyes big and luminous. "Lord Jesus, we's depending on you."

The door flew open, and Seema hurried in, followed by Sydney, who looked pale but important, if the set of his young shoulders meant anything. He slammed the door behind him and cleared his throat. His voice started as a squeak but grew stronger.

"The Cap'n says for all ladies to stay below deck, and I'm here to guard you." He took his stand next to the door with his pistol ready.

Seema put her hands on her hips. "Yeah, sure, little man." Another loud explosion rocked the floor beneath the cabin, and she put her fingers in her ears before running to drop on the cot beside Mama Penn. A low moan came from beneath her bowed head.

"Now you don't go worrying yo'self, girl. Mr. Thorpe told me Captain Bloodstone ain't been defeated yet by a Spaniard, or any other enemy for that matter. The Lord's going to protect him and us." Mama Penn rocked to and fro. Her low prayers and praise flowed incongruously beneath the battle raging above their heads.

Travay leaned to look out the porthole, but the fighting was on the other side of the ship, a fact for which she was most thankful. The cabin rocked with multiple explosions, and Travay screamed. Particles of dust and splinters sifted down around them from the deck above. Would the walls fall in on top of them? Smoke filled Travay's throat, and she coughed. The sounds of running feet, shouts, and curses filled her ears. She fell on the bunk and pulled a pillow over her head. What if Captain Bloodstone did suffer his first loss? What would happen to her?

※ ◡ ◊

Lucas's stern battle countenance, which made most of his crew tremble, brightened into a tight-lipped smirk as the *Blue Heron* jostled around the heavier galleon, dodging its shots but getting in several from their own ports. It soon became evident the Spanish ship was no match for the smaller, more maneuverable brigantine. So much for their one hit on his deck—they would not get another.

"Look, she's listing, Captain. We must've hit one below the waterline," a pirate cried from below.

Finally, a white flag, hoisted above the smoke, signaled the ship's surrender.

The *Blue Heron* drew alongside, splitting the still oars of the galley. Expertly thrown grappling hooks secured the Spanish ship to the brigantine. Lucas swung over the narrow strip of sea, along with his crew, with one hand on a rope and the other on a cutlass. His men knew his rule: No unnecessary killing. Most of them would obey. But not Pitt. He slashed a Spanish sailor to the deck— then found himself face to face with Bloodstone.

"Muster the prisoners," Lucas commanded in a steely voice.

With a smirk, Pitt waved his sword and rounded up the prisoners near the stern.

Lucas stepped around bodies strewn about the smoking deck. Slippery red patches of blood made spidery patterns across the planking with every roll of the galleon. He stopped before the Spanish crew. Most of them were wounded and bleeding from injuries hastily wrapped with torn parts of uniforms. But the hard faces under the silver helmets that turned toward Lucas still blazed with bared teeth and flinty eyes.

The conquered captain stepped forward, his nostrils flaring and his whole body at stiff attention. His once handsome Spanish uniform of red, white, and gray now showed the distress of battle with rips, burns, and splattered blood. He removed his deplumed helmet and placed it under his arm, then withdrew his sword and offered it to Lucas, hilt first. The man's proud stare faltered and his upper lip, lined with a thin mustache, trembled. Was he thinking how a captured captain would be executed first?

"We will not harm you or your men now that you've surrendered. We practice no Inquisition here." Lucas spoke to the man in passable Castilian but was unable to keep the last words from rolling out between gritted teeth. Had his own mother and father been given the same mercy?

The man stumbled back at the tone of Lucas' last sentence. His right hand reached for his sword, no longer there.

Lucas tossed the confiscated weapon to Sinbad, who stood several feet away.

The captain bowed his head and crossed himself. Some of his crew did the same.

"Take enough men and go below to free the galley slaves and search for valuables," Lucas shouted across the deck to Thorpe. How many would be left of all those who may have been executed or drowned during the capture? His gut rolled, knowing it was the custom of defeated Spanish ships to kill the chained slaves rather than see them freed.

The chosen men tumbled down into the ship's smoking belly like a pack of rats. The Spaniards cursed and moved as if to start fighting again, but swords flicked under their chins and held them at bay.

Lucas knew his crew was in a hurry to search for treasure. And treasure they did find. They brought three ornately carved chests and deposited them with heavy thuds at his feet for later distribution. But he was more interested in the galley slaves that emerged from the bowels of the ship. Ragged, gaunt men, with hopeless lines and pallor etched across their faces, raised their arms to the sunlight and blinked watery eyes as they climbed on deck.

An older man, gray-headed and bent with labor, stopped before

Lucas. "Your men told us you are English?"

Lucas's heart warmed as he looked at the man. "Yes, we are English, from Charles Town. And you are no longer slaves." He glanced at Thorpe, who also stared at the men. Would they ever forget their own terrible two years as galley prisoners?

Pale, emaciated faces gained color as they comprehended the words. Several shouted toward Captain Bloodstone. "Thank ye, Captain, thank ye. Thank God."

Lucas addressed them. "You are now free from these Spanish pigs, and you are welcome to join my crew on the *Blue Heron* until we get to Charles Town. And there are berths on my ship in the future if you still have a taste for the sea."

"Charles Town?" The men smiled and nodded. One hollered, "Good, Captain. Some of us got folks there."

A leggy Irish lad of not more than eighteen stepped forward. "Yes, and we'll be glad to serve you any way we can, Captain."

"You who were once called slaves will have no duties on my vessel for now. Enjoy your freedom and rest. Our ship's surgeon will see to your wounds." He grimaced as he saw the infected marks of beatings on several of the men.

The men shouted and clapped.

Thorpe came up beside the captain, brushing away smoke with his hand. "This ship is taking on water fast, sir."

They both stepped away just in time as more flames broke through the deck. "Abandon ship!" Lucas cried.

His crew had already tied the treasure chests with strong ropes and drawn them across the water. Lucas, the freed slaves, and the Spanish prisoners, with pirates at their back, scrambled onto the *Blue Heron*. They watched the burning ship they'd left behind begin to sink into the sea. A great wave rocked their vessel even as they steered away as fast as possible.

Thorpe laid his hand on Bloodstone's shoulder as the captain turned to walk across the deck.

"Captain, you're wounded!"

"It's only a nick."

"Let me get the doc to look at it."

Lucas shook his head. "In a few minutes, Thorpe. I want to speak to the Spanish captain first, in private. Send him to me below."

"Aye, aye, sir."

The Spanish leader soon arrived at Lucas' cabin. Thorpe ushered him in and left to guard the door.

The man whipped off his helmet, clicked his heels together, bowed, and spoke in his native language almost too fast for Lucas to translate.

"Capitan Pedro Juarez at your service, Capitan Bloodstone. We are grateful for the mercy you have shown us and our crew. I hope this meeting is to tell me what your plans for us are." The man's alert brown eyes acknowledged Lucas, then darted around the cabin. His thin, carefully trained black mustache twitched.

Lucas swallowed the distaste in his mouth and replied alike in Castilian. "If you and your crew cooperate, I will drop you off on an island I know your ships pass on their way to the Spanish Main. With food and water, of course, enough to last you until you are rescued."

Captain Juarez's eyes widened. "That is very noble for a pirate, Captain Bloodstone. Perhaps there is something I can do for you?" The man's face hardened with anticipation.

Did the man expect a greedy request? If so, he was in for a surprise. Lucas indicated a chair for the man and took a seat himself, trying to hide his loathing for all Spaniards and what they represented. "I want to ask you about an English vessel that one of your ships took in battle seven years ago. It sailed from Charles Town to Jamaica."

"Seven years is a very long time, Capitan, and we have many different crafts sailing these seas. Do you know the name of the Spanish ship?"

"The *Conquistador*."

The man's bearded chin jerked up, then quickly lowered. But Lucas had seen the flash of recognition. His heart ricocheted against his ribcage. Could the man know something?

"I only want to know about the English ship they took, the *King's Lion*."

Juarez cleared his throat. "What is your interest in that particular vessel?"

"My mother and father were aboard."

The man took a deep breath. "You mean you are only trying to find out what happened to your *madre y padre*? That is the only information you are looking for? And for any I can give, you will set me and my crew free as you said?" He raised his dark brows and stared at Lucas.

"Yes."

The Spaniard leaned back in his chair. "Your luck is unbelievable, Captain Bloodstone. It happens I was an officer on the *Conquistador* until about six and one-half years ago, when I was given my own ship—which, I am reminded, you just burned and sank." He scowled.

Lucas' nostrils flared. His gut rolled, and bile blanketed his throat. Was he facing the murderer of his parents? Heat flushed through his body. His hand closed on the hilt of his sword.

The Spanish captain evidently saw the change, for he stiffened and stood, groping for his own absent sword.

Lucas took a slow, labored breath and moved his hand back to the table. He motioned for the Spaniard to be seated again. "The loss of your ship was your own fault. We gave you a chance to surrender without bloodshed. As far as what happens now, I give you my word: I will not harm you or your crew if you cooperate. I want information."

The captain sat, his back stiff. "Information about your *madre y padre*?"

Lucas nodded. "Do you remember an older learned gentleman and"—Lucas' voice cracked—"a gentle woman with golden hair and the greenest eyes you might have ever seen?"

The captain blinked. "Like yours? Yes, I think I do remember such a couple. But only because it was the last ship we took while I was an officer on the *Conquistador*. The gentleman—I promise you, not at our hands—died clutching his chest soon after the ship was taken. And the gentle lady, yes, I remember the hair and the eyes." He hesitated.

Lucas' breath gushed from his chest. His beloved father dead, and what about his mother? He sprang up and took the captain by the neck, ignoring the pain in his injured arm. "You will tell me whatever you know or I'll—"

"She did not die, and no one harmed her, I swear it by *la Virgen Maria*," the man croaked, his eyes bulging. Lucas removed his stiff hands from the Spaniard's jugular, but he still stood over him, trying to recover from invisible iron fingers that clutched his own throat. *My sweet mother in Spanish hands!*

"What did happen to her? Why would she have been spared? If you lie to me ..." Lucas spat out, opening and closing his fists.

The Spaniard rubbed his neck and took a ragged breath. "If I remember correctly, she admitted she had been born Catholic, and the capitan said she would make a fine governess for his young daughter."

A ray of hope blazed across Lucas' heated brain. Yes, born Catholic, but became a Protestant like his father. He had to swallow to speak. "Which captain? Tell me his name and where he was from." Lucas sat, never taking his eyes from the captain's.

"El Capitán Quinton Ramondo. And all I know is we sailed from Cádiz. I don't know where he was from, whether his family was in Spain, or whether he had an estate in the colonies like many of our titled families." Captain Juarez twisted his neck from side to side and uttered a slight groan.

"If you are lying to me"—Lucas leaned close to the man and ground out the words—"I'll come after you. This time there will be no mercy."

The captain expelled a heavy breath. "Come now, Capitan Bloodstone, I did swear by the Blessed Virgin, did I not? And why would I not be happy to give a man any information I might have about his dear mother?" He cocked his head. "It is not likely you will sail into Spanish waters to look for her, now is it?"

Lucas stood in dismissal, but the Spanish captain had one more query. His dark eyes glittered.

"Please, answer me one question, Capitan Bloodstone. How do you English expect to sail with any speed when you don't have galley slaves to push you through windless seas?"

Lucas' lips tightened as he thought of all the prisoners the Spanish forced at their oars with frequent beatings and little food. "We have an old proverb in England: 'Those who sail without oars stay on good terms with the wind.'"

The man gave Lucas a black layered look, turned on his heel, and marched to the door where Thorpe waited to escort him back to the hold.

Long after the Spaniard left, Lucas sat staring into the gathering darkness, oblivious to the throbbing of his injured arm. His father had been a good man. Lucas had loved him dearly. How sorry he was knowing he'd never see him again until heaven.

But his mother. Could she be alive? Hope flamed into reality. "Yes, by all that is in me, I would sail into any waters to rescue her."

❧　❧

Around sundown a few days later, Lucas stretched his bandaged arm gingerly and looked out over the blue waters of the southern sea. In a few more days, they would be in Charles Town, and it couldn't happen soon enough. Even after he'd marooned the Spanish sailors, supplied with food and water, on a small island he knew to be in the lane of Spanish merchant ships, his brigantine was still crowded to capacity with the galley slaves he carried to freedom. His crew chafed at the bit to get somewhere they could spend their winnings, and squabbles erupted daily. Thorpe was kept busy mediating problems. Meanwhile, always just below the surface of Lucas' mind, he found himself formulating, and discarding, plan after plan of how he would find his mother. That is, if she still lived. With each new sunrise, hope grew stronger in his breast.

"Captain, how is your arm?"

The lovely passenger he'd rescued from the sea walked up the steps to the quarterdeck. Alone.

He frowned. "You must never walk about this deck unescorted, milady. I thought I made that clear." He looked into her questioning gaze and couldn't maintain his stern expression.

Travay cocked her chin. "I couldn't stand it below deck another minute." She turned and gazed across the rippling waves, painted pink and purple by the setting sun. She leaned against the rail near him.

He tried to ignore the lovely contours of her face and the waves of hair, pinned up with tendrils escaping and blowing in the evening breeze.

"You really must return to your cabin, milady." He forced his voice to sound firm when all he wanted to do was take her in his arms.

And why not? She has come to you in this one private spot on the ship.

The thought came out of nowhere. Lucas shook his head, but he couldn't tear his attention from her as she looked up at him from under dark, silky lashes.

"And what if I refuse?"

Warmth and surprise spread through him. Was she a vixen like Seema?

"Then I'll just have to escort you." He reached for her elbow with his good arm, but she slipped from his grasp. As she did, she stumbled. He caught her around the waist, and she fell against him. A curl brushed against his cheek, and he breathed in her lilac scent. He groaned. The softness of her form against his chest was more than any man could resist. At least he told himself this as he turned her around to face him. He lifted her chin with his thumb and saw again the spattering of freckles and the sapphire eyes that could drown a man. He heard her intake of breath. Her thick lashes fluttered down. Her lips trembled. He bent and gently brushed them with his own. For a moment she went limp, then turned stiff as an oar.

"How dare you—you pirate!" She moved to slap him, but he caught her wrist. She stomped his foot instead and escaped from his grasp. She ran back the way she had come, her skirts flying behind her.

He strode to the end of the deck to make sure she went down the steps toward the cabin, then went back to the rail and shook his head in disbelief. Shock rolled over him for far more than the kiss still burning his lips. Her freckles had been the first thing to jar his memory, then the clear blue eyes and quick temper. The stomping of his foot finally left no doubt of who she was. Only God in heaven could have thought of bringing her back into his life. Was it just chance or coincidence he happened to be below fishing when she jumped off a cliff in Jamaica? Reverend Wentworth would say that when we are a part of his family, God has a part in anything we consider a coincidence.

CHAPTER 5

How could he ever forget the favorite punishment of his childhood playmate—the love of his boyish heart and enemy of his sanity? She had stomped his foot many times.

A long scar on his back burned as assurance of her identity. He closed his eyes and was immediately back in Charles Town, the fourteen-year-old son of indentured parents.

Eight-year-old Travay Allston had plucked at his sleeve in the stable entrance. "Lucas, please, please do saddle up Miss Rosey. Mr. Poole won't mind. He knows I miss her since he bought her from us." She flipped her dark, gold-splashed braids behind her shoulder.

"Go on, little miss. He would have my hide if anything happened to that filly."

"You know nothing will happen. I used to ride her. She does fine with me. Please, Lucas."

She turned startling blue eyes up to him and pursed her lips into a rosebud. She knew how to get to him. For the three years, he and his parents had served as indentured servants on the Pooles' plantation, which sat next to the Allston estate, Lucas had not been able to deny the lovely child anything she wanted. He often suffered punishment for his weakness. Neither the Poole nor the Allston families approved of the friendship between him and Travay, and it always cost him.

He groaned, remembering the fateful ride and the jumping accident. The filly had to be put down. And Lucas had taken the worst beating of his life from old Sir Poole, with young Roger Poole smiling as he leaned against the barn, watching. That was the worst beating until his galley slave days.

Lucas stretched his shoulders to relieve the stinging on his back. One of those scars was from Poole's beating for giving in to Travay Allston. She always spelled trouble.

❧ ☙

Travay rushed toward the steps down to the cabin, then passed them, blinking away tears of frustration. Or was she in shock? She didn't know what to call it, but she couldn't breathe, and her legs felt wobbly. She certainly didn't want to face Mama Penn like this. How could she let a low-down pirate kiss her? She stopped at the rail and clasped it for support, hoping the strong lapping of the waves against the side of the ship would slow her heart. The startling kiss still tingled across her lips. She took a moment to catch her breath and compose her thoughts.

"I hope milady fares well today."

Travay whirled around. First mate Byron Pitt stood before her in the spotless attire of a gentleman. The sides of his blond hair, pulled into a queue, glistened as if oiled. He swept off his three-cornered hat and bowed. A strong, fruity scent, reminiscent of slightly spoiled fruit, wafted across the sea breeze. The man had overdone his perfume.

"I am well, thank you."

His dark brown eyes searched hers. "Are you sure, milady?"

He must have seen the kiss. Warmth flooded her cheeks.

Pitt frowned and replaced his hat. "I feel I must warn you, and every other lady he comes in contact with. Our Captain Bloodstone is not a gentleman. Actually, he is no more than an escaped indentured servant and a lying, womanizing pirate."

Travay cocked her chin. "And who exactly are you, Mr. Pitt?"

"I am the third son of Baron Von Heflin. But I have fallen on bad times, milady."

"Really? And how did you end up on a pirate ship, pray tell?"

"That is a long story, milady, but one I would delight to share with you at some opportune time." As the sun slipped below the horizon, he looked around and took a step closer. "May I escort you to your door perhaps?"

"No, Mr. Pitt, thank you." Aware of the descending darkness, she started to go past him. Before she could move, he threw out a hand and blocked her way.

"May I say one more thing, milady?" He moved closer and spoke in a low voice. "If you ever have need of my services, my help in any way, don't hesitate to let me know."

His heavy breathing and the way he devoured her with his dark, unreadable eyes troubled Travay. "I'm sure there will be no need, Mr. Pitt." Did he think she was in danger from the captain? Or should she be more wary of Mr. Pitt? She edged around him and hurried to her borrowed cabin.

❧ ❧

When Sydney skipped up the quarterdeck steps the next day, Lucas turned from studying the choppy turquoise sea and smiled at the boy.

"Look, Cap'n Bloodstone. Seema dropped this when she was hurrying across the deck and I, well, I picked it up 'fore she knew she dropped it." He held out a small leather coin purse. "I think she musta taken it off our leddy guest."

Lucas fingered the small rawhide purse with its drawstring and nodded. Before he opened the neck, he knew he would find his initials scratched inside. He had made it for Travay for her eleventh birthday, just before he ran away from the Charles Town plantation.

"What you be thinking, Cap'n?" Sydney's voice drew him back to the present.

"I think you're right, lad. This probably came from our guest. Thank you for bringing it to me."

The boy started away, but Lucas called after him. "Sydney, this was empty when you found it, correct?"

"Oh, yessir! I would never take nothing from a leddy like our guest."

Lucas nodded. "Find Seema and send her to me, will you, lad?'

"Yessir, Cap'n." And off he went.

Seema appeared on the quarterdeck a few minutes later. She smiled and swung her hips as she came toward Lucas. She was an attractive woman with a sun-kissed complexion, shiny black hair around her shoulders, and the fire of her Spanish blood evident in her manner. At Mama Penn's insistence, he had bought her off the slave block in Kingston. He had come to regret it when she made bold plays toward him, and to at least one other crew member—first mate Byron Pitt. Lucas had threatened to leave her in Kingston.

He had to admit, in one way it was good she was considered Pitt's girl now. He didn't have to worry about the rest of the crew bothering her. If he could just get her to Charles Town and to Reverend and Mrs. Wentworth's household, with God's help, those two would straighten her out. Like they had him.

"You sent for me, Capitan Bloodstone?" Her dark eyes flashed a welcome, and her full lips stretched into a warm smile.

"Seema, where did you get this?" Lucas pulled the coin purse from the folds of his shirt.

Her face paled. "I don't know what you are talking about. I have never seen it before."

"Don't lie to me, Seema. I happen to know you took it from our lady guest. My question is, did you take anything else?"

Seema's hand flew to a locket around her neck.

"Let me have the locket. I won't ask for the coins you've kept, but I must have the jewelry."

She untied the ribbon and threw the ornament at him. "I don't see why you took that uppity one on board. She is going to be nothing but trouble."

"No more than you are, I expect." Lucas dismissed her, and she sashayed away, but not before she gave him one long look under her thick, dark lashes.

Lucas opened the familiar golden adornment with its secret catch. He found exactly what he expected: a miniature of Travay's mother.

That evening after supper, Lucas paced the top deck, trying to decide when and how to show the purse and locket to Travay, as well as the pearl knife found on her person when he rescued her. These personal possessions of hers could bring back her memory. Then perhaps she could tell him what had happened to her in Kingston. But how would she feel when she discovered who he really was—and what he had become?

Wonderful kiss or not, nothing could ever work out between them. They had always moved in different worlds, and now those worlds were even farther apart.

His brows set in a straight line, Lucas left the quarterdeck and descended to Travay's cabin. What had she been doing in Jamaica, and from whom was she fleeing? He needed to know. He knocked on the bolted entrance and waited.

Mama Penn opened the door. Lucas cast a quick look around—Seema was not present. Good. Travay sat on his bed with one of his books open before her. A ray of the setting sun through the porthole crowned her in golden light. His heart thudded against his ribs.

When Travay looked up and saw him, she ducked her head and closed the book.

"I need to talk to you, Tr—milady." Lucas pulled out a chair and faced her. Mama Penn headed toward the door, but Lucas stopped her. "No, you stay, Mama Penn. You can hear anything that's said." *And make sure I keep my distance from this most lovely woman.*

Lucas glanced at the volume Travay still held in her lap. He smiled to put her at her ease. "What were you reading?"

A tremor started up Travay's back, and warmth rose in her cheeks. Was it because she remembered the wonderful way his lips had touched hers the evening before, or was it for the serious expression on the captain's face? Maybe it was because of the dynamic vitality he exuded. She turned to the woman. "Yes, please do stay, Mama Penn." Her voice sounded stilted even to herself.

Mama Penn sat in a chair in the corner, as far away from the two of them as she could get in the small quarters, and folded her arms across her ample bosom.

Travay held up the book so Lucas could read the title, *The Reasonableness of Christianity*. Whatever did the captain have to say? Surely he had not come to see what she was reading. "It is by someone named John Locke."

"Yes, a minister friend of mine loaned it to me. Have you ever heard of Locke?"

Travay laid the book on the bed beside her. "I can't say that I have, or at least I don't remember." She met the captain's glance and alarm darted through her. It couldn't be apprehension she sensed in his demeanor. Not this man who roamed the seas as the infamous Captain Bloodstone.

He drew a deep breath before he responded. "I have something I want to show you, milady." He pulled a small leather purse, a pearl-handled knife, and a gold locket from his sash. He laid them on the table one at a time. "Do these belong to you?"

Travay touched the handle of the knife. She picked up the small bag and stared at the locket. Her heart jumped in her chest so hard it pained her. She swallowed. "Yes, yes, I believe they are mine. Where did you find them?"

"Does that really matter? I am hoping they will trigger your memory. Do they?"

"Yes, things are coming back now. The knife was given to me by my father when I turned twelve. This little purse was made for me by a childhood friend, and this locket—" She clutched it to her heart, and her face crumpled. "Oh, my God, my mother, my sweet mother. She is gone, is she not?" Tears pooled in her eyes and flowed down her face. She looked first at the captain, then at Mama Penn.

Lucas leaned forward. The concern on his face softened his strong profile. Mama Penn stirred in her chair. "Lord Jesus, we need your help," she whispered.

Travay fell back on the bed. The blood drained from her face. She bit her fist as memories flooded back: her father's death, then her mother's remarriage and death after her stepfather moved them to Jamaica; her stepfather gambling away the plantation—and her hand in marriage. She remembered how she fled the house on Arundel, followed by Sir Roger, and how she'd had no choice but to make the terrible jump over the cliff and into the Caribbean. She sat up and uttered a dreadful cry.

❧ ☙

Lucas lunged toward her and pulled her into his arms. She rested her head on his chest as hoarse sobs racked her body. Something deep inside him exploded and shipwrecked all his arguments against involvement with her. He couldn't trust himself to murmur a single comforting word. His arms tightened around Travay. What had brought that alarming cry from deep within her? What memory—or what person?

Slowly the sobs subsided. Travay hiccupped and lifted her tear-stained face from Lucas' shoulder. She looked up at him from under thick, wet lashes, and it was all he could do not to press his mouth to her trembling lips. He released her, and she sat on the bunk.

Mama Penn came and helped Travay lie down. She pulled a blanket over the trembling form. "She's gonna be all right now, Cap'n. You'll see. I'll take good care of this little lady. Don't you go worrying none."

Lucas stumbled away, his mind swirling like a hurricane. His deepest desire was to tell the young woman on the bunk that he had loved her since their childhood days and wanted to take care of her the rest of her life.

Travay's weak voice arrested him at the door. "My name is Travay Allston. I have an aunt in Charles Town. Please help me get to her."

"By all means, Miss Allston." His throat felt raw from the effort it took to keep his voice steady.

He entered his borrowed cabin and kicked the door shut, trying to rip from his heart the powerful feelings Travay had reawakened. How could he let his thoughts, his emotions, get so out of hand? He had nothing to offer her. Besides, when she discovered who he was and what he had become, she would surely hate him. He felt like smashing something. Instead, he sat down, and soon a strange peace came over him. Was Ethan Wentworth praying for him? He hoped so.

There were still questions he wanted Travay to answer. What had happened in Jamaica? He shook his braids and frowned. Maybe he should forget the questions, avoid her, and just deliver her to her aunt in Charles Town. And maybe she'd never discover who he was and be shocked at the privateer he'd become. Although he was a Charles Town merchant when not at sea, to her he would be nothing more than a pirate.

❦

Travay slept long and hard for almost two days and nights, hardly eating anything Mama Penn tried to tempt her with whenever she awoke. But a morning arrived when she sat up and asked Mama Penn, "Do you believe there is a God? I don't."

The woman's eyes widened, and her back straightened. "I sho do, Miss Travay. How cum you say such a wicked thing?"

Travay ducked her head. She knew exactly what she could answer, but she didn't want to further shock the good-natured servant. How could God have allowed all the bad things that had happened to her, that had left her without loving parents and made her dependent on a wicked stepfather? Only by a desperate act had she been saved from a disgusting forced marriage. She shut the chilling memory of the cliff from her mind and arose from the bed. Weakness washed over her, and she wobbled.

Mama Penn grabbed her elbow. "Now, lit'l lady, you gotta take it slow after the shock you've been through, sleeping the days away and not eating 'nuff for a sparrow."

The memory of the captain's strong arms holding her flashed into Travay's mind and sent a tingle all the way to her toes. Did he have compassion? But what man could have a sprinkle of compassion and still be a pirate? It was most likely lust, not empathy. She tried to force him from her thoughts, but somehow he stayed at the edge of her mind.

She sat down and ate her first hearty breakfast in two days. The captain's presence hung about her as Mama Penn helped her dress and did her hair—his eyes that flashed when angry, his strong arms, the way his lips had brushed hers that time on the deck. These thoughts made her cheeks burn, and she turned her face away from Mama Penn's quick eyes.

Was he thinking about her? Was that why she couldn't seem to banish him from her brain? She had to face him again sometime so she might as well get it over with. She walked over to the trunk of clothing—some of the captain's ill-gotten gains, no doubt—and searched for a suitable dress. She hated wearing someone else's clothes, but what choice did she have? She found a blue silk dress that seemed to be her size. "Mama Penn, where could the captain have gotten this chest? Was some woman captured who owned these beautiful dresses?"

The older woman stopped straightening up the cabin and turned to Travay. "Most likely she was rescued and returned home, and the trunk found later. Some pirate probably thought to take them dresses to his wife or daughter, but the captain confiscated it."

Travay dropped the dress in her hands. How many women had the captain rescued? A better question: How many had he kissed like he kissed her?

CHAPTER 6

Lucas traversed the quarterdeck, trying not to go back to the cabin and check on Travay again. Her continued stupor worried him. If she didn't get back to normal soon, what could he do? The doc said she'd be all right, to just give her time. But what did he know about sheltered young women like Travay? All he'd ever treated were pirates and women of the night in the various ports they frequented.

"No change yet with our lady?" Thorpe stepped up on the quarterdeck.

"No, I don't think so." Bloodstone stopped pacing and leaned across the rail with his face turned away from his lieutenant.

"You, uh, like her?" Thorpe pulled a pipe from his pocket and took time lighting it with two small pieces of flint.

"I do not know what you are getting at, Thorpe. We rescued her. She is a guest on our ship. We are glad she got her memory back, and we will deliver her to her aunt in Charles Town next week. End of story." Bloodstone looked into his lieutenant's face with dismissal and tried to control the quiver of his eyelid.

A voice from behind them interrupted.

"May I join you, gentlemen?"

They turned as one man.

Travay Allston stood before them, thinner and paler but as beautiful as Bloodstone had ever seen her. She clutched her blue ruffled skirts against the breeze that snapped the sails. A few curls escaped her upswept hairdo and blew softly about her face.

Both men whipped off their hats and bowed.

Lucas smiled. "It's good to see you up and about, Miss Allston."

"Thank you, Captain Bloodstone."

"Yes, it is good to see you looking so well, Miss Allston." Thorpe fidgeted with his hat, then turned to the captain. "I guess I had better get below and see about the crew." He left grinning.

Travay turned to look at the crowded deck below. "I am glad you released the galley slaves. What a terrible sentence it would be for any man."

"I know very well, having once served at the mercy of the Spanish in the bowel of one of their ships for almost two years."

She turned wide eyes on him. "But what happened? How did you end up there?"

Lucas looked out to sea. How long would he be able to keep his real identity secret from her and from most of the crew, who only knew him as Captain Bloodstone? "It's a long story, milady— one which I doubt you'd really be interested in hearing."

"On the contrary, I would like to hear it. Were you a runaway indentured servant like Mr. Pitt told me?"

So Pitt was up to his usual methods, trying to discredit the captain. Thankfully, the majority of the crew didn't believe the first mate—most of the time. But would Travay? He examined the lovely face lifted toward him. A frown creased the ivory brow. Reverend Wentworth would say, "The truth is better than untruth. One lie will require another."

He looked back out across the white-capped waves. He would tell her some of the story, even though he hated to dredge up the memories. And if she guessed who he really was, he'd just have to face the consequences. "My parents suffered financial losses in England because of their faith and chose to go to Charles Town as indentured servants rather than to debtors' prison. Their master made our lives very hard. When I was sixteen, he sent the two of them to his Jamaican sugar plantation, but the ship was captured by the Spanish."

"Oh, my."

Lucas glanced at Travay. Her lips tightened, and her shoulders slumped. His gut turned. She was thinking of the Inquisition. He stiffened. "I have never found out exactly what happened to them, but I intend to, if it's the last thing I do." Why muddy the water with the facts the Spanish captain had revealed? The man may have been lying.

⁂

Travay gripped the railing to steady herself. The captain's face had turned gray. His jaw became granite, and a muscle jumped in his neck. No wonder. She closed her eyes a moment to block out thoughts of the horrible Inquisition his parents might have suffered. "But how did you end up in a Spanish galley?"

"I ran away after my parents disappeared. I tried to get to Spain to seek information, but I was captured and sent to the galley."

The scars. Captain Bloodstone was not a criminal, but a victim. But it was only his word. Could she trust him?

"Then what happened?"

"Later, a pirate ship took the Spanish ship I was on, and that's how I—"

"Ended up in this terrible pirate trade?" Travay couldn't keep the scorn out of her voice. "Why didn't you leave that pirate ship? Surely you had chances. But you joined them instead." How had she ever thought he was handsome or compassionate? Her father had died at the hands of pirates, and that was when her life and her mother's life had changed forever. "I can't get to Charles Town and off this ship soon enough."

Lucas turned a stiff face to Travay. "I am a privateer, not a pirate, Miss Allston, and I have things to attend to. Please go back to your cabin. You are not safe wandering aboard this crowded ship."

"Gladly." The coldness in her voice matched his.

As Travay made her way back to the cabin, Pitt stepped out from among the crew and blocked her way. His cagey brown eyes devoured her. Today he was half-dressed, with strong brown arms and chest exposed and a sweat cloth tied around his brow, holding back his blond hair. A scent of sweat and his overdone perfume sickened her.

"May I escort you back to your door, milady?"

"No. Thank you. I'll be fine."

He continued to stand before her amid catcalls from the watching crew.

Her stomach lurched, and her heart jumped into her throat as he stepped close enough for her to feel his hot breath touch her cheek.

"Get back to work, Pitt." The captain's voice rang loud and clear from the quarterdeck. "And all the rest of you, too. Sydney, escort Miss Allston to her cabin."

Sydney ran up from behind the crew and stood beside Travay.

Pitt smirked and stood back to allow them to pass.

❧ ☙

The next evening, Lucas began to sense in the pit of his stomach that something was going on between his crew and the galley slaves. He had given the slaves liberty on the ship, and the crew was none too happy having to pull all the chores. He was sure that was it, and he thought about dividing the work now that the released men had had a week of recovery. Anything to keep the peace until they landed in Charles Town.

But just after supper, before the captain could make any kind of announcement, fighting broke out, due in part to the rum some of the crew had slipped from the stores. It escalated to fist and sword fights. It was all Lucas, Thorpe, and Sinbad could do to break it up. There were quite a few injuries for Edwin Bruce to attend to.

Lucas found the doctor below deck in the sick bay, stitching up a wound. "Do you think you could send Mama Penn and Seema to help tend the wounded?" Bruce asked him. "You know Sydney is also here as of yesterday. But he's young, and surely he'll kick whatever is getting him down."

Lucas looked at his surgeon, who was none too good for drink himself, and knew he'd better send the two women—or else he might lose crew members. Not to mention Sydney.

He walked over to the pallet on which the boy lay tossing with a fever. He stooped down, a frown creasing his forehead. "Sydney, dear boy, I am so sorry you're sick. We are going to do everything we can to get you well. You hear me?"

The boy opened bleary eyes for a second. "Thank ye, Cap'n Bloodstone."

❧ ❧

During the fighting, Travay lay on her bunk, trying to block out the sounds. Loud curses and ungodly shrieks filtered through the walls. Was this what hell was like? Her lips curled, and nausea rose in her throat. Thank God she would soon be with her aunt in Charles Town. She hoped she never saw another pirate ship.

After it quieted down and Mama Penn and Seema were sent for, Travay turned over in the bunk and wished for sleep. But something sinister in the warm air fought her. It seemed the room had grown darker than usual, even with the windows the captain's cabin boasted. The porthole on the opposite wall beamed with a sliver of light. She turned her head and concentrated on it.

She had almost dozed off when she heard the cabin door open. Assuming it was Mama Penn and Seema returning, she kept her face to the wall.

She took a long sleepy breath. A jangle near the table and a scent of sweat and rotting fruit tugged at her consciousness. She frowned, turned over, and opened her eyes. Byron Pitt stood over her. In the ray of moonlight, the muscles in his shoulders glinted as if oiled. She bolted upright and opened her mouth to scream, but he bent and clamped a hand across her mouth.

"Don't do that, milady." His voice was husky. "This can be a pleasant time for both of us, or just one of us if you don't cooperate. Besides, everyone's down on the lower deck, dealing with the injuries." With his other hand, he cast the blanket from her. His lustful eyes traveled over her form, clad only in her nightgown. He pulled her up to his chest. Travay could see the sweat on his upper lip and feel his hot breath on her face and neck. His body odor and overdone cologne turned her stomach. She beat her fists against his arms and his head, but he clasped her even tighter, arching her back into his embrace. He removed his hand from her lips and crushed his mouth down on hers. She pounded against him and pulled his hair. He grabbed her hands and twisted them behind her.

Dear God, if you are there, help me.

He lifted his head a moment. "Come on, you are enjoying this as much as I am, milady, and we have much more to come." A throaty laugh escaped his lips, and a chill traveled down Travay's spine despite the warmth in the cabin and the heat emanating from his body.

She gasped a ragged breath and screamed, but he lowered his mouth on hers again. He loosened his hold on her momentarily, and taking advantage of his lapse, she managed to raise a knee and kick hard into his groin. He swore and fell back, doubled over.

Sobbing, Travay scrambled over him toward the door. It flew open and almost hit her.

Lucas stood in the entrance, his sword drawn. He looked at her and then at Byron, who managed to straighten up. A menacing growl came from Lucas' throat.

Pitt staggered up from his bent position and managed to grab his rapier from the table. He emitted a bellow like a mad bull and licked his lips. "Now let's see who will captain this ship." He lunged toward Lucas.

Travay crawled to Mama Penn's pallet in the corner and lit the lamp with shaking hands. Then she covered herself with the blanket and shrank back in the corner as far as she could while the furious battle waged. She lost sense of time amid the sounds of clashing swords, grunts, and heavy breathing as the two men crashed around the lamp-lit cabin, once almost stepping on her, and finally fought out the door, up the steps, and onto the deck.

Shaking uncontrollably, she crawled to the door and pulled herself up to bolt it. She turned, leaned her back against it, and prayed her second prayer in years. "Dear God, please help me get off this ship and help Captain Bloodstone not be killed." She slid down to a sitting position.

She did not know how long she sat pressed against the locked entry as sounds of the deadly conflict moved back and forth across the deck above. The stamping feet and clashing swords jarred the ceiling. Crew members had evidently joined the melee, for she could hear them yelling, laughing, and crying for blood. She put her hands over her ears and lowered her chin, trying not to throw up. She wondered if Mama Penn and Seema were safe.

Finally, silence came. Her body quit shaking, and a haze crept across her mind.

Heavy footsteps crossed the deck, bounded down the steps, and approached the cabin door. Her head flew up. She clutched the blanket and couldn't breathe.

CHAPTER 7

"Travay, are you all right?"

At the sound of the familiar voice, she sucked in a needed breath and offered a silent prayer. Captain Bloodstone—thank God. Groaning with her bruises, she pushed herself up and unbolted the door.

"Are you hurt?" The captain stood there in the lamplight, bleeding from a nick on his left shoulder and the side of his neck. But safe, strong.

Travay fell into his arms with a sob.

Lucas kicked the door shut. She clung to him, shaking, and weeping.

"Travay, did that swine …" His voice sounded like a growl.

"No, no," she mumbled against his shoulder.

"Then why are you crying so? Everything's going to be all right. Pitt's not dead, but he won't be bothering anyone for some time."

Travay wiped the tears from her face. She reveled in the warmth emanating from him and breathed in his manly scent. She sighed—what she was about to say shocked her, yet she knew it was the truth.

"I was afraid you … you might have been killed," she whispered.

He tipped her chin up with his thumb and made a noise between an exhale and a groan. In slow motion, he bent and touched her lips with his own. He pressed her so tight against him, she gasped. He cupped her head with his hand, entwined his fingers in her hair, and turned her face up to within an inch of his. She melted into his embrace. His mouth crushed down on hers. Her whole being filled with joy like she had never known.

Suddenly, he ended the kiss, and his strong hands gripped her shoulders, moving her away. He stepped back, and his face seemed to turn to granite. "Miss Allston, I'm sorry. Will you forgive me?"

Forgive him? She gasped for breath and prayed her knees would not give way. Then reality struck her benumbed mind. How could she feel this way about a pirate? Fie! She fought a double battle to either fall back into his arms or slap him across his taut cheek. She opted for the second and raised her hand.

He grabbed her wrist.

A knock sounded at the cabin door. Lucas moved in front of her and opened it.

He spoke to the two standing there, shielding their view of the room. "Thorpe, get Mama Penn back up here from the sick bay. Sinbad, get Pitt off the deck and into chains. Send the doc to sew up his face."

"Aye, aye, Cap'n," both men replied.

Lucas went out the door, and Thorpe said, "Is milady hurt?"

"No. She's unharmed."

Thorpe's next words, spoken quietly to Captain Bloodstone, nevertheless reached Travay's ears. "Pitt'll remember this night every time he shaves."

Travay bolted the door, ran to the bunk, and fell onto it. Confusion battled in her mind, but a wonderful warm glow from Lucas' touch still thrilled her. She tingled from her head to her toes. Nothing in her life had prepared her for the kiss she had just experienced. *With a pirate.*

She shot straight up, then cringed. How could she have responded like that to a pirate? But that thought didn't stop her racing heart. She pulled her knees up and wrapped her arms around them. A new plan had to be made about Captain Bloodstone or she'd be lost, as her mother would have said. He most definitely was not a gentleman in any sense of the word, she reasoned, or she wouldn't be in such a bewildered state.

The next day, after visiting Sydney in the sick bay, Lucas stood on the quarterdeck, facing north toward Charles Town, trying to get Travay's face and the memory of their kiss out of his mind. He should never have kissed her like that. She was not like the women in his past. And he was probably on the verge of making a complete fool of himself. Why should she ever feel about him as he felt about her? He wasn't in her class. And she thought him nothing but a pirate. It would be best if he stayed away from her until they made port. He hoped Reverend Wentworth was praying for him. *Please pray a lot, Ethan.*

Thorpe joined him. The lieutenant took out his pipe and tried to light it, cupping his hand around the bowl. "If this breeze holds, we should soon enter the Gulf Stream that flows beyond the Florida Keys, and we should be in Charles Town a few days later."

"Sure should. If this wind isn't a promise of a coming squall." Lucas leaned over the quarterdeck railing and yelled, "Raise our colors!" Below, a crew member ran the English flag up the mast.

Thorpe finally lit his pipe and took a deep draw. The current of air blew away the smoke as he exhaled. "What are your instructions, Captain? We've got a bit to take care of when we dock in Charles Town this time."

"Yes, more than usual, Thorpe. But I know you'll take care of everything like you always do when I revert back to my Charles Town merchant identity." He smiled at his first lieutenant. "Here's the lineup for home port. After we unload our hold, you will pay off and release the crew and galley slaves. When you release Pitt and Knox and pay them off, tell them we don't want either of them back on board the *Blue Heron*."

"Aye, Captain, and good riddance, I say. You know, of course, Pitt has sworn to make you pay for his face. Guess he's worried the womenfolk won't gather around him quite so fast anymore with that scar you gave him. It's going to be a dilly."

Lucas shrugged. "I want you and Sinbad to escort Miss Allston to her aunt's house, which I understand is just off Bay Street. Take Mama Penn with you. She's told me she would like to stay with Miss Allston. Maybe the aunt can use a good cook and helper. On the way, take Seema to Reverend Wentworth's. Tell him I'll see him later."

"Aye, Captain."

"And Thorpe,"

"Yes, Captain?"

"Two other things." A frown crossed Lucas' brow. "I've got to believe Sydney is going to make it through the strange sickness he's come down with and accompany me back home. He was worse than this when I pulled him off the street two years ago."

"I'm with you on that score, for sure. And the whole crew, I'll wager."

"The other thing. I haven't told you, but the Spanish captain gave me some information about my parents."

Thorpe turned and stared at Lucas. "Can you believe him?"

"That's what I don't know, but he says my mother could still be alive. And I'm trying to figure out exactly how and where I should go look for her."

"You know I'm with you every step of the way, Captain."

Warmed by Thorpe's reply, Lucas added, "I'll let you know when I've come up with a plan. But you know it will be dangerous."

"Wouldn't expect anything less." Thorpe dumped his pipe against the railing, blew on it, placed it back in the fold of his shirt, and left.

Travay made her way to the quarterdeck, and Lucas braced himself. He couldn't help but admire the way she moved with such natural grace, even on the bobbing deck. Her bouffant skirts swayed in time to the ship's rhythm, and her upswept hair glistened in the morning sunlight.

"Good morning, Captain." She stood beside him, her demeanor cordial. That and nothing more.

So she was going to ignore what had happened. Fine. It was for the best. "Good morning."

He breathed in her sweet lilac scent and smiled. She had used the Castilian soap he had sent along, confiscated from his last Spanish ship conquest along with the dress she wore. The blue satin garment with its petticoat layers hugged her tiny waist as if it had been made for her, and her curls, though pinned, bounced about in the fresh sea breeze. One curl escaped to flutter about on her creamy neck. It begged him to touch it. Lucas had to look away.

He leaned over the deck rail and pointed north. "Keep watching the horizon. In the next day or two, unless we hit a calm, we might see some of the outlying keys of Florida."

❧ ❧

"Oh, my, are we truly getting close? Charles Town won't be far then." Travay tried to keep her gaze from the captain's broad shoulders and his strong, tanned hands gripping the rail. She scanned the horizon and listened a moment to the recurring snap of the sails and the water capping against the hull. Was her heart beating faster because of the nearness of Charles Town or the nearness of the captain?

She turned toward him, and his scent of the sea and leather pleased her. His white wide-sleeved shirt puffed about in the breeze under his rawhide baldric, and the thick dark plaits of his hair spread out over his shoulders. She turned away, remembering her new plan—cordial, just cordial, until they reached Charles Town and the end of whatever was going on between them. She would go on with her life, and he would go on with his pirating.

"Should be docking in Charles Town in a few days, if this northwest wind continues and doesn't turn angry." Lucas wet his finger and held it up in the breeze.

As he did, Travay saw the bend in the little finger on his right hand.

Her breath caught in her throat. Memory crowded upon her.

A boy and his indentured parents had come to live at the Charles Town plantation next to her father's rice plantation when she was a child. She remembered the day she had met him fishing in the pond between the two estates. He showed her how to put a worm on a hook. That's when she had noticed his bent little finger. She had asked him about it like any child would, and he had laughed and said it ran in his family. Now the story he had recently shared of his life fell, brick by brick, into place. And there was the color of his eyes—how had she missed that? She had never known anyone else with such distinctive green eyes.

He must have noticed her staring at his hand. He moved it out of sight.

She raised her brows. "Lucas Barrett, could it really be you?" Her voice trembled.

Lucas sighed and looked down at his feet before raising his eyes once again to hers. "Yes, it's me, Travay. I wondered when you'd recognize me." His shining gaze locked onto hers for a wonderful moment.

Standing beside the strong, attractive man, playmate of her childhood, Travay's palms turned clammy, and shock raced across her belly. The new plan seemed an ocean away. Could this be a man she could trust after all, even though he was a pirate? He had certainly fought a life and death battle to save her from Byron Pitt. Heat rose in her cheeks as his kiss also came to mind. She pushed the memory away. She needed to know more about this man and what had occurred over the years since their youth.

"You said your parents were captured by a Spanish ship and that's why you ran away. But I seem to remember another incident about the time you disappeared."

꧁ ꧂

Lucas scowled and leaned over the railing.

"I never got a chance to apologize for what happened," she continued. "It was my fault entirely for pushing you to saddle Sir Roger's prize mare for me."

"I should have known better."

"But who could know the horse would miss the jump and break a leg?" She leaned to peer into his face. "And that Sir Roger would blame you? I am so sorry."

"It's over. Long over. Let's forget it." He took a deep breath. "But if your apology is sincere, I have a favor to ask of you."

"A favor?" She cocked her chin.

Lucas gripped the rail in his strong hands. "No one on the ship knows my real name but Thorpe and Sinbad. Will you continue to call me Captain Bloodstone as long as we're on board?"

Travay stiffened. "Oh, yes. I almost forgot. You are a pirate, and you don't want anyone knowing your real name. What are you doing? Living a double life, deceiving others in addition to piracy? She stamped her foot and glared at him. "You know, I was glad when you escaped from the Pooles' indentured service. I knew what a rogue your master was, and now I've learned how much worse his son is. But how absolutely horrible that you've used your freedom to become a thieving, lawless pirate instead of a merchant." She tossed her head and clamped her mouth shut.

Lucas gritted his teeth. "I'm sorry you have such scorn for my occupation, Travay, which is *privateer*, not pirate. But may I remind you that if I had not been in that bay to rescue you, pirate that you believe I am, you'd be at the bottom of the Caribbean right now? As would your horse."

Travay glared at him with burning, reproachful eyes. "I should have known you would bring that up, to remind me I should be forever in your debt."

A wave of heat rose from Lucas' midriff and scalded his face. He didn't care if he hurt her or not. "If you were not so spoiled, Travay Allston, you would be more appreciative of someone saving your life."

She sputtered, bristling with indignation. "Well, I refuse to be in debt to a thief, a liar, and a low-down pirate." She turned to go.

Lucas grabbed her elbow. What she really needed was turning over his knee, something she surely had missed growing up so stubborn and unthankful. Instead, he drew her into his arms so tight the air whooshed out of her lungs. She surrendered without a word, shocking him. Her breath feathered his chin. He looked at her soft, full lips, and she closed her eyes. He fought a terrible battle, then groaned and pushed her back. As he released his hold on her, her knees buckled. He caught her and looked into her stunned face, heard her labored breathing.

I love you, Travay. I've always loved you.

Her eyes swam with tears. "Let me go." She ducked her chin, and a tear spilled down her cheek. He flicked it away with his thumb and willed his heart to quit bruising his ribs. He made sure her legs no longer threatened to fold before he released her.

"I don't want you in my debt, Travay."

She jerked away from him and stumbled across the quarterdeck and down the steps.

He slumped against the railing, willing sanity to settle back over his fire-blasted mind. Reverend Wentworth would be proud of him today, if not yesterday.

※ ※

Travay gasped for breath as she flew through the cabin door and fell onto the bunk. Thank heaven the room was empty. She turned over and crossed her hands over her heaving chest. She'd never been held like Lucas had held her. Why did she allow a pirate to take her into his arms? The conceit of the man. The shame of her response. *And the ecstasy!*

Yes, she had wanted him to kiss her again. In his arms, she was filled with an amazing sense of completeness. But it was all a lie. It had to be. No pirate could have any place in her life. Not even one who had been a childhood friend or who called himself a privateer. Privateers, her father had told her, usually had a letter of marque from the king that permitted them to attack and plunder the ships of England's enemies. But he also told her many of them attacked ships of any nationality that might carry treasure. Had her father not been killed in just such an attack as a passenger on an English ship attacked by Dutch privateers?

She pressed her eyelids until the tears stopped. Her heated emotions wrestled with the memory of Lucas taking her into his arms so fast she lost her breath. But why didn't he kiss her? He definitely intended to—she was sure of that. What had stopped him? How many other women had he kissed? She lay on her back and stared at the ceiling. How many other women had shared this cabin with its pirate owner? Even Seema, perhaps? She had seen the way Seema looked at him when she thought no one would notice. And Lucas was, after all, a pirate, whether he called himself a privateer or not. What difference was there between the two?

Travay sat up and looked around. As her confused emotions becalmed like trees after a hurricane, one fact remained clear in her mind. Never had she dreamed of such feelings as Lucas' embrace aroused. Both heat and ice traveled through her veins. She needed to stop thinking about the childhood playmate she'd looked up to and tormented at every opportunity. He was gone forever, replaced by one who called himself Captain Bloodstone.

Seema walked through the door and slouched down in a chair at the table. She tossed her thick black hair across one shoulder and pointed a finger at Travay. Her dark eyes shot daggers.

"I saw the captain hold you in his arms, Miss Uppity. How could he not, when you threw yourself at him?" She smirked.

Heat traveled up Travay's cheeks, and then pride stepped in. "How dare you speak to me like that! I did not *throw* myself at him. But I'm sure whatever I do—or what the captain does, for that matter—is no concern of yours."

Seema's lip curled. "He's besotted with you, no doubt."

"I don't care what he is. All I want is to get to Charles Town and off this ship as soon as possible. He's nothing to me." If that were true, why did her heart scream something different?

"I don't believe that any more than you do." Seema's eyes narrowed. "I saw the way you melted into his arms. You couldn't resist him."

Travay stood up and put her hands on her hips. "I did not do that. He forced that embrace." She busied herself picking up around the cabin, wishing Seema would slink back to wherever she'd come from. Instead, the girl stepped in front of her with her head thrown back and her full lips in a tight line.

"I give you fair warning, milady. Make no plans for Captain Bloodstone. He's taken." Then she flounced out the cabin door.

Travay sank onto the bunk. So Lucas was exactly what his line of work indicated—a womanizing pirate.

She turned her face into the pillow and wept.

CHAPTER 8

The next night, Travay was thrown out of her bunk by the rocking ship. The keening sound of the wind and the heavy pounding of the waves against the hull alarmed her.

Mama Penn burst into the cabin. Travay had not heard her leave. "They say one of them hur'canes is blowing up from the south waters and coming 'bout as quick as you kin say scat."

"What do we need to do?" Travay couldn't keep the tremble out of her voice.

"You stay right here in this cabin, milady. Don't even think about going out on that deck, no matter how bad it gits. I'se got to go down in the sick bay and tie down the sick men so they won't be tossed to the floor."

"But can't I help you?"

Mama Penn eyed her and seemed to make up her mind. "I guess you'll be about as safe there as here. Maybe more. And Sydney will be glad to see you if he's awake."

"I've missed him. Thorpe told me the boy was sick but advised that I not visit because it might be contagious." Travay grabbed up a shawl. "I would love to check on him."

As they left the cabin, Travay locked arms with Mama Penn, who clutched the railing with her hand. With her free arm, Travay tried to keep her billowing skirts from toppling them both as they made their way across the tossing deck and blowing rain to the lower-level hatch. As they stepped down into the sailors' hold and then to the sick bay, the stench of sickness and unwashed bodies assailed Travay's nose. Her stomach roiled.

A small, forlorn figure in a makeshift bed in the corner drew

Travay's attention. Sydney. She walked over and looked down at him. He opened his eyes but couldn't seem to focus, he was so sick.

"He's come down with a strange fever, milady." Mama Penn laid her hand upon his forehead and shook her dark head tied up in a red scarf.

Travay's heart caught in her throat. She knelt down and took the boy's hand in hers. Suddenly he turned to her.

"Muther! I knew you'd come back. Why did you go 'way?"

Travay's gaze shot up to Mama Penn. The woman wiped away a tear.

The boy tossed aside the dirty blanket and looked up at the rain-soaked boards above. "Please, Muther, won't you sing our little song for me? I can almost hear it now." The ship rolled in the storm, and Travay had to hold the thin body on the cot. He reached arms around her neck. She blinked away tears and began to hum a song her mother had taught her. Soon she began to sing the words to the lullaby, gently rocking the thin, hot body clinging to her. She closed her eyes.

Mama Penn worked around the beds, tying the now quieted men to their bunks. Travay did not notice the towering, rain-soaked form that came to stand at the door to the sick bay.

❧ ❦

Lucas could scarcely believe what he saw. Travay knelt beside Sydney's cot, rocking him in her arms and filling the foul-smelling room with the sweet sounds of an angel. All ears seemed to be tuned to the heavenly singing coming from Sydney's corner.

"Oh, Captain Bloodstone! I'se glad you's come." Mama Penn cast hurting eyes toward the two in the corner and then continued her work among the sailors' cots.

For a moment, Lucas couldn't move. The sound of the storm raged above deck, and the ship tossed about under his helmsman's steerage, but here was an island of peace. Not finding the women in the cabin had drawn him to the sick bay.

Travay glanced at him but didn't move. Tears coursed down her cheeks. A spasm coursed through the boy's body, and she bowed her head to look down at him. Lucas rushed to her side. He knelt and gently unwound the thin arms from around her neck, then laid Sydney back on the cot. In death, the sweetest look of tranquility rested on the young face.

Lucas' heart crushed against his ribs and choked off his breath. He closed the eyelids over the unseeing eyes and rocked back on his heels, shaking his head.

❧ ☙

Groaning, Travay stumbled to her feet and ran across the room. Later, she didn't even remember climbing the rain-swept steps of the sick bay to the upper deck. She barely recognized Seema standing at the top as if waiting for her.

The heavy wind and rain whipped Seema's clothing back and forth. She reached out a hand to Travay as if to guide her, and Travay latched onto it. Then they battled their way across the deck, hanging on to the railing and trying to keep upright as the ship rolled with the waves.

Suddenly, Seema wrenched her hand away and pushed Travay. That was all it took. Travay hit the deck and slid to the other side as the ship tossed in the strong wind.

Her full skirts billowed and then soaked up the driving rain like a sponge. She grasped for something, anything to stop her slide across the tilting deck. A huge wave washed over the railing and left her sputtering for air. She knew she must find something to grasp or the wave would take her back with it. She found a thick black boot.

❧ ☙

Bounding up the steps, Lucas saw Seema push Travay. At that moment, he could have thrown the slave woman over the railing without regret, but he knew he had only moments to save Travay from being washed overboard. He reached her and stopped her roll on the deck by grabbing her flapping skirt while holding onto the nearest rail. When Travay wrapped her arms around his boot, he slowly bent, pulled her up from the deck, and clasped her to his side.

"Put your arms around my waist, Travay, and lock your hands." For once, she obeyed without hesitation. Her soaked skirts added great weight, and the blowing rain almost blinded them both, but Lucas half dragged her the length of the railing toward the cabin hatch. Once, they both fell to their knees. Finally, they reached the steps, and Lucas staggered down them, still holding Travay to him. He kicked the cabin door open and slammed it shut behind them.

Travay loosened her grasp around his waist and sank onto the floor under the weight of her drenched skirts. With one hand, she pushed back the wet hair blinding her and looked up at Lucas. "Thank you for saving me." Then her lips tightened. "Once again, I find myself indebted to you." Her voice sounded rusty as a nail, and her eyes were cold.

Lucas' jaw hardened as he looked at her. She was the most spoiled, ungrateful woman he had ever had the bad luck to know. "Travay, tie yourself down on the bunk until the storm's over. Don't even think of venturing back out on deck. Do you hear me?" The ship climbed another wave and started down the trough. Lucas grabbed a chair tumbling toward him. He pushed it against the wall and stabilized it behind the heavy chest. He did the same to other loose items knocking about the cabin.

Travay, holding on to the edge of the bunk, marveled that he never seemed to lose his footing. Then she remembered Sydney. The boy had died in her arms. A wail escaped her lips.

"Are you all right?" Lucas swung toward her, holding on to anything that wasn't moving in the rolling ship.

"Sydney." Her lips trembled.

Lucas touched her shoulder. "Thank you for what you did for the boy, Travay."

Tears flowed down her cheeks. She pushed his hand aside and screamed at him. "Go away. What was a young boy like Sydney doing on this pirate ship? I hate this ship. And I hate *you!*"

She saw him recoil and wished she could take back her last words. But she couldn't. Instead, she swiped her wet cheeks with the sleeve of her gown. "Just get me to my aunt in Charles Town."

"Yes, ma'am. That's the plan." Lucas ground the words out between his teeth and made his way back to the door. He jerked it open and slammed it behind him.

CHAPTER 9

T ravay sat on the porch of Merle Allston's townhouse in Charles Town the morning after her arrival. She wore a light green shawl Mama Penn insisted she wear against the early morning spring air flowing in from the Atlantic. The African woman had chosen to come with Travay to her aunt's home, and Aunt Merle welcomed the household help.

The heady scent of narcissus at the edge of the walk filled Travay with well-being. Life seemed filled with promise now that she was safe in Charles Town. But life had taught her, if nothing else, that promises couldn't always be counted on. What appeared at first a shining opportunity might end in bitter disappointment.

She drew a calming breath, squared her shoulders, and glanced over the edge of the walled flower garden. Between the palmettos, she glimpsed the ocean beyond and the sky joining with it in a blue haze. Immediately, Lucas invaded her thoughts. Again, she saw him recoil when she'd told him she hated him. Fie! How could she hate the man who filled her dreams? Where was he? Would he stay docked in Charles Town long or head back out to sea and his infamous buccaneering? When the thought of his handsome, chiseled face brought back the memory of a kiss, she shook her head and clenched her eyes shut.

"Are you having a pain of some sort, Travay?"

Travay's eyes popped open. Her aunt stood at the corner of the porch, looking at her with concern. Travay had not noticed Merle walk up from the side of the house after her inspection of the roses just beginning to form buds. She cast about for something to say. "No, no. I'm fine. I was just wondering, thinking that the pink satin will probably be fine for the Drake soiree." Her aunt had given her several hand-me-down gowns since Travay had nothing except what Lucas had given her on the ship.

Merle climbed the steps and sat in the wicker chair beside Travay. "I have an idea for a new gown for you, dear, and I'm going to find the money to get it. I think I have just enough in the savings from my little sachet business."

Travay had been surprised to find her aunt had a small business she'd developed from her love of gardening. Roses, zinnias, lavender, mint, and other blossoms Travay could not name grew in every square inch of the garden surrounding the house. After harvest, they hung in bunches to dry in the carriage shed, which Merle used as her workshop. An elderly African servant helped with the gardening. His wife embroidered the small sacks for the dried petals and worked as housekeeper. The two lived over the carriage house and always smelled of lavender and mint, which Travay loved. "Oh, Aunt, I don't want you to have to go to extra expense for me. Truly, I am just so glad to live here with you. That's enough. We can just add some lace or ruffles to the dress, and it should be fine."

"No, your birthday will be soon after, and I had already planned to do something special for you. After all, you'll be eighteen and the perfect marriageable age. So don't worry about the cost. I am sure Esther, my seamstress, will treat me right. She's sewed for me many years."

Travay lowered her head. She had not dreamed, when she arrived from Jamaica, that her widowed aunt would have any worries about money. After moving from Charles Town to the islands upon her remarriage, Travay's mother had little contact with Merle, who had been married to Travay's uncle on her father's side. But Travay had kept up a writing relationship with her interesting aunt who was also her only living relative.

Merle relaxed in her chair. "My husband had the same addiction as many other colonial planters—gambling. He may have lost the plantation, but I am not penniless—not yet, my dear. And a new dress you shall have."

"I really wish you wouldn't, Aunt Merle." Travay sighed. Her aunt always seemed happy and at peace, but had she given Travay the full picture of her financial situation?

"Had your father lived, or had your widowed mother not married Karston Reed, your coming out this year as a prosperous planter's daughter would have shown this colony a thing a two. And, I might add, we would have had all the eligible gentlemen at the door, trying to win your hand." Merle smiled and gave Travay's arm an energetic pat. "You're so pretty, you can still have a herd begging for your favor. Why shouldn't we just go ahead and introduce you with a beautiful gown? The right marriage could secure your future." Then she added confidently, "And I assure you, Charles Town has not forgotten the Allston name."

Her aunt stood. "But enough of this serious talk. We have to get ready for your first Charles Town ball."

That night, Travay laid her head on her pillow, finally excited about the coming soiree. They had spent the day looking at fabrics and patterns that now danced through her mind. She heard the clip-clop of horses' hooves and the rumble of carriages on the cobblestone street below her window. She had not heard such sounds from her Jamaica plantation window the past four years. Instead, she'd gone to sleep listening to the humming of crickets and the trade winds rustling the curtains—sleepy sounds she'd grown used to. She yawned and surrendered to slumber.

She was on Arundel, and Roger Poole stood in front of her, reaching for the horse's reins. She had to get away! With a terrible sob, she whacked her whip on the filly's trembling rump. But then she saw the cliff. Arundel's front legs came up, and her tossing head knocked Travay in the forehead. They leaped out into sheer nothingness. Travay screamed.

"Travay! Travay, wake up!"

Her aunt stood over the bed. Mama Penn flew through the door, huffing and puffing as if she'd run up the entire staircase.

Tears gathered in Travay's eyes and flowed down her cheeks as she looked at them both. "I am so sorry. I was having a bad dream."

Mama Penn leaned over the bed and looked into her face. "I sez you was. Was it that cliff again?"

Travay nodded.

"What cliff?" Merle looked at Mama Penn, then Travay.

"It was just a bad dream. Please, both of you go back and get your rest. I am so sorry I awakened you." Travay sighed. She had not told her aunt all the details of how she'd left Jamaica. She hated to even think about it, much less talk about it.

Mama Penn fluffed Travay's pillow and then lumbered out the door. Finally, her aunt also tiptoed away.

❦

Lucas sat in his small merchant's office on the second floor of a building at the end of the Charles Town dock. A wooden block on the edge of his table repeated the sign on the closed door: Sutherland Mercantile Company. One of Lucas' favorite people sat across the desk, Reverend Ethan Wentworth. Lucas had come to know the Presbyterian minister and his wife, Hannah, on his last trip from London. They had requested passage in such a desperate way that he found he couldn't refuse them. Ethan had once sailed the sea himself, as a privateer. On that long sea voyage, Lucas had come to embrace the Wentworths as true friends. Lucas also came to know their God as his Lord and Savior.

"Lucas, you haven't told me everything about this last voyage, have you?" The minister's gray eyes carried no accusation. In his late twenties, Ethan was a few years older than Lucas. With his strong physique, he looked more like the seaman he once was than a minister who spent long hours at his texts. This was what had first caught Lucas' attention when they met. He also differed from the English clergy Lucas had known in his youth in several other ways. For one, Wentworth believed in a God who had the power to change things, including pirates.

Lucas leaned back in his chair with his arms behind his head and threw his booted foot up on the end of the desk. "How is it you can read me like a book, Ethan?"

Wentworth chuckled. "Some would call that a gift from God, my man. Suffice it to say that I discern a new light in those remarkable eyes, and I suspect it might have something to do with the opposite sex. Are we talking about the young woman you sent to us, Seema, by any chance?"

Lucas jerked his boot back to the floor and sat up. "Hell's bells! No! I can't believe you even had such a thought. I sent that vixen to you to straighten up if there's any hope of it."

"There's always hope, as long as there's life, Lucas." The minister cocked his chin. "Just like there was hope for you before you saw the light." Again, Ethan's eyes held no reproach for Lucas' outburst of pirate vernacular. "If not Seema, then who? There is a woman somewhere who has sparked your interest. Am I right?"

Lucas stood and looked out the dirt-smudged window at the harbor below. Numerous ships bobbed alongside each other. Sloops, two-masted and square topsail schooners, ketches, brigantines like his *Blue Heron*, and a medley of lesser vessels bumped against the long dock. He didn't speak for several seconds.

"So you've got it that bad?"

"No, a thousand times no." Lucas came and sat back down. Would the minister understand if he told him about Travay? Yet, to speak of her would be like opening an old wound, one that reached back to his childhood. Three weeks in Charles Town had hardly dulled the edges of his pain.

"Why is it I get the idea that the thousandth and one time will be yes?"

The man was uncanny. Lucas had often thought it since he met him. Ethan seemed to have some kind of supernatural power, maybe from God, to get Lucas to unload his heavy heart.

"Yes, there was another young woman who took passage on

my ship from Jamaica." He told the story of his rescue of Travay and his coming to recognize her as his old childhood playmate. And her pure hatred of pirates.

"Well, your pirate days are over, are they not, my friend? Wasn't this last voyage the adventure to end all such adventures?" Ethan's piercing look struck Lucas' heart.

"I thought so until that Spanish captain told me about my father's death and that my mother might still be alive."

"I am sorry if that is true about your father, Lucas. But he could have been lying about both your parents to get you off his back."

Lucas slammed his fist on the desk and then looked an apology toward the minister, who had jumped in his chair. His voice softened. "Yes, I've thought of that, Ethan. A lot. But I think he was telling me the truth. I can remember my mother saying that Father had a weak heart. Even as a boy, I knew she worried about him. And as far as the captain taking mother to be a governess, she was a born teacher and wonderful with children. Almost anyone could see that. And she was a real lady, from the nobility herself. In fact, she still has a brother in England I've never told you about, Lord Graylyn Cooper. I've never met him, but she often talked of him."

"I'm sorry I never met your mother, Lucas. And I can see how those qualities might have indeed caused the Spanish to spare her. But what is your plan? How can you possibly hope to find her, much less rescue her?" The minister lowered his voice. "If she still lives."

"That's what I must find out." Lucas leaned toward Ethan and looked him straight in the eye. "Tell me, wouldn't you try to do the same if it were your mother?"

"Yes, yes, I suppose so. I will pray for your wisdom and safety." Then a very serious look crossed the minister's face as he stood to leave. "I would hate to see you hanged at low tide as a pirate, Lucas, even if you do have a letter of marque right now. England's alliances and enemies can change overnight." He paused and breathed deeply. "And it would break Hannah's heart and mine. Did you know there's to be a hanging next week?"

Lucas flinched and then smiled a brittle smile. "Just keep praying, Ethan. I put a lot of stock in your prayers and Hannah's. How is she, by the way?"

The thick atmosphere lightened.

"She is doing well in this longed-for spring weather and new life bursting out everywhere we look. And having Seema here to help after the baby arrives is really an answer to prayer. Thank you for sending her to us. Hannah has taken her under her wing. I believe one day you'll see a real change in that young woman."

"That's good news, Ethan. If anyone can effect a real change in Seema, it will be your wife." Lucas chuckled. Seema would be a handful, even for the kindhearted, hardworking, and wise Hannah.

Ethan turned at the door. "Actually, I am talking about Seema's coming to trust the Lord as you have, Lucas. You know man can only be an instrument in God's hand for that work." Ethan lingered a moment. "By the way, are you going to the Drakes' ball? I know you aren't considered nobility here, but there's always a shortage of single men, even if they are wage earners like merchants." He grinned. "If they're not suspected of being pirates, that is.

Lucas waved an invitation from his desk. "I guess John Sutherland should make an appearance."

❧ ☙

Travay stood at the mirror in her bedroom as her aunt and Mama Penn adjusted the satin folds of the lovely new azure gown with its ivory Chantilly lace at the dipped neckline, along the bouffant sleeves, and hem.

Merle clapped her hands, and a wide smile lit her face. "This color brings out the blue of your eyes, Travay, and the shine in your curls. I knew I was saving the lace for something special." Then she turned to the black woman. "Mama Penn, would you please bring the box that I laid out this morning on the top of my dresser?"

"Yes'm." She left, and her heavy steps echoed down the hall.

"Aunt Merle, if you're not going, how can I travel alone to the ball?" Travay's brows knit as she looked at her aunt in the mirror.

"Now don't you worry. Everything is taken care of, even your escort for the ball. Our dear family solicitor, John Hawkins, has agreed to come by for you in his lovely carriage. Said he'd be delighted."

Travay turned to stare at her aunt, surprised at this news. She vaguely remembered him coming to their plantation to see her father in earlier years. He seemed old then. "But he's old enough to be my grandfather, Aunt Merle."

"Yes, he is, but he's known by everyone in Charles Town, and he is the very best one to introduce you. If it hadn't been for his wisdom and quick action, Travay, I might have ended up on the street when George passed."

"I wish you were going, Aunt."

Mama Penn returned and handed a small box to Merle.

"Well, you know I feel pretty young, but all that standing, not to mention dancing, would be a little much." Merle opened the velvet box. "Here, let me clasp this around that pretty neck."

Travay gasped at the glistening pearl and diamond necklace her aunt held up. Surely it was worth a fortune. She bent her head for her aunt to fasten it in place. The pearls glowed against her neck as if they held a life of their own. The interspersed diamonds caught every sparkle of light and winked the colors of the rainbow when she glanced in the mirror.

"I saved this piece my mother left me, and one day I want you to have it. So why not enjoy it now? Here are the matching earrings."

Tears gathered in Travay's eyes. "Oh, Aunt Merle. You are too good to me." Travay affixed the tiny pearl earrings.

Mama Penn stood looking out the window to the street. "Yo gentleman's carriage is here, chile."

"Go and greet Mr. Hawkins, Mama Penn. Take him to the library. Tell him we'll be there in a cat's whisker." Merle bent and patted Travay's blue ruffled skirt, which surrounded her like a cloud. Soon every ruffle was in place.

When Travay and Merle entered the library, their visitor looked up and laid down the book he'd been thumbing through. His attention flew from the older woman to Travay behind her. He caught Travay's eye and smiled.

Heat spread over Travay's cheeks at his quick perusal. Her escort was not the solicitor John Hawkins, but a handsome young man in a British military uniform, his blond hair tied neatly back in a queue.

Merle had stopped in her tracks and stared. "Oh. Are you John's grandson? I didn't know he ever married or had a child." Merle stopped. Pink overspread her face.

"He never did, and he doesn't. I'm his nephew—to be exact, his great-nephew." The man bowed to both Merle and Travay and stepped forward. "Captain James Hawkins, of His Majesty's Royal Navy, at your service." Merle lifted her hand to him. He took it and bowed again.

"Captain Hawkins, you do have John's coloring. I remember him when he was younger, and you certainly do favor him. May I present my niece, Travay Allston."

The captain turned to Travay, and a deep smile lit his tanned face. "How do you do, Miss Allston? I trust you do not regret my uncle's sending me in his stead?" His cobalt eyes twinkled, set off by his navy blue military dress coat with its gold buttons and white facing.

Travay smiled and extended her hand. "How do you do, Captain Hawkins? I hope you don't regret coming in your uncle's place." She withdrew her hand when he held on a little long.

Merle handed Travay a silk wrap, and the couple walked to the waiting coach. Mama Penn followed. A man in spotless red livery bowed and opened the gilded door. The carriage glowed in polished oak, with golden trim outside and red-and-gold satin inside. Captain Hawkins offered Travay his hand, and she stepped up and sat. He climbed in and sat across from her.

Mama Penn reached in to help arrange Travay's gown and preserve its yards of fabric from the slightest wrinkle. The ruffles spilled across the carriage and over the captain's shining black boots. "Now chile, you dance but don't you get overtired. Sit out some, you hear?"

Travay smiled and placed her blue lace reticule and matching fan in her lap. Why did she feel this evening might change her life? For no reason she could fathom, a chill traveled up her spine.

※ ❧

Lucas dusted the finishing touches of powder on his periwig and spread the white paste on his face to hide his tan. He glued a fake mole on the left side of his smooth chin, pulled on shiny dress shoes with wide buckles, and pushed a perfumed handkerchief up his sleeve. Lastly, he placed the pince-nez in the breast pocket of his green silk topcoat. He leaned toward the small mirror, gave one more adjustment to his white silk cravat, and turned around.

Dwayne Thorpe grinned at him. "You're the real thing, Lucas. A perfect colonial fop. No one in their wildest imagination could think of you as Captain Bloodstone who sails the southern seas."

Lucas bowed toward Thorpe, who was dressed as his footman, and forced his voice half an octave higher. "Let us go, my man, and astound every forlorn maiden in search of a rich husband." He winked and added in his normal deep voice, "And infuriate every pushy mama and grandmama who wishes a title with the riches."

On the way to Sir Oliver Drake's townhouse, Lucas' thoughts wandered and, as usual, ended up with Travay's face haunting him. Thorpe had assured him he had delivered her to her aunt's home, which overlooked Charles Town Bay. Lucas had ridden by it and decided she must be in good hands. Not many could afford the bay houses—and one with such a large garden as well. He pushed further thoughts about it away and set his mind to being the epitome of a colonial merchant. He pulled the lace-edged handkerchief from his sleeve as the carriage rolled up to the townhouse entrance and placed the pince-nez on his nose.

In spite of their careful planning, they somehow arrived late.

"Mr. John Sutherland," the servant at the door announced as Lucas entered. He acknowledged the introduction with a brief wave of his handkerchief and looked around the room.

"How good of you to come to our little soiree, Mr. Sutherland." Lady Drake, his hostess, came forward beaming. She extended her hand and glanced at the far wall, where several young ladies stood whispering behind bright silk fans.

Lucas bowed to his hostess and headed past the ladies, ignoring their giggles. As he skimmed over them with the slightest of smiles, the glasses almost slid from the bridge of his nose. Travay stood apart next to a window. The azure gown enhanced her ivory skin and silky hair, and when she turned her eyes to him, he almost spoke her name. Instead, he adjusted the pince-nez, gave her a slight bow and moved away, trying to breathe again. She had only glanced at him and then spoke to an English captain standing at her side. A pain crossed his gut as he remembered her last words to him before leaving the ship. Did the most beautiful woman in the world, who constantly invaded his dreams and often his daytime thoughts, actually hate him? He prayed not. Even if he never spent another moment alone with her, he did not want her to hate him.

Lucas leaned on an ivy-entwined column that led to the entrance of the dining room and watched Travay unobserved. She was the vision of his dreams in her gown, which flowed out from her small waist like a pale-blue cloud. The pearl and diamond necklace at her throat gleamed in the candlelight and caught Lucas' eye. It was a stunning piece, and it confirmed to him that Travay's aunt was well able to take care of her. He breathed a sigh of relief and then looked at the man who was obviously her escort. Who was he, besides a captain in His Majesty's Navy? Travay seemed taken with the man, or at least she was looking into his face and smiling like she'd never smiled at Lucas. The blond man stepped closer to Travay and leaned to speak to her. She laughed. Heat traveled up Lucas' neck and a new, prickly feeling unsettled him—the knife-sharp pangs of raw jealousy.

The hostess approached the couple. She drew the captain away with her, and Travay gave him a tiny wave, then turned her head to see the latest arrival enter the hall. She stiffened, and her face turned white as a snowflake. Lucas followed her frozen stare. The butler's voice rang out the introduction.

Sir Roger Poole. In his finest silks and satins.

CHAPTER 10

Bile rose in Lucas' throat at the sight of his childhood enemy. Gone was the chubby boy Lucas remembered—he had grown into a vain man. Several of the young women against the wall took notice and tittered behind their fans.

Poole gave a small tug to his perfectly knotted white cravat and scanned the room. He stiffened, and his eyes widened when he saw Travay.

She turned away and hurried past Lucas into the dining room.

Sir Roger followed. "Travay, my dear, how delighted I am to see you alive and well." That egotistical voice had no effect on Travay's retreat. She flew through the dining room doors onto the veranda, with Poole close behind.

Lucas followed Sir Roger and stopped at the door within hearing distance. What an odd thing for Poole to say. He was glad to see her *alive*? Leaning forward, Lucas saw Travay turn and confront Poole. Anger contorted her lovely face.

"How dare you follow me out here, Roger, when I never want to see your face again. Didn't you get the message in Jamaica when I risked my life to get away from you?"

So her flight over the cliff was from the trussed up snake Roger Poole. Lucas' gut twisted. Everything in him wanted to grab the man by his silk collar and pound the life out of him. Not even Reverend Wentworth's face popping into Lucas' mind lessened the desire to do the man harm. He took a ragged breath and stayed concealed.

Sir Roger moved closer to Travay. "But my dear, you can't possibly mean that. Don't you realize I've loved you since you were just a little girl, running around like a tomboy with that no-account Lucas Barrett? I must say, you look absolutely stunning tonight—no evidence of that tomboy at all."

❧ ☙

Travay swallowed hard trying to stop the choking sensation rising in her throat. "I detest even the sight of you, Roger Poole. I have prayed I would never see you again!" She threw the words at him like stones.

He looked at her with a sardonic expression and took a step closer. His strong form and fast breathing chilled Travay. Any other woman might have appreciated his handsome face and apparent wealth, but she detested everything about him, even the smell of him. Despite having bathed, dressed in finery, and undoubtedly used an expensive perfume, the man's own scent rose above it all and sickened her.

"Have you forgotten, my lovely one, that I still own our old Charles Town plantation that was next to your own, before your illustrious stepfather lost it? And, of course, I also now own the Jamaican plantation. Oh, and I am so sorry to tell you, but your dear stepfather has … succumbed. Just a month after you disappeared, in fact. But, be assured, I am here to take care of you."

Her stepfather dead? Her eyes narrowed. "How did he die, Sir Roger? Did you kill him?"

"Oh my dear, no. I am no murderer." Sir Roger cleared his throat. "Actually, he, uh, died in a duel over a gambling debt. But not with me, of course. I actually liked the man." He flipped a handkerchief from his sleeve and touched his nose.

She inched back from him until her back pressed into the veranda trellis. "I guess you did. You won everything he owned." *You even thought you had won me.*

"My dear girl, I won those plantations fair and square, even though they were gambling prizes. But let's not talk about it." He

❧ 90 ☙

leaned toward her. "I have a more pleasant surprise for you. You are going to see a lot of me in Charles Town now."

She frowned at the self-satisfaction on Sir Roger's face. No surprise from him could be pleasant.

He moved closer, blocking her escape. "Let me introduce myself to you." He gave a bow. "The newest Charles Town Council Member at your service."

Travay gasped. He took advantage of her momentary shock and pulled her into his arms.

She balled two fists against his chest and tried to push away, but he only leaned in closer. His overdone perfume made her nauseated.

"I think it best you release the lady, sir."

A man stood in the patio entrance. His eyes, hard as steel, bored into Sir Roger's back. His voice carried authority and sounded familiar to Travay. But no, she was sure she had never seen the man prior to his entrance tonight. She'd hardly glanced at him—a fop if there ever was one. She didn't even remember his name.

Sir Roger turned with a sneer on his lips, and his hand moved inside his maroon silk waistcoat. "Really? And just who are you?"

"A friend of Lady Drake, my lord. John Sutherland."

❦

Lucas raised his voice half an octave and played his role to the hilt. He even gave a small bow, though what he really wanted to do was smash his fist into the smirking face of Roger Poole.

At that moment, the veranda door opened, and the hostess sailed out. "Oh, there you are Sir Roger. And John." She looked at Travay. "And Miss Allston, I believe?"

Travay nodded and took a breath as Sir Roger stepped back. Had the woman seen the exchange from the window?

"Sir Roger," the hostess continued, "I have several guests asking about you and your new appointment. Won't you come talk to them? And Mr. Sutherland, perhaps you can persuade Miss Allston to dance with you? Her captain seems to have been captured by others." She held out her hand to Sir Roger, who had no choice but to offer his arm and escort her inside. At the door, he turned to give a black look at the man who had interrupted.

Lucas adjusted his pince-nez and stepped toward Travay. "May I have this dance, Miss Allston?" How he wished his smile, his presence, could wipe the desolate expression off Travay's face as her eyes followed Sir Roger and the hostess through the door.

❧

Travay nodded and allowed John Sutherland to escort her back inside to the dance floor. Her mind in a dark fog, she stumbled in the minuet steps more than once. She was thankful her partner was adept and alert. He certainly didn't move like a soft fop, more like a swordsman. And he had a much more pleasant scent than Roger Poole, spicy with a touch of lemon. But what was she going to do now that Roger had found her? No one knew better than she his determination to get what he wanted. Now that he had more power than ever before, how could she have a moment's peace?

A face from two months earlier floated into her troubled mind. Captain Bloodstone—Lucas Barrett. How many times had he rescued her? That was a man who would not back down from a threat. But he was assuredly back on the seas, doing what he did best: pirating. And likely remembering her last hateful words. If only she could take them back. She sighed deeply, drawing her partner's attention. His green eyes behind the pince-nez startled her. She blinked. She must be transferring her thoughts of a long-gone pirate to an overdressed colonial merchant.

When the minuet ended, Captain Hawkins appeared at Travay's side.

John Sutherland bowed and adjusted his pince-nez. She noticed his hand for the first time. How could a tradesman who sat behind a desk most days have such strong, tanned hands? And though his face was white with fashionable paste, a bronzed, corded neck bulged from his cravat.

The man moved away, and Captain Hawkins led her toward the table of refreshments.

❦

Lucas could hardly breathe while dancing with Travay. When her escort led her away, he went to the sidelines and breathed deeply. He could not take his eyes from her, and he knew better than to dance with her again. She seemed lost in deep thought—troubling thoughts by the set of her brow. He was glad of it, for if she had not been so preoccupied, she could have recognized him.

He was sure Roger Poole had everything to do with Travay's unease. But this was not Jamaica. The scoundrel might have gotten away with forcing his attentions on her there, but he couldn't do the same at Charles Town. Here British order ruled—at least most days—even for Council Members. He smiled and relaxed a little.

To make his hostess happy, he danced with several of the young women lining the wall and found more than one of them hinting under fluttering lashes for a walk on the moonlit veranda. But Lucas had little interest, and he rejected the idea of leaving early. He would not leave Travay at the soiree as long as Roger Poole stood next to the laden refreshment table. Although Poole was talking with Lady Drake, his eyes followed Travay's every move.

Travay danced several sets with the captain and quite a few other young men. They stood in line, and Lucas couldn't blame them. She was easily the most enchanting woman on the floor.

Lucas chose another dance partner. At the right moment, he asked his partner, a giddy girl of no more than sixteen, about the English captain.

"Oh, he's Captain James Hawkins, old Mr. Hawkins' nephew and new in our midst." She giggled. "And believe me, all of the belles are hoping for a dance with him, even if he may not be in port long." Then wistfully, "That Allston girl seems to have captured him for the rest of the evening. But, after all, he is her escort."

"Do you know why he was posted to Charles Town?"

"Oh, yes. My papa says Captain Hawkins has been sent by the king to stop the pirates in our southern seas. Isn't that exciting?" Her eyes glowed with admiration.

Lucas stiffened. "I suppose so. We can wish him good hunting."

After the set, Lucas bowed farewell to his partner and walked to the table laden with food, where he filled a plate.

Sometime later, he looked up to see Travay and her escort heading to the door. Lady Drake hurried toward them from another part of the ballroom. "Leaving already? But the night is still young, Captain Hawkins."

"Yes, it is, but I am due to sail early in the morning, milady. And this young lady," he bowed toward Travay, "says she has danced her limit for the next two months. We thank you for a wonderful evening. It has been delightful." His face creased into a warm smile, and he turned to help Travay with her wrap.

Travay nodded to the hostess. "Yes, thank you so much, Lady Drake, for inviting me."

"Young lady, I hate to see you go, but I expect a few other young guests are smiling behind their fans, as dance partners will now be more available." The hostess leaned over and gave Travay a quick hug.

Wolfing down another miniature sandwich, Lucas let his eyes sweep over Travay. He would not soon forget how lovely she looked tonight. He would have a good memory for his coming weeks at sea.

As the door closed behind the pair, Roger Poole approached his hostess. "You say she lives with an aunt on the Bay?"

❧ ❧

On the carriage ride back to town, Travay tried to keep up a polite conversation with Captain Hawkins, but her heart sat like lead in her chest. Roger Poole had found her.

The captain said something to her. She glanced at him and realized he was awaiting her response. "Oh, I am sorry, what did you say?" She had trouble keeping her concentration on the conversation. Sir Roger's leering image kept intruding in her thoughts.

He smiled, reached over, and patted her hand with his gloved one. "I didn't realize how tired you must be. I heard your servant tell you to sit out some sets, but you didn't have a chance, did you? I said I am sorry I won't be in Charles Town longer this first trip."

She searched for a reply. "What did you hope to do here, Captain?"

Now he really grinned at her. "Why, if I could be here longer, I would be delighted to get to know you better, Miss Allston." He leaned to glance into her face.

Heat warmed her cheeks, but she avoided his gaze. "You did say this is your first trip here?"

"Yes. I am sure I will be back in a few months with some prizes."

Travay longed to arrive home and make it to her bedroom, where she could release the full grief of her burdened heart. But she still tried to keep up her part of the conversation. "What sort of prizes, Captain?"

"Why pirates, of course. The king has commissioned the HMS *Greyhound*, a fully outfitted man-of-war, to chase, confront, and arrest any pirates, or privateers acting as pirates, found in these southern seas. I have the honor to command her." He lifted his chin as his voice rose with confidence.

She stiffened, then shut her eyes and dropped her head back against the seat. A certain pirate with long black braids and emerald eyes rose larger than life behind her clenched eyelids.

"Miss Allston, are you all right? Did my talk of pirates frighten you?" The captain reached for her hand.

Travay lifted her head and set her countenance into a calm pose. "No, of course not. Pirates … are just part of colonial life, are they not?"

When they arrived at Merle's house, the captain jumped down from the coach and helped her alight with a firm clasp to steady her. He continued to hold her hand as he escorted her to the door. There, he released it and bowed.

"Miss Allston, I can't tell you what a pleasure this evening has been. Just the right send-off for a captain in His Majesty's forces headed out to sea on a dangerous mission. May I call on you when I return?"

She considered the fine, chiseled features of Captain Hawkins. He had been a perfect gentleman, and he'd helped keep Sir Roger at bay at the ball. Perhaps he could do so again one day. But how dangerous would he be to Captain Bloodstone? Lucas was probably on the high seas now, unaware a British man-of-war would sail from Charles Town harbor with the morning tide with orders to rid the waters of pirates, or privateers acting as pirates, the man had said. Would Lucas' letter of marque protect him from this new thrust against piracy?

Tired, she replied as if in a dream, "Yes, I think you may call again, Captain Hawkins. And I wish you a safe journey." *If not success.*

Later, after pacing the floor with her heavy thoughts, Travay dropped into her canopied bed in the wee hours of the morning. Fear for Lucas' safety gripped her mind and kept her from relaxing. Hope tried to rise in her heart that he had given up piracy, but had he?

Another question burned in her mind: Should she tell her aunt the whole sordid story about Roger Poole and his pursuit of her? She had tried to block from her mind the night she'd jumped from the cliff into the Caribbean. She had only told her aunt about her stepfather's mistreatment and her decision to come to Charles Town. Perhaps Sir Roger would not be able to discover where she and her aunt lived, at least for a while.

She punched her pillow and turned over, hoping for sleep, but a face came into her mind: John Sutherland's. Lady Drake seemed to accept him as a well-to-do Charles Town merchant, perhaps a good catch for someone's older daughter. But Travay remembered the way he danced, so light on his feet like a swordsman, even though he was a big man. And his strong, tanned hands were hardly the hands of a merchant who sat at a desk. A soldier, perhaps. Just before sleep overtook her, she saw again the surprising color of his eyes. The man had eyes like … Lucas.

CHAPTER 11

The following morning, as Travay concluded the finishing touches to her toilette, a carriage pulled up below, in front of the house. She hurried to the window and drew aside the curtain as a man stepped from the carriage. She gasped.

Sir Roger Poole had found her.

She pressed her lips into a tight line and tiptoed into the hall. Stopping behind a planter at the top of the stairs, she leaned forward to hear what Roger might have on his mind. She hoped her aunt would tell him that she would sleep for some time after her late night at the ball.

When the knocker sounded, Mama Penn's heavy steps trudged from the kitchen to the door. Sunshine flowed through the entrance as she opened it.

"Good morning. I have come to see Lady Merle Allston. I am Sir Roger Poole." He handed the servant a card and stepped across the threshold. Travay shivered with dislike at the sound of his voice as well as his pompous attire. His flamboyant green jacket and breeches fit like a glove, and he boasted a white silk shirt with a lace cravat and more lace at his wrists. He also wore a full brown wig that curled to his shoulders.

Mama Penn took his hat and cane, muttering as she turned to take the card to Mrs. Allston.

Travay smiled at the woman's distinctive harrumph. Roger Poole could not fool the African woman, who was wise in the ways of worldly men.

"Who is it, Mama Penn?" Travay's aunt came up from the parlor and stopped mid-stride to stare at their visitor. Of course, her aunt would be surprised at what seemed like a fine-dressed gentleman coming to call. Travay shook her head. He was no gentleman.

"Hello, do I have the pleasure of greeting Lady Merle Allston? Let me introduce myself. I am Sir Roger Poole, and I've come to talk to you about your niece, Travay."

The man bowed. Merle extended her hand and smiled.

Travay's stomach roiled.

When the two withdrew to the parlor, she slipped silently down the stairs and positioned herself in the shadows beside the parlor door. Her heart pounded against her ribs

"I am so honored you were able to receive me, Madam." Sir Roger proceeded to tell Travay's aunt who he was, being sure to mention his ownership of estates in Charles Town and Jamaica.

"Yes, I do remember that the Pooles had an estate next to my husband's brother here in the Charles Town area. Are you part of that family?" Her aunt sounded impressed.

"Yes, but I've lived in Jamaica the past ten years. In fact, since my parents were lost at sea." Finally, as if saving the best for last, Roger bragged, "You may also be interested in knowing I am the newest member of the Charles Town Council."

"Oh, and are you—and I suppose you have a family of your own—planning to live in Charles Town now?" Merle asked.

"I am, although I have no family to speak of. That brings me to my reason for visiting this morning." He cleared his throat. "I came to speak to you about your niece, Miss Travay Allston. Since our Charles Town estate was next to her father's, we grew up together, and I also was acquainted with her mother and her stepfather later in Jamaica." He paused and assumed a sympathetic countenance. "Before they passed."

"Her stepfather has passed too?" Merle's voice sharpened with interest.

"Yes, I'm afraid he died some weeks ago. And, sad to say, he left nothing of an inheritance to Travay."

"Oh." Her aunt's voice dripped with disappointment.

Travay leaned against the wall. She felt only relief at her stepfather's death. Now he could not hunt her down and force his will on her. She grimaced. The same could not be said of Sir Roger. She peeped around the door at him.

"Your niece and I know each other very well. In fact, I ... wondered where she had gotten to until I saw her last night at the Drakes' ball." Sir Roger paused and glanced around her aunt's sparse parlor. He moistened his lips. Travay knew exactly what the man was probably thinking—that her Aunt Merle, and hence Travay, had limited financial resources.

"I am glad you and Travay are acquainted." Merle's voice rose with something new—hope. Then she added, "Travay has a number of acquaintances."

Travay shrank back and bit her lip, worried her aunt might be fooled by his act.

"I will come to the point, Lady Allston. I've decided it is time for me to settle down and have a family. I have loved Travay since we were children, and I would like to ask her hand in marriage. I can give her a secure future."

He stood and paced across the room. Travay pressed deep into the hall shadows.

When he stopped his parading, he took a seat closer to her aunt and leaned toward her. "I know Travay will come of age soon and can decide for herself, but I felt led to come to you with my suit first. Please tell me, is there any hope for me, dear Lady Allston?"

Travay stiffened. Her hands tightened into fists. *Aunt Merle, don't let this snake fool you. Tell him no, no, no!*

"Well, I will certainly talk with Travay later, but she's not available at the moment."

Merle's voice sounded too kind. Had he deceived her? Travay blinked back hot tears. She started to slip back up the stairs when Sir Roger's next question stopped her step in midair.

"May I call again tomorrow or later this week and see Travay?"

Her aunt's answer came after only a brief hesitation. "You may call again the day after tomorrow, on Friday. Come to tea at four o'clock."

"Thank you, my good lady. Thank you. I look forward to Friday."

Travay fled to her room, tears scalding her cheeks. She would tell her aunt the whole story about Roger Poole. And Merle would want to protect her. But she knew Roger well enough to know nothing her aunt could do would stop his pursuit. He would do whatever it took to break down all hindrances to anything he wanted. If only Lucas were in Charles Town, he'd know what to do. Even the English captain might have been some help. But he had sailed away on the morning tide.

Lucas pored over the new map of the Spanish trade routes. "Thorpe, this map is great. How in the world did you come by it?"

Dwayne Thorpe smiled. "I was busy last night with important things while you danced the night away with the Charles Town belles. Somebody had to keep his head."

Lucas threw a quill at him, which he ducked. "How soon can you get up a good crew for the *Blue Heron*?"

"A couple of days for a crew *and* supplies."

"You're a good man, Thorpe. Get Sinbad to help. We'll sail with the tide Friday at dawn." Lucas stuffed another breakfast roll into his mouth.

"Aye!" Sinbad shouted from across the room.

"Sinbad's been ready for weeks." Thorpe picked up the quill from the floor and placed it on Lucas' desk. He walked out the door, toward the dock and ale houses, with Sinbad's big form swaying by his side.

As soon as he could finish dressing in his merchant garments, Lucas—in his white wig and pince nez—visited Reverend Wentworth's small house at the edge of town. Seema opened the door to his knock. Her eyes glittered with what he was sure was some kind of secret. Had she guessed who he really was? And had she kept up her relationship with Byron Pitt? He frowned. If the answers were yes to both questions, she could cause problems. Pitt would love to know about Lucas' Charles Town disguise.

Seema lowered her lashes. "The minister and his wife have just finished breakfast and have gone out to the garden."

Lucas strode past her to the back of the small plot where his friends sat on a shady bench.

"Good morning," he said, taking Hannah's hand when she offered it and bowing. "I came to say goodbye and ask your prayers for our voyage. We sail at first tide Friday."

"So you are going on your search?" The minister's voice lowered as his gray eyes glanced back at the house, then to Lucas' face. "Are you sure this is the best thing, the wisest thing to do, Lucas?"

"I'll never rest unless I find out what happened to my mother, Ethan, and whether my father truly did succumb."

"Then we will pray for God's help and protection to guide you on your way, dear friend."

Hannah nodded and shielded her eyes from the morning sun as she studied Lucas' face. "We certainly will."

The pregnant young woman reminded Lucas of his own sweet mother's character and faith.

He smiled at her. "When I see you again, I expect there'll be another member of this family in a cradle."

"Oh, yes, just a few months away now. Thank you for sending us Seema. She will be a great help when the baby comes. And I am working with her. God has such a great plan for her life, but she does not know it yet."

"I do hope you are right, Hannah. If anyone can influence that young woman for the good, you can." Lucas took his leave and hurried back to his mercantile office.

If Seema did see through his disguise and even told Byron Pitt, what of it? There was nothing the man could do. On Friday, the *Blue Heron* would sail for the open sea—without Pitt or his buddies.

CHAPTER 12

Travay rushed into her room and washed her tear-stained face. Her aunt would soon come, and she needed to collect herself. She took a deep breath. A knock sounded at the door, and the familiar voice called out, "Travay, dear, are you up and dressed? I've some news for you."

"Yes, I'm up and dressed. Do come in, Aunt Merle."

"You will never guess who just visited. Sir Roger Poole! He said you two are well acquainted." Her aunt's brows rose.

Travay sank down on the edge of her bed and hung her head. "Yes, I am acquainted with Roger Poole, unfortunately."

Merle pulled the dressing table chair close to the bed and sat. "Why unfortunately? The Pooles are known to be a family of means and he's ... asked for your hand in marriage, my dear."

Travay looked up into her aunt's face. "No! No! Never!"

Merle drew back in her chair and crossed her arms. "Travay, I think you'd better tell me what this is all about. Why such angst about this man? He might be a good catch for someone."

Travay clenched her fists and licked her dry lips. "Aunt Merle, I did not tell you about Sir Roger Poole because I never wanted to think about him again. But I see I must tell you what happened in Jamaica."

"Yes, my dear, do." Merle leaned forward and reached for her niece's hand.

Travay told the story of her stepfather's gambling and Sir Roger Poole's pursuit. When she described jumping off the cliff on horseback, Merle gasped, drew her fan from her pocket, and fanned furiously.

"And a—a pirate rescued me, a Captain Bloodstone, who eventually brought me safely to Charles Town." She did not tell her aunt he was also a childhood playmate named Lucas Barrett. She was already exhausted from going over the disturbing story.

Merle stopped fanning, and her face turned pale. She stared, aghast. "A pirate? Are you telling me everything? Were you … hurt, my child?"

"No, no. I was not the only woman aboard, Aunt Merle. In fact, there were two others. As you know, Mama Penn was one of them, and she watched out for me like a hawk."

"Good. Well, I will do all in my power to help protect you from this scoundrel. But we must be wise as serpents. Did you know he is now a Council Member?"

"Yes, he was sure to brag about that the first thing at the Drakes' ball." She looked at her aunt and frowned. "What does that mean, Aunt Merle, the fact that he is a Council Member? Does that give him the right to force me to marry him?"

"No, but we will have to be most careful in how we receive and deal with him. As a Council Member, he does wield a great deal of power. Even though I cannot see right now how he could use that power against us." Her aunt looked around the room and sniffed.

"Receive him? Deal with him? What do you mean?" A shudder traveled up Travay's spine.

"It means he is coming here to tea Friday, and you and I will have to receive him."

"Oh no! Do we have to? Do I have to be present? Can't you just tell him my decision?"

Her aunt took a deep breath and straightened her shoulders. "I think you will need to receive him, but I will be by your side. The Lord will help us deal with this man, rascal that he is. Hopefully, it will be the last time you or I have to deal with him. Let's pray about it right now."

Travay sighed and knelt beside her aunt, who had dropped down beside the bed. Doubt rose in her mind. God had hardly helped her in the past. Would it be different now?

※ ♪

Thursday evening, Lucas prepared the finishing touches of his Captain Bloodstone identity and other details for the early morning departure of the *Blue Heron*. He tried to suppress a strong desire to see Travay before he sailed. Failing, he dressed in dark clothing, hid his braids under a hat, and slid a knife into his waist sash.

He slipped through the shadowy deserted streets as silently as a fox to the house where Travay and her aunt lived. He scaled the garden wall and dropped onto the soft ground beyond. Staying crouched for a moment, he listened. A swing squeaked in the middle of the garden. He stood and looked around the bushes. Travay sat in the falling twilight, swaying gently in the wooden seat, her long curls moving in the evening breeze. It was just the picture he needed to take with him. She was safe, happy.

Then he heard the sobs.

Lucas stepped out of the shadows.

Travay gasped and froze.

Lucas removed his hat and came closer. "Is anything wrong, Travay?" He softened his voice, but it still cut the silence like a rapier.

She wiped tears from her face. "Oh, Lucas, he's found me again. Roger Poole. I never told you, but he was the one I escaped from in Jamaica."

Lucas spat on the ground. "That pompous devil. He'll have a difficult time forcing his way in Charles Town."

She stood.

He longed to take her in his arms, and he had to compel his mind and voice to work. "Surely you have nothing to fear from him here, Travay." He saw her chin tremble, and he uttered a groan, then drew her to him.

"That's what my aunt thinks, but—"

He bent and kissed away the tears, then trailed down to her trembling lips. He touched them as if asking permission then claimed her mouth in a desperate, burning kiss. She resisted for a moment, but then her lips parted and yielded in a way he had only dreamed. The kiss deepened, and fireworks exploded in Lucas' head. He tried to release her, but her knees started to give way. He held her shoulders and looked into her eyes, his breathing ragged.

"I came to say goodbye."

She reached for the swing rope and cleared her throat. "You mean you are leaving Charles Town?" The tremor in her voice touched him.

He swiped his forehead with his hand, and then clamped his tricorne back over his braids. "Yes, I sail with the morning tide."

She stiffened. "Where are you going? Back to pirating?" She spat out the last word.

"I have one last quest, Travay. I don't have time to explain, but trust me, it's for a good cause."

"Good cause? Pirating for a good cause? Of course, that's probably always been your excuse. But how can you justify plundering ships, killing people?" She moved away from him and almost fell into the swing.

He reached out to steady her. "This is war, Travay. Spain persecutes the Protestants with their Inquisition and must be stopped. Every ship we take reduces the gold to finance their sins against humanity."

The rack, the thumbscrews, the Iron Maiden. And after all that torture, if the victim didn't recant or reveal the hiding place of other believers—buried alive or burned at the stake. Lucas' spine turned icy. Had his dear mother suffered those horrors when the Spanish took her captive? His gentle mother with golden hair and green eyes like his own, the one who had prayed with him beside his bed as a child and comforted him from all his fears.

Travay pushed his hand away. "And that same gold lines your pockets, of course. Go ahead with your pirating, Lucas. Why should I care? Do you know how you will end up? I do. They'll hang you at low tide in Charles Town harbor."

He looked into her blazing eyes for a long moment, then turned and hurried back the way he had come.

※ ※

Travay stared after him and touched her burning lips with her finger. No matter what she said, she did care. *Dear God, don't let him be hanged.* "Lucas!"

Crickets beginning their nocturnal song drowned out her cry. She rushed through the rows of her aunt's flowers in the direction he'd gone. Twice she had to stop and release her gown as it caught on thorns. Her search ended at the estate wall. She put both hands against it as if she would push it down.

"Lucas!"

She hadn't even told him goodbye. And she hadn't warned him about Captain Hawkins' new mandate against piracy.

Tears filled her eyes. She left the garden and trudged to her room as if dragging a bag of rocks behind her. She undressed and climbed into bed, her lips still smoldering from his kiss. She groaned and tossed. Finally, the dread of having to receive Sir Roger Poole the following day blocked out every other thought.

Roger Poole arrived promptly at four o'clock. His green coat and white cravat were made of the finest silk, his white breeches of imported satin were without a wrinkle, and every curl of his long brown wig was in place. Travay refused to meet his eyes as Mama Penn left him at the open parlor door. Her aunt greeted him with a smile and an extended hand.

He bowed over Merle's hand and then stared at Travay, who barely nodded her head and did not offer her hand.

Tea became a formal, stiff affair, with her aunt and Sir Roger carrying on polite conversation between bites of cake or fruit and sips of tea. Travay answered when spoken to, but offered no other remarks. And her stomach was in no shape to eat. She kept glancing at her aunt, willing her to get it over with.

Finally, Merle said, "Sir Roger, I regret to tell you," she glanced at Travay, "but Travay is not ready to marry. I'm afraid you would be wasting your time pressing your suit."

Well put. Travay now met his eyes and nodded to let him know it was her exact wish.

"Really?" He chuckled nastily, took another grape from the tray, and popped it into his mouth. "I think you will want to reconsider this decision, Travay." He touched his napkin to his lips and smiled at her.

She turned her face away.

Sir Roger looked around the room and then leaned back in his chair. "You like living here, do you, Lady Allston?"

Merle's back stiffened. "Yes, of course. It's been my home since I was a bride."

Travay's heart jumped into her throat. What did Sir Roger have up his sleeve?

"Actually, the truth be told, your husband lost this house gambling, did he not? I found out you were a tenant here and bought the house from your current landlord this week." He reached for a cucumber sandwich wedge and stuffed the whole thing into his mouth, then another, while looking from one of them to the other.

Merle gasped and laid a hand over her heart

Travay's eyes hardened, and her breath burned in her throat.

"I want to be a good landlord, but surely you know what you are paying monthly is far below what this house is worth." He wiped his mouth with a napkin and then grinned at them.

Travay glanced at her aunt. She had had no idea Merle did not own the house. Then she looked back at Sir Roger, her expression thunderous.

Merle looked him straight in the eye, her face pale. "What are you saying, Sir Roger? Surely, as a gentleman—"

"He is no gentleman, Aunt Merle." Travay's icy voice chilled the room.

Sir Roger retained his affability, but there was a distinct hardening of his eyes. "Yes, I see you are getting my drift." He took the last piece of cake, pushed it in his mouth, and smiled at them while eating it.

Travay stood and ran from the room.

※※

Lucas looked out over the wide expanse of ocean, now bathed in late afternoon light, and breathed in the fresh air. How good it was to be back on the high seas for almost two weeks now. The *Blue Heron* was in excellent form. Thorpe and Sinbad had managed to round up a crew a little better than average. But every evening, thoughts of Travay and that last kiss in her garden flowed back into Lucas' mind. He'd dreamed she would kiss him back like that, but he'd never dared hope. He shook his head to force the memory away. If there was ever a hopeless relationship, one between the two of them would be it. "Give it up, Captain," he whispered.

"You talking to yourself?" Dwayne Thorpe strolled across the quarterdeck and propped his arms on the railing beside Lucas.

Lucas ignored the question. "Dwayne, what do you think about the tip from that half-drunk sailor at Antigua?"

"Well, I think we made a good choice to try out the new route he told us about."

"But we've not seen a Spanish ship since we took his advice." Lucas had begun to wonder if it had been wise to act on the tip. As far as the crew knew, the *Blue Heron* traversed new waters in search of treasure ships. Only Thorpe knew Lucas had another motive, to learn more about the line of merchant ships owned by the Spaniard Quinton Raymundo—the captain who had captured Lucas' parents' ship seven years earlier.

"*A sail!* A sail on the starboard!" The lookout's yell rang across the decks.

Lucas lifted his eyeglass and focused on a small shadow on the horizon. A ship emerged, and just behind it, another. Cannon blasts now rumbled from the same direction.

"What is it, Captain?" Thorpe leaned over the railing searching the horizon.

"Take a look."

Thorpe took the eyeglass. "I'm not sure what I'm seeing."

"Yes, you are. It's an English merchant ship with a Spanish galleon bombarding her."

Thorpe lowered the eyeglass and shot a glance at Lucas.

"We will offer assistance to the English, of course, Thorpe. Give the order to sail straight toward the melee."

"Yes, sir."

Fifteen minutes later, Lucas saw the Spanish ship turn about toward the *Blue Heron's* advance. He could now see the ship's massive size, with its many galley oars and guns, and he knew why the small English merchantman had tried to flee.

"What do you think, Captain?"

"I think that English captain is shouting praises to God and the Spanish devils are uttering curses that they have to turn their attention to us."

Lucas shouted to the gunners below, "Ready the guns! Aim for the main masts. Avoid the low shots that might hit the galley slaves."

Blasts from the *Blue Heron* burst toward the Spanish ship and its masts.

One of the masts on the galleon exploded and folded down to the deck, its canvas in flames. Screams and curses echoed across the waves.

As the smoke cleared, a joyous shout sounded from the deck of the English ship. They lowered their white surrender flag, raised the English jack, and positioned their guns to hit any part of the ship they could. The captain, with his eyeglass in hand, waved at Lucas as the *Blue Heron* easily sailed around the ungainly galleon.

The return fire of the Spanish ship cracked the mizzen mast of the *Blue Heron*. It fell to the deck, missing Lucas by inches.

The battle raged as the sun began to set, with the Spanish ship taking heavy blows from both sides. The ship began to list. Flames licked up its sides. Screams and oaths filled the air.

Lucas slammed his fist on the railing as he thought of the galley slaves trapped in the belly of the great ship. He prayed they would escape. His mind ran in all sorts of circles, trying to think of a way to help them. He yelled for Thorpe and Sinbad.

Voices on the deck below caught Lucas' attention.

A sailor laughed. "If the English captain has any sense, he'll high-tail it out of here while he's got the chance, just like me and you are going to do."

Lucas looked down below the quarterdeck where two sailors talked. Why weren't they at their posts instead of near the longboat? He frowned. The two had kept to themselves most of the time they had sailed. They were never openly hostile, but there was something secretive about them.

"Get back to your posts, men," Lucas shouted at them and then turned back toward the Spanish ship. A couple of minutes later, a loud explosion rocked the *Blue Heron* from deep within its hold. Flames shot up into the falling darkness.

"What in tarnation?" Lucas turned as Thorpe and Sinbad bounded up onto the quarterdeck.

"Captain, our powder's been set off!" Thorpe's face was drained of color.

Another loud explosion threw all three of them to the deck. The next one sent them flying into the sea. Screams filled Lucas' ears as the dark waters of the Caribbean sucked him into oblivion.

CHAPTER 13

An icy chill woke Travay. She sat up in bed, drew the covers close, and looked at the moonlight pouring through the window. She slipped from the bed and made sure the window was fastened tight, listening for any sounds that may have woken her. Only the ticking of the clock on her dresser floated on the air.

As she climbed back into bed, a memory skittered across her mind, something her mother had once told her about waking suddenly for no known reason: "Travay, if you ever awaken in the night, wide awake as if sleep has just flown away, it could be one of God's angels alerting you to pray. That's what I always do. I pray until sleep comes again." Remembering her mother's faith caused a familiar pain in her heart.

She lowered her head onto her raised knees. Pray? For whom? For what? That Roger Poole would drop off the ends of the earth? But it was not Roger Poole's face that filled her mind. It was a tanned face with a firm jaw and blazing eyes.

Lucas. She wondered where he was now. He'd been gone for nearly two weeks—long enough to be far out at sea. Did he need prayer? She doubted it would help—warning him hadn't. And who would hear her if she prayed, anyway? She arose, put on her robe and slippers, and walked quietly downstairs to get a glass of milk. As she passed Mama Penn's small room beside the kitchen, she heard a rocker moving back and forth and soft mumbled words. Mama Penn was praying. Travay flattened herself against the hall wall and listened.

"Only you knows, Lord, only you knows what's gone wrong with Captain Bloodstone, but I gives myself to prayer."

When the words stopped, Travay knocked softly on the door. She heard the lumbering form of Mama Penn rise from the chair and come to the door.

"Chile, what you doing up at this hour? And looking pale as some ghost."

Travay hugged her arms together. "Mama Penn, I just woke up. I don't know why. And I heard your prayer. Do you think something has happened to Captain Bloodstone?

The older woman drew Travay into her small room and sat her down in the only other chair in the room, then she sat in her rocker.

"Yes, chile, I thinks the Lord woke me up to pray for the captain. And maybe he woke you up, too, if you care for him. Do you?"

Travay burst into tears. "I don't know. How can I care for a—a pirate?"

"I'se told you Captain Bloodstone ain't a reg'lar pirate. No sir. Trust me. I'se seen the reg'lar kind and he ain't it."

"Well, what is he, if not a pirate? I know he says he's a privateer, but there's scarcely a hairsbreadth between the two, my father used to say."

"Yo father a seaman?"

"No, he was a rice planter before he was killed."

"What hap'nd yo father?"

"Pirates killed him on his way back from a trip to England. Can you see why I hate the word?"

"Yes'm, I guess I kin." The woman rocked silently for a moment or two. Then she pinned Travay to her chair with a long stare into her face. "The truth be that you do have feelings for the captain. Ain't I right?"

"I don't know. I don't know, Mama Penn. I'm trying not to." Travay looked away from the kindly face of the African woman.

"Well, the good Lord, he's gonna work it all out. You watch and see." She stood. "Now, I'se gonna go get you a glass of warm milk and shoo you back to your bed, young lady. And don't you go to worrying 'bout Captain Bloodstone. I done been praying, and he's got two other fine friends, besides the Lord, to help him when trouble comes."

"You mean Dwayne Thorpe and Sinbad?"

"Yes'm, that's exactly who I mean. Them two will watch out fo' the captain. I'd bet my life on it."

The following morning, Travay awoke with heaviness pressing on her chest. She took longer than usual to dress but finally went down to breakfast.

Her aunt eyed her. "My dear, you look like you've given up this battle even before we've begun to fight."

"Aunt Merle, how can we win against Roger Poole? He holds all the cards in the deck, and he knows how to play every one of them."

"I don't know. Let's withhold judgment until our meeting with Sir John today. He's been busy seeing what can be done. And I still have a card or two of my own to play."

Travay looked at her aunt and wondered what card she could possibly have that would trump Roger Poole's threats. Their rent would double the first of the month. Her aunt couldn't possibly sell enough sachet bags to make up for the increase.

Later, in the solicitor's office, Travay sighed and heard the same from her aunt's lips as Sir John told them Roger Poole would not give an inch.

Unless, of course, Travay accepted his marriage proposal.

"You know he's in his right to charge whatever rent he wants to and can probably get the higher rate—if not from you, from someone else. Too bad there is such a housing shortage in the colony. I am most sorry." He leaned back in his chair and steepled his hands, frowning.

Merle took a deep breath. "Well, we're not out on the street yet. Not by any means."

Travay looked at her aunt and wondered what she meant.

The next day being Sunday, Travay agreed for the first time to accompany Merle to the Anglican Church she attended. The bells tolled throughout the city as they strolled down Church Street to the house of worship with its high steeple. Travay looked up at it as they drew near.

"What did you say about the steeple being so high, Aunt Merle?"

"I said when the city was planned, some of the founders had strong faith they'd brought with them from the reformation in Europe. They determined that no other building should be taller than the church, so they made sure to raise a tall steeple."

The imposing building with its lofty façade and Grecian portico hardly seemed inviting to Travay, but she followed Merle up the steps and into the sanctuary. The scent of pine oil greeted Travay in the chancel. Merle led the way to her family's enclosed pew. They sat on well-worn silk cushions for which Travay was thankful, as the service proved to be lengthy. The scriptures read from the Psalms encouraged her, as did the hymns. The minister's message from John 14, delivered in a strong, bold voice, touched Travay and lifted her spirits. She would work harder at not letting her heart be troubled. Not even by Roger Poole.

As they walked home, the sweet smell of roses and early summer flowers fluttered in the breeze. The sunshine on the cobbled street and birdsong filling the trees brought a measure of peace.

"Aunt Merle, thank you for encouraging me to come today. I feel better."

"Of course you do, my dear."

They passed along Bay Street with its hodgepodge smells of the waterfront—fish, wet wood, and drained salt marshes. In the harbor, sloops, brigantines, schooners, and merchant ships bobbed in the Sabbath quiet. Soon they came to Merle's own garden gate, and harsh reality settled on Travay again. What were they going to do about Sir Roger Poole?

Later that day, Aunt Merle came into Travay's bedroom with the worn velvet box Travay had seen before.

"I had hoped to pass these on to you, but if they can keep

you out of the clutches of Sir Roger Poole, then I'm all for selling them." She opened the box, and Travay's breath caught in her throat. The diamond and pearl necklace and matching earrings caught the sunlight from the window and sparkled on the black velvet.

"Oh, Aunt Merle, your family jewels I wore to the ball!"

"Yes. I kept them well hidden from Mr. Allston after he began to gamble, and I think he actually forgot about them."

"But I hate for you to sell them."

"Never you mind, my dear girl. The Lord will provide us with a good buyer, and we should get enough to keep us here for several months while we look for other lodgings if there are any to be had. Anyway, it's not as if we could pick up and leave in a day, even if someone offered us temporary lodgings. I would have to abandon all my precious furniture and family heirlooms." Merle shook her head. "Unless there's no other way, I won't do that. So we have to sell these."

Travay lowered her chin and sighed. "Of course, Aunt Merle."

The next day, Merle took the jewels to Sir John and asked him to find a buyer discreetly, keeping her ownership confidential. Within the week, he brought her enough money to meet their needs for several months, if they were careful.

"I was pleasantly surprised that the buyer had this ready cash. He said he was acting for someone else who would be happy to get the set for his wife-to-be."

Merle looked at Sir John and sighed. "I'm sure you got the best price you could in this rushed sale. Please don't ever tell me who bought them. I don't want to find myself looking for them at a ball or at church."

Merle and Travay searched for new lodgings, but it turned out to be an impossible task. They found a townhome whose owner had gone back to England for a year, but it was far too expensive, while a tenement they located at the edge of town proved unfit for humans.

One day, they ended their search in Sir John's office. He welcomed them warmly. "Find anything yet?"

"No, but we are not giving up hope." Merle sat down near the window and took off her worn kid gloves.

Travay sat in a chair beside her.

"That's the spirit. And I am going to ring for tea. By the way, I just received some strange news about our merchant, John Sutherland. A couple of sailors are telling a story around the taverns."

Travay lifted her head and gazed at Sir John. She remembered the merchant with the startling green eyes that had reminded her of Lucas.

"I don't know whether I believe it or not. Seems so unlike Sutherland to me. It's been said his ship went down in the Caribbean a few weeks ago, and him with it. The two sailors said there were no other survivors besides them. And here's the real shock. They said Sutherland was really Lucas Barrett, who became known as Captain Bloodstone when sailing the seas. Can you believe that? They said he attacked an English ship and as far as they were concerned, got what he deserved from a Spanish ship that surprised him. The two sailors said they barely escaped before the *Blue Heron* sank."

The room spun under Travay. She fell from her chair to the floor in a faint.

"Travay!" Merle jumped up and knelt beside her.

"I'll get some smelling salts." Sir John rang the bell pull, and a servant appeared. He soon returned with the needed bottle. The solicitor waved it under Travay's nose.

She sat up. "I—I don't know what happened." She looked from her aunt to the solicitor. What must they think of her? But Sir John's words echoed in her heart.

The *Blue Heron* sunk? Lucas dead? Tears gathered in her eyes, and she averted her face. Sir John gave her his hand to help her rise. She took it gratefully.

Her aunt spoke. "Well, I am sorry to hear this about John Sutherland, if it is true. He seemed like a nice young man."

As soon as Travay and her aunt each drank a cup of tea, they left for home.

The ride back had been one of heavy silence. As the carriage bore them home, Travay tried to silence the terrible words echoing in her mind. *Lucas attacked an English ship. Lucas is dead. Lucas is dead.* She couldn't comprehend it.

Aunt Merle held firmly to Travay's arm as they walked into the house. Travay knew her aunt was mulling over the whole fainting episode, probably with questions on the edge of her tongue. If Travay could only get to her room before they started.

Merle stopped her at the foot of the stairs. "Have you told me everything about this Captain Bloodstone, alias John Sutherland?"

Travay turned to look in her aunt's kind face. Her resolve crumpled, and she fell into Merle's arms, sobbing. "Oh, Aunt, I can't believe he would attack an English ship. And he was—he was my friend. His real name is Lucas Barrett. He was my one real defense against Sir Roger."

"Really?" Aunt Merle's tone suggested she was reading a lot more into the answer than Travay intended. She handed Travay a handkerchief. "Well, well." She patted her niece's shoulder. "We'll just have a time of prayer about all this. We still have God on our side, now don't we?"

Later, Travay dutifully knelt with Merle beside her bed and listened with a doubtful heart to her aunt's fervent prayer.

"Lord, we have heard bad news about a friend. Show us if this story is true. If it is not, show us the truth. If Captain Bloodstone, John Sutherland, and Lucas Barrett are one and the same, and he is still alive, protect him and help him escape whatever danger he is in. Help him make it back to straighten out the record."

Amen. Yes, Lord, if you're listening this time. Travay climbed into bed and finally slept.

The next day, Travay found nothing that could take her mind

off the terrible story now circulating in Charles Town.

That afternoon, Sir Roger showed up at tea time. She and her aunt had no choice but to admit him—he was their landlord, after all. He had heard the tale about Lucas.

"Well, well. So our old friend Lucas Barrett was leading a double life, was he? Tell you the truth, I didn't think he had such audacity in him. Captain Bloodstone, no less, as well as John Sutherland." His voice oozed with mockery. He sipped his tea and looked at Travay over his cup. "I wondered what became of him after he ran away from our plantation. Heard later he might be sailing the high seas as a pirate. I've done some investigating. That's how I found out this man is—was—Lucas Barrett. Sounds like he got what he deserved."

Travay set her cup and saucer down so heavily tea spilled onto the polished tabletop. She blotted it with her napkin.

Merle stood. "Excuse me. I'll get a cloth to wipe that up and a fresh napkin for you, Travay."

Sir Roger's gloating eyes bore into Travay's. He leaned forward and placed his hand on hers. "You will marry me, Travay. Eventually."

She brushed his hand away like an insect. How she hated the smooth confidence that rolled off his lips.

Merle returned. Mama Penn came behind her carrying a thick cotton cloth. The servant swiped up the spill and huffed in Sir Roger's direction, then left.

"What do you think about Travay's childhood friend?" Sir Roger addressed his question to Merle.

Merle just looked at him, her lips in a tight line.

"So she hasn't told you the whole story? We three grew up together. Lucas' parents were indentured to my father." Sir Roger's voice was as silky as a spider's web.

"And you and your father were most wicked to him and his parents." Travay spat the words out.

"Come now, Travay. We were as good to our servants as anyone else. But enough of this subject. Would you and your aunt care to attend the Carters' ball with me next week?"

"No. We would not." Travay's quick answer stung the air and momentarily set Roger Poole aback.

He blotted his lips, then went on smoothly. "Well, if you change your mind, there's a free month's rent for you two next month."

Merle's face hardened. "Sir Roger, you are no better than a low-down scoundrel."

He stood and prepared to leave. "Maybe so, but that's the offer. I expect you can use the extra money?"

Mama Penn stood dark as a thundercloud in the hall, holding Sir Roger's hat and cane. He took them and turned back to the two women, ignoring the glowering servant.

"And I forgot to tell you, if you *don't* attend with me and be very cordial while attending"—he looked directly at Travay and licked his lips—"the next month's rent, instead of free, will be doubled." He left whistling.

Travay stamped her foot. "Oh! That man!"

Merle sighed and sank onto the sofa.

Mama Penn came in and picked up the tea things. Her large eyes flashed when she spoke. "That's a bad man. A bad man. And I don't believes one bit o' that story about Cap'n Bloodstone. He's good man, and I don't believes the Lord has let him die either. Hadn't I done gone and did prayer warfare for him since the Lord told me to?" With that said, she began to hum as she shuffled out of the room.

Travay's heart jumped with hope but settled down like dust as she saw her aunt's pale face contract into tight lines.

"Travay." Merle took a long, labored breath. "I believe Roger Poole is rotten to the core, and we must reconsider what we should do with our remaining funds. I am now convinced he will never stop until he's forced his will on you—on us."

"But what else can we do, Aunt Merle?"

"We can return to England and to the one relative I still have."

CHAPTER 14

Lucas fought his way up through a dark tunnel. Gusts of fire licked at him when he pushed too hard. Something wrapped around his head tightened and pained him. He tried to move his hand to his head but couldn't. At times, he became aware of light and the sound of birds chattering and their wings flapping. How long he'd been in this strange state, he didn't know. Times of light and darkness passed over him in waves. Then the throbbing in his head became softer. And finally, during a time of light, a wonderful smell assailed his nose.

Light flickered across his eyelids. He heard sounds of someone busy about a fire. Warmth touched his face. He managed to barely open his eyes. At first, he squinted at the light. Then he saw Sinbad cooking over a fire with Thorpe close by. The savory smell of fish cooking stirred his memory. He tried to make a sound.

His two friends began to eat the fish. Finally, a groan escaped his parched lips. The two men dropped their food and rushed to his pallet.

Sinbad stooped down and looked at him, uttering a sort of happy grunt. He gently lifted Lucas' head and placed a split coconut to his lips. Lucas opened his mouth and received a sip of the sweet liquid. Sinbad smiled. Lucas took more sips, then opened both his gritty eyes and looked at the huge dark man.

"You gonna make it, Captain. You gonna make it. Just keep taking them sips." Sinbad's gruff voice sounded wonderful to Lucas' ears.

Thorpe leaned down closer. "Wonderful to see you back with us, Captain. We believed you would make it." His voice cracked.

Lucas tried to sit up but fell back on the sand, groaning.

Thorpe touched his shoulder. "Now don't you try to get up yet, Captain. You have been down for almost a week, and you got to take it real easy. We've kept you alive by pouring coconut juice into your mouth."

A smile started on Lucas' dry, cracked lips. "You are a hard taskmaster, my friend." The voice hardly sounded like his own, but before his heavy lids closed, he noted the happiness on the faces of his two friends.

The next day, Lucas was able to sit up. He gingerly touched the cloth wrapped around his head.

"You got a mean hit from a plank of the ship before you went under the water, Cap'n."

Lucas looked at Sinbad as the memories came back. The battle with the Spanish ship that was attacking an English merchant. Then their own ship exploding.

He winced as he remembered flying through the air and hitting the water like he'd hit a rock wall.

"I don't remember a thing after I hit the water, except feeling as if my very life were being sucked down into a dark hole." He glanced around and saw the blue Caribbean lapping a white sandy shore. How had the two men gotten him here on what appeared to be an island?

Thorpe sat down on the palm leaves beside him. "Sinbad dove and found you after you went down. When I fought back to the surface, I saw him pulling you toward a large piece of our deck floating just beyond us. We all three got on that decking, and the sea eventually spit us out right here on this beach. It was a miracle we survived, Lucas. Nothing less than a miracle. My mama would say somebody was praying." Thorpe chewed on a pine twig.

Lucas smiled. The man had undoubtedly lost his trusty pipe in the sea.

He turned to Sinbad. "So you saved my life, my friend. I am grateful. I thank both of you." When he looked out across the blue

Caribbean, his face hardened. "We will get off this island, and I will find out who sabotaged the *Blue Heron*."

Lucas tried to stand but found he was weak as water.

"You got to take it easy, Cap'n. Now don't you go fretting yourself." Sinbad stood. "We are going to take care of you till you get well."

Lucas grinned as best he could with chapped lips, but he did lie back on the palm leaf pallet and soon fell asleep.

Every day his strength grew, especially with the good diet of fish, mango, bananas, and coconut, which his friends gathered for him.

One thought never left Lucas' mind: Who had sabotaged his ship? Even Sinbad and Thorpe agreed that the two pirates Lucas had overheard talking had acted strange most of the voyage. Lucas was determined to learn the truth, just as he knew he would learn the truth about his mother.

A few days later, as the three of them sat eating their midday meal, Thorpe dropped his fish and stood. He pointed toward the ocean and whooped. A white sail appeared on the horizon, slowly growing larger as they watched.

❦

Travay agreed to sail to England once she realized Merle had made up her mind to use a large chunk of their funds to buy passage. Merle picked out a few of her heirlooms to take with them—the rest would have to stay. They packed within the week and advised the solicitor of their plan.

When Sir Roger came next, he eyed the trunks lining the hall.

"Well, dear ladies, where are you off to?"

Travay ignored him.

Merle stopped packing and faced him. "I still have one relative in England that I think might take us in, Sir Roger."

"Is that so? Well, well. Let's see. What can I do to help you change your minds?"

Travay turned to him, her lips tight. "Absolutely nothing."

Still smiling, he looked at her. "In that case, let me do one thing for you, ladies." He looked around. "I will hold this house and your furniture for you."

Travay looked at Merle whose eyes flickered in surprise then clouded with distrust.

"I'll hold it for say, six months." He took a snuffbox from his jacket and placed a pinch in each nostril. "Just in case you find you need to return to Charles Town."

Now Merle's face changed from cautious to hopeful. "Would you really do that, Sir Roger?"

Travay knew her aunt hated to leave her furniture for John Hawkins to sell—because they might *have* to return. But Travay also knew Sir Roger too well. What wicked plan did he have in mind?

❧ ❧

Travay leaned across the railing of the merchantman, heading for England. She wished the tightness in her chest would abate. Her heart still refused to admit Lucas could be dead. Every hour the small ship carried her farther away from the life she'd known in the new world and the possibility of seeing Lucas again—if he still lived.

She missed Mama Penn, who had chosen to stay and cook for John Hawkins, who was delighted to have her. He had also given a place on his estate to the gardener and his wife. Though her heart was heavy, Travay found comfort in thinking that at least she was rid of the leering face of Sir Roger Poole. But what if her aunt's relative refused them shelter? What would they do?

The second day at sea, Travay stood on deck looking back at the western horizon wondering if she would ever see Charles Town or Lucas again when a cry came from the lookout.

"A sail! A sail!"

Merle came up and laid her hand on Travay's shoulder. "My dear, until they decide what type of ship is coming toward us, we had better go below deck. You know these waters are full of pirates."

Pirates? What she would give to see the face of one particular pirate. She cast the hopeless thought behind her and followed her aunt below deck.

The two sat in their small cabin amid all the shouts and stamping feet above them. Prayers flowed from Merle's lips.

A cannon blast found its mark and shook the ship so hard they both almost fell to the cabin floor. Travay screamed.

Merle stopped praying and stifled a cry herself. "My goodness, Travay, has our ship been hit? But why have our own cannons not fired?"

Travay heard more scurrying feet and curses from above, and the boat seemed to come to a standstill. She looked out the porthole and saw another ship fast approaching. Checking its colors, she gasped. The Jolly Roger. Had their merchant ship surrendered?

Soon they heard the grappling hooks singing through the air and sinking with thuds into the deck above—next, a steady stream of boots and strange voices.

A loud knock banged on their cabin door. Merle motioned for Travay to stay seated and went to open it. The merchant captain stood with his hat in his hand and a sad expression on his face. Another tall, grinning man stood just behind him—a pirate, judging by his gaudy clothing, as well as the pistol and two swords swinging from his baldric. He wore a red scarf under a yellow plumed hat. He looked at Merle and frowned, then leaned in and saw Travay. The grin returned to his swarthy face and deepened.

Their captain held his hat in one hand and swiped sweat from his face with the other. I am so sorry, madam, but we have been waylaid by pirates. They are taking all our stores but also have demanded that you and the young lady be escorted to their ship with your trunks. If we don't comply, they will blow us up."

The pirate beside him stepped forward and mimicked a bow. "Captain Bart at your service. Yes, we need both you ladies to board our ship with your trunks. Your captain was wise to surrender, rather than lose his ship and you."

Within the hour, Travay and Merle found themselves and their trunks aboard the pirate ship *Talon*. Where it was heading, they did not know. The crew treated them with respect as they boarded, and they were given a large, well-furnished cabin. They were even told they would dine at the captain's table for their meals. How strange if they were prisoners.

Travay sank onto the large bunk and fingered the colorful quilt covering it. "It seems like too nice a cabin for a pirate ship. And everything looks new, doesn't it?"

Merle sat at the table in the center of the room, her lips pressed together. "Yes, much too nice." She glanced at Travay. "Just before we boarded, I overheard one of the crew say, 'Did the captain get the two ladies we were supposed to get?' Then he saw us and clamped his mouth shut."

Travay's eyes met her aunt's. Then she stood and stormed toward the door, her skirts bouncing. "How dare Roger Poole! It has got to be his doing. I will confront this captain and get the truth."

Her aunt's voice stopped her. "That may not be wise, Travay. We can't know for sure, can we? Some of this crew might have just seen us boarding the merchantman in Charles Town and heard their captain's plans to pursue us with the idea of holding us for ransom. Of course, he'll be disappointed if he does."

Travay trudged slowly back to her bunk, shaking her head. "I hate Roger Poole. No wonder he offered to hold our house." She gritted her teeth. "What can we do, Aunt?"

"We'll play our cards carefully. A lot can be learned at a captain's table."

They both sat stiffly at dinner that night. The table was spread with various dishes and fruits. Captain Bart himself had even cleaned up and seemed in a jovial mood.

"Eat up now, my dear lady guests. We would hate for you to grow pale and weak." He laughed, and his lieutenant beside him laughed too.

Travay spoke up. "Captain, I demand you tell us what you plan to do with us. Why did you bring just the two of us off the merchantman? Where are we headed?"

He glanced at his second in command and then met Travay's eyes. "Why my dear, haven't you figured that out?" He pointed a thick, dark finger at Merle. "I am sure she has."

He picked up half a chicken from a platter and began to pull the meat off and push it into his mouth with his fingers. Travay turned her head in disgust.

"There is no one anywhere who will pay ransom for us, Captain Bart." Merle's voice was cool.

The captain stopped chewing. "You don't say? Now that's not what I'm thinking. I expect we'll find someone back in Charles Town who might—or perhaps someone in Jamaica." Then he burst into loud guffaws.

So Roger Poole *had* planned the whole thing. Travay lost her appetite, but she finally took a few bites when prodded by Merle, who whispered, "My dear, we must keep up our strength."

In the late afternoon the next day, Travay stood on the deck with Merle, getting some fresh air. Suddenly, one of the crew, a boy of seventeen or eighteen, came running up to them and jerked off his grimy hat. "The Cap'n, he says you must get below deck. A ship's a-coming and we don't know what kind it is. It don't look friendly at all." Fear, stark and vivid, glittered in his eyes.

Merle turned to him. "Do you think we will be in a battle, or will we outrun it?"

The young man twisted his hat. "I kinnot say, ma'am, but it's my strong hope we outrun it."

CHAPTER 15

Lucas awoke and groaned as a rat scurried across his chest, down his leg, and dropped to the floor. He rubbed his eyes, wrinkling his nose at the sickening odor, and remembered where he was. He was in the hold of the pirate ship, the *Fortune*, that had sailed into a secluded cove on their island for careening and had rescued him, Thorpe, and Sinbad.

Lucas glanced around his prison cell in the stinking hold. Some rescue. This was where refusing to sign ship's articles had gotten him. Both he and Thorpe rejected the evil code of operations lived out by the bloodthirsty Captain Edward Low, better known as Ned, and his crew. Sinbad, however, did sign and winked at Bloodstone while doing so. The big man intended to intimidate the rest of the crew and make sure Lucas and Thorpe didn't starve.

"Captain, you having bad dreams again?"

Lucas peered across the blackness toward Thorpe's voice, in the cell next to his. "Yes, and I'm mad enough to do about anything to get us out of this hellish hole."

"I'm with you, Captain. I'm with you. And you know Sinbad will help any way he can."

The hatch door above opened, and a shaft of light flooded down into the soggy darkness.

"It's me, Cap'n." Sinbad's large form descended the creaking rungs. He carried a loaf of bread, and a flask hung about his neck from a cord. "I got some good food this time, Cap'n. No weevils." He handed the food to Lucas and the flask to Thorpe.

"Thank you, dear friend." Lucas smiled at the man, and he and Thorpe devoured the bread and washed it down with the flagon of water in short order.

Sinbad sat back on his haunches. "Cap'n, I got some news. The *Fortune* is preparing to enter into battle with a smaller brigantine. The lookout saw its sail in the dawn, and we gave chase. We're about to get into firing distance."

Lucas gave the man his full attention. "What flag does it fly, Sinbad?"

"The Jolly Roger."

Thorpe frowned. "Why would Captain Low trouble fellow Brethren of the Coast? And why waste time on a small pirate vessel when it is the Spanish ships that carry the treasure?

"He's just that wicked, Thorpe." Lucas had heard the tales of Ned Low's inhumane cruelty. "Nothing is sacred to him, and no one is safe from him. He's the kind to destroy any ship for the wicked pleasure of killing and torturing its crew."

He turned to look at Sinbad. "I know you're watched, but when the fighting begins, try to get the key to our chains."

"Yes, sir, Cap'n."

Lucas knew when the battle began and how short was its duration. As he and Thorpe heard the shouts of victory and the hooks being thrown from the *Fortune* toward the other deck, they also heard Sinbad returning to the hold.

He came quickly to them and unlocked their cells.

"I found the quartermaster breathing his last and managed to get his keys," the man exclaimed, and he went to work unlocking their leg irons.

As the *Fortune* crew boarded the smaller ship and got busy with cutlass and knife, Lucas and Thorpe slipped up on the deck and took swords from fallen sailors. They pretended to join the attacking crew on the beleaguered ship but actually worked to save the lives of the other ship's crew.

The attacked crew battled valiantly and killed several of Low's pirates, but they were outnumbered. The last survivors, including their captain, were soon backed into a corner as fires burst up from below deck. Lucas, breathing hard but with every muscle ready, stood with Sinbad and Thorpe beside the captain, guarding the survivors from Low's men.

Captain Low, circumventing the now numerous blazes on deck, swaggered up before Lucas and the wide-eyed victims. Never did a man look more like a demon from hell, with his clothes blood splattered, his straggly hair and watery eyes wild, his sword dripping. The fires behind him seemed like part of his attire and suited him well.

"I see you have rounded up our victims, and for that I thank you." Low mimicked the voice of a gentleman, as he was known to do before some of his most cruel acts.

"Why would you want to kill these men, worthless as they are? Why not just maroon them on an island for a much slower death?" Lucas prayed his appeal to the evil imagination of the pirate might work.

"Well, yes, that would take longer to die, but why should I bother when I can kill them now after we have a little fun with them?" He waved his sword menacingly toward the men and licked his lips.

Terror registered on the faces of the captured men, all of them bleeding from wounds.

"Captain, look what we found below on this here *Talon*." The pirate crew dragged two women across the bloodied deck and threw them at Low's feet.

Lucas' face paled under two week's growth of beard. Blood crawled cold to his heart, then flung back in a burning tide, leaving a red haze before his eyes and a taste like brass in his mouth. Travay and her aunt, their faces carved in terror.

Shock, then hope, lit their countenances as they recognized him.

Ned Low spat tobacco juice on the deck beside Travay. "I see you recognize the young one, and she you. What is she to you?" He took his lusting eyes off her long enough to glare at Lucas.

Lucas, his color returning, didn't move a muscle. "She's my very own sister. And I ask for her life and that of my aunt with her." His voice was casual, but his eye twitched in spite of his effort to prevent it.

"Sister, huh? Now why should I believe that? Lover is more like it, and as captain, I can have my pick of women captives." He looked back at Travay and licked his lips.

"I can't allow you to do that, Captain. Not my sister."

Captain Low growled and swished his sword toward Lucas. "And what will the notorious Captain Bloodstone do about it? Do you dare challenge me, Ned Low, to a sword fight?"

"Yes. But first, you must agree that whoever draws first blood will win the two women's safety."

"Rules? You, my prisoner, dare quote rules to me?"

Captain Low swung his filthy sword over his head and yelled, "Whoever *lives* takes all, my ship and these women."

The bellows of the raucous crew deafened Lucas' ears. The men stamped and clapped, ready to see more blood spilled, even their captain's. They gave way and made a circle around the two men.

"I will quarter you and hang your head from my mast." Captain Low swished his sword toward Lucas and cursed when he missed him.

Thorpe and Sinbad dashed to Lucas' side. Thorpe whispered hoarsely, "Don't do it, Lucas. The man is mad and has unnatural strength. What will happen to them if you lose?"

Sinbad growled.

Lucas didn't hesitate. He planted his feet firmly on the deck, thrust his sword toward Low, and whispered to the side, "I won't lose, but if so, you and Sinbad must kill them both before this demon from hell and his crew can get to them."

Travay's stomach threatened to spill its contents. The smell of smoldering fires and fresh blood, even now red on her hands from the soaked deck, churned acid up her throat. The ungodly faces of the growling crew made her think of how hell must look and sound with its demons dancing around the Devil himself.

"Travay, pray like you have never prayed." Merle's whisper made Travay swallow the nausea and follow her aunt as she crawled as far away from the battle as they could.

God, if you are up there. Save us. Save Lucas.

CHAPTER 16

Lucas sidestepped from the second blow of Captain Low's sword, aimed to sever his arm. The air swooshed just beyond Lucas' left shoulder.

Around and around the smoldering deck, the two circled, clashing steel until sparks flew like lightning in a summer storm. Lucas, weakened from three days in the hold, had all he could handle keeping Ned Low's sword at bay while sidestepping the fires breaking through the deck and jumping over the bodies of slain pirates. Meanwhile, the ship took on water.

The crew followed the battle, jumping about and screeching like lunatics.

Lucas, his breath coming in short spurts, gathered his strength and stormed toward his enemy.

Backing away from Lucas' punishing sword, Low stumbled on the bloody deck. Lucas quickly knocked the sword from his hand and stuck his blade tip to the sweating man's throat. A trickle of blood ran down into his filthy shirt. He fell to his knees.

The raucous crew clapped and yelled, "Kill him. Kill him."

"No." Lucas stood over the now pale man, ragged breaths bursting from his taut throat. "I'll do exactly what I tried to get him to do with the prisoners—lower a longboat."

The pirate captain was hauled into the small boat by the same crew he once commanded, and the boat was lowered to the water. He cursed his crew and all aboard, shaking his fist at them before grabbing the oars.

"He better get away from this sinking ship fast." A crew member looked over the railing then back to Lucas. "And so had we."

Lucas wiped the sweat from his brow and sought Travay's face among the huddled prisoners behind him. Relieved breaths sounded from the five captives. But where were Travay and Merle?

Sinbad and Thorpe gathered at Lucas' side.

Thorpe leaned toward him and whispered, "The moment you won, the ladies rushed below deck to gather what they can of their possessions before this ship goes down."

"There's not a moment to spare. Go after them, Thorpe."

Thorpe hurried away, but Sinbad stood with Lucas as he prepared to address Low's ragtag, blood-splattered crew.

"I've won the ship and the safe passage of all prisoners. If anyone harms them, he will have me to answer to. Understand?" He scanned the dark, dirty faces in front of him, pointing his sword melded to his fist at them. "Now, abandon ship!"

"Yessir, Captain," voices rang out. The crew scurried back aboard the *Fortune,* dragging whatever of the ship's stores they could.

Thorpe escorted Travay and Merle aboard, and another sailor dragged their trunks after them.

As the *Fortune* sailed away, Lucas approached Merle and Travay, who watched the *Talon* upturn and sink beneath the waves.

Merle turned to Lucas. "Captain Bloodstone. I want to thank you for saving our lives and delivering us from that monster."

Lucas gave her a slight bow and looked at Travay. Where were her thanks?

She stared at him, tears streaming down her cheeks. "Lucas, we—we heard you were dead."

Was that relief on her face?

She fell into his arms. He drew her to his chest and cupped her chin tenderly in his hand.

"Do you really care, Travay?"

Before she could answer, an excited pirate rushed up, and Lucas released her.

The man bowed to the ladies and extended his hand to Lucas.

"Sir, I'm Bart, once captain of the *Talon*. I don't know who you are, but we thank you. Who hasn't heard the tales of Ned Low's savagery? Thank you for delivering us."

"Captain Bloodstone, privateer in His Majesty's service. At what port would you like us to drop you and your men?"

Bart smiled, showing yellowed teeth. "Jamaica will be fine, Captain." He winked. "Or as close to there as you can get. I've got to give the bad news to the *Talon's* owner. He's a gentleman with wealth, but he's not going to like this tale."

Thorpe walked up. "What are your orders, Captain? Where do we sail?"

"Get our bearing and head for Jamaica."

Grumbling broke out amid the crew, who preferred heading into Spanish waters to hunt treasure ships. But after one look at Lucas, and Sinbad's glaring dark presence beside him, they scurried to their posts.

⁂

Travay and Merle fell onto their cots below deck after washing up as best they could.

"Thank God," Merle said. "Thank God, we made it through that, that—"

"That hell," Travay supplied. She turned to look at the ceiling. "Is that how God and prayer work? He keeps Lucas alive so he can rescue us?"

"Travay, child, I am not about to try to explain how all this has happened. I am just thankful to still be alive and not in the clutches of that fiend Captain Low." She turned on her cot. "And I thank God for Captain Bloodstone—I mean Lucas. He risked his life for us, for you."

The older woman sat up to peer into Travay's face. "What are your feelings for him, Travay?"

"Aunt Merle, he is a pirate. What feelings can I possibly have?"

She closed her eyes, signaling an end to the conversation.

But nothing could erase Lucas' face from her mind, her heart. Even with two or three week's growth of beard and his clothing looking and smelling like a pigpen, she could not deny how her heart had sung to see him alive when they were thrown at Captain Low's feet. But he was still a pirate. Maybe a rung or two higher than Ned Low, but a pirate even so. Would he ever give it up? She sighed and drifted off into a fitful sleep borne of shattered nerves and exhaustion.

A few hours later, when Thorpe came to bid them to the captain's table, Travay shook her head, and Merle asked that a tray be sent down to them.

❧ ☙

Lucas invited Captain Bart to his table that evening.

The man's dark eyes searched Lucas' face. "How did you and your men become prisoners of the notorious Ned Low?"

Lucas held his knife in midair over the meat on his plate. "After my ship was sabotaged and sunk a few weeks ago, two of my men and I ended up on a deserted island. Low's *Fortune* came to the island for careening. We were glad to get off the island, but when Thorpe and I refused to sign articles, we were thrown in the hold." Lucas turned back to the beef with vegetables and hard bread.

"So you lost your ship. I can sympathize." A shadow passed over his face. He glanced around the table but then looked directly at Lucas. "You say it was sabotaged?"

Lucas nodded.

"I heard a couple of pirates we picked up some time back bragging about that kind of thing—something about sinking the *Blue Heron.*"

Lucas dropped his knife. Thorpe choked on his mouthful of bread and coughed.

"When I overheard them, I threw them off my ship at the next port. If they would do that to one, they might try it with me." Bart stopped and raised questioning brows toward Lucas.

"The *Blue Heron* was my ship." Lucas' voice had turned hoarse.

"And I know just the two," Thorpe ground out.

"So do I." Lucas stared at Captain Bart. "What port did you leave them in?"

"One of the Bahamas. Didn't much care where I left them, to tell the truth."

After dinner, Lucas walked up on the quarterdeck, breathing deeply of the salty air, enjoying the last of the sun feathering his face. The sails billowed out in a fresh, new wind, and the sloop skimmed across the sea. He offered a brief prayer of thanksgiving for having a ship to sail again. Looking out across the turquoise waters turning red in the sunset, anything seemed possible—even finding the Spanish captain who possibly took his mother prisoner.

If he could only find out what truly happened to her, then he would leave privateering forever, maybe. He might even be able to forget the loss of the *Blue Heron*. His gut told him Byron Pitt was involved in the ship's destruction.

His next thought drove all other thoughts from his mind. Travay was just below deck. He could feel her presence on the ship. Eventually, they would talk again. He worried about how she was coping with the whole ordeal but thanked God that he had saved her from a sentence worse than death. He remembered her terror when she was thrown at the feet of Ned Low. He grimaced and slammed his fist into his palm at the thought of where she would be now had he not won the sword fight?. How had the two women ended up as prisoners on a pirate ship anyway? He needed to know the story and to get them safely home.

❦ ❧

As twilight fell, Travay grew restless. The long afternoon nap had refreshed her, and she longed to stretch her legs on deck. She looked over at Merle, who had fallen asleep after their dinner. Softly, so as to not disturb her aunt, Travay slipped a shawl around her shoulders and made her way from the cabin. Her steps turned toward the quarterdeck.

She heard the thick thud of Lucas' fist and saw his face contort as if in pain.

She stopped and would have gone back, but Lucas turned at that moment. Her breath caught at the sight of his handsome, clean-shaven face and fresh shirt. A red sash held a cutlass at his side. His plaited hair was pulled away from his tanned, square face in a queue. He stood with his back to the sunset, which cast a golden glow about him.

He bowed when he saw her. A smile flashed across his lips, and he held out his hands to assist her up the steps.

She ignored his offer. She had to find out what his plans were. Would he remain a pirate, or had he had enough close calls? But before she could ask, he spoke.

"Travay, how did you and your aunt end up on Ned Low's ship?"

"We left Charles Town for England, and our ship was waylaid—twice, actually."

"England? Why were you and Merle headed to England?"

She looked into his eyes. "To get away from Sir Roger Poole's demand that I marry him."

"Poole? But how could he wield any kind of power over you in Charles Town?"

She hated even discussing Poole and abruptly asked, "Where are we headed, Lucas? I have to know." She kept her voice level and avoided looking at his face. She leaned on the railing a good three feet from him, but still her hands grew damp, her breath short.

"Is that all you have to say?"

He sounded harsh, and she glanced back at him. "Oh, and thank you for saving us from that awful pirate, Captain Low."

He stepped close and gripped her wrist. "You have no idea

what I've saved you from, or you'd be a lot more thankful."

She tried to remove her arm from his grasp, but his fingers clamped down.

"Oh, Lucas, I am thankful, but I want to talk to you. To find out where we are headed." She looked into his eyes. "Please let go of me."

He blinked and released her.

She turned away, hoping he couldn't hear her heart slamming against her ribs or see the heat climb her neck in the gathering shadows. Just from his touch and one glance into his eyes, she had almost lost control.

"What do you want to talk about? I am dropping Captain Bart and what's left of his crew off at Jamaica, and then I had planned to take you and Merle back to Charles Town." He stopped and took a deep breath. "It seems we've done this before."

Lucas gazed back out to sea and the golden sun slipping farther toward the horizon, lighting the sky in varying shades of rose and lavender.

"Yes, but it seems so long ago since your rescue in Jamaica." She pushed away a wave of sadness that seemed to drag at her mind and her strength. She moved closer to him. "Lucas, what are you going to do with your life? Haven't you had enough pirating?"

He turned to her. "Not just yet. I have one more adventure I must attempt. Besides, I assure you I am not a pirate. I am a privateer." He caressed her face with a look that raised warmth in her cheeks. His smile maddened her.

So he planned to continue his wild, dangerous way of life. Tears gathered in her eyes. But her hands balled into fists. She stepped up to him and pounded his chest.

He drew her into his arms so tightly she could not move, then lifted her chin.

"What? Tears for me?"

Travay found her strength and pushed away from him. "Lucas Barrett, after I get off this ship, I never want to see you again.

Go on and be a pirate, if that's what you want, and don't say it's privateering." The last words ended in a sob. She turned and rushed down the quarterdeck steps, her silk skirts swishing behind her.

She pushed open the door to the cabin, where Merle still slept. After putting the bar in place, Travay dropped down onto her bunk. She took a deep breath and battled angry tears and a feeling of helplessness. Fatigue gripped her, and she slipped out of her dress and climbed into the bunk, falling asleep almost at once.

Something dark and sinister moved into the cabin through the porthole. Travay fought it in her sleep. The blackness settled over her like a cloud until she found it hard to breathe. She moaned. The thing lifted, but suddenly she found herself back on Arundel, her legs pressed close to the horse's heaving sides. She could feel the wind and raindrops blasting her cheeks, smell the salt air, and hear the breaking of the tide on the cliff wall below. She brought her whip down hard on the filly's rump, and they sailed over the cliff into gray nothingness.

Travay screamed.

❧ ❧

Lucas stayed on the quarterdeck after Travay left in anger. He had insisted on taking the night watch, knowing sleep would be hard to come by with Ned's and Bart's crews on board. Anything could happen. He was tired to the bone, but thoughts of Travay pounded in his mind. One refrain kept repeating. *I love her. I love her, but I must try once more to find out if my mother still lives.*

And there was a difference—a big difference—between a pirate and a privateer. But he had kept his letter of marque, his license to attack ships belonging to England's enemies, stored on the *Blue Heron*. Now, both the ship and the letter were at the bottom of the sea.

A heart-wrenching scream came from below deck. Then another. He bounded off the quarterdeck and all but slid down the hatch steps. Travay or Merle? In three strides, he stood before their cabin entrance.

"Travay! Merle!" He pounded on the door. Then he heard sobs. Lucas' blood rushed to his head, and he prepared to knock down the door. Sinbad and Thorpe moved down the passage behind him, shaking the sleep from their heads.

"Captain Bloodstone, we're fine." Merle's voice called out to him over the sobbing, which began to subside. The door opened, and Merle stood there clutching a brown robe about her shoulders. She inclined her head toward the far bunk.

Travay sat up in the bed with her head on her bent knees, still sniffling.

"She just had a nightmare. That's all." Merle lit a small lamp.

Lucas caught his breath. "Are you all right, Travay?"

"Yes," was the muffled response. She lifted her head. "It was the cliff again."

He gritted his teeth. If he ever got his hands on Roger Poole ...

He approached her bed. She drew the blanket about her shoulders and looked up at him with glistening eyes and wet lashes.

"I guess it's not surprising to have nightmares after what you've been through today." He stopped, his heart hammering in his chest. She was beautiful with her red-gold hair tumbling down her back. There was more he wanted to say, but the words stuck in his throat.

"Of course. That's just what I told her." Merle came to stand close to Travay. "I think she'll be fine now." The older lady glanced back at the door and saw Sinbad and Thorpe, naked to the waists, their hair tousled. "We are sorry we woke up the ship."

"No bother." The two men echoed each other and turned back up the passage.

Lucas tore his eyes away from Travay and prepared to follow the two men.

At the door, Merle came to his side. "Lucas, I know this is not the kind of seaworthy ship to make it to England, but we really would like to visit a relative I have there. Can you help us make it to a ship returning home to England?"

"Yes, I will do all I can, but our best bet is to find one in the Charles Town port."

Lucas avoided any more private conversation with Travay until they docked in Kingston, Jamaica. In the brief stop at the island to set Captain Bart and his men ashore and to take on supplies, Lucas also managed to leave several of Ned Low's most problematic crew members drunk in the taverns. He preferred to sail with a skeleton crew he could trust.

Travay and Merle did not ask to leave the ship, to his relief. He could protect them much better on board. Perhaps Travay didn't want to go ashore and stir up painful memories.

The next morning, at first tide, they were back at sea and heading north by northwest to Charles Town. He would find the best passenger ship for Travay and her aunt in Charles Town if they still wanted to go to England.

The second day out, an albatross took up station on the bowsprit, his great wings at rest in silver splendor. A crew member said it was a good sign, but Lucas felt a steel-like thrust in his gut as if the words were in error.

Around midnight, Lucas awoke with a start, all his senses alert. He pulled on clothing and headed to the quarterdeck where Thorpe stood watch. The night was clear and the wind steady, though chill for the time of year.

"Any sign of a storm?" Lucas leaned over the railing and scanned the dark horizon.

"No, but I'm uneasy for some reason." Thorpe pressed his lips together. "Don't know why. Sky's been clear all night. No thunder. Nothing on the horizon."

"Do a sounding."

Thorpe motioned to a young guard on the lower deck who had been listening.

"Aye, sir." He took up a slender rope with a heavy weight attached to one end and cast it over the railing, giving it time to sink the length of the rope. "No bottom, sir."

Still, uneasiness gripped Lucas' insides. He took up the spyglass and turned it southeast, directly into the wind.

Then he saw it—a glimmering flash at the horizon, so fast he wanted to discount it. But when he saw it again, he knew it was no illusion. He handed the glass to Thorpe, who turned pale as he looked. "It's a blow. A big one, Lucas."

On the horizon, a slice of light formed a line between the ocean and the sky. Lightning slashed across it. They had only a brief window in which to prepare.

Lucas leaned over the quarterdeck railing and shouted, "All hands on deck."

Thorpe bounded down the steps yelling the same thing.

As the men clamored from their hammocks, Lucas and Thorpe shouted orders: "Prepare a storm anchor! Lash everything double tight. Rig all sails for storm! Batten down the hatches!"

Within five minutes, the storm was visible to all hands, a beast that rumbled toward them, blowing wind and fire. Thick darkness denser than midnight soon settled over the ship, broken only by streaks of lightning. Thorpe and Sinbad threw overboard all but the most necessary supplies to lighten the ship.

Lucas plunged down the hatch and yelled through the door to Travay and Merle's cabin. "We're heading into a big tempest! Tie yourselves to the bunks. And pray."

He scuttled back up the steps and plowed across the deck toward the ship's helm, holding on to whatever he could grasp. After lashing himself to the wheel's pedestal behind the young helmsman, Damon, Lucas reached around him to grip the wheel just below Damon's clenched hands. It would take both of them to steer through this deadly storm. Lightning split the sky, and the wind drove waves as high as the sails.

In front of Lucas, Damon shivered so hard his words came out choppy. "Cap'n, w-will w-we s-survive this blow?"

"Yes." Lucas ground out between stiff lips. "With God's help."

A sulfurous smell from the lightning, which was much closer now, blanketed them. The helmsman stiffened with fright, and Lucas forced his voice into steely hardness.

"Focus on the next wave, the next blast of wind, my man."

The sheets of rain lashing them hid huge waves seeking to flip the ship over. Both men groaned as they tried to hold the ship against the hurricane force winds.

※ ※

The riotous roar of the storm caused Travay, tied to the berth, to quake. The spittle dried in her mouth when the ship shot to the top of colossal crests then dropped into the torturous troughs below.

When she could get her breath, Merle offered prayer after prayer in the thick darkness filling the cabin. Travay shrieked every time a bolt of lightning cracked and flashed fire across their porthole, lighting the cabin with an unholy luminosity. They could not escape the cold water that sheeted through the small opening and seeped down on them from the deck above, driven through the boards by the blowing rain and the swells lashing the ship. It puddled on the floor and splashed from one side of the cabin to the other as the ship lurched. Soon they were drenched.

※ ※

With his hands gripping the wheel from behind the helmsman, Lucas searched through the driving rain and caught glimpses of Thorpe and Sinbad who had ropes tied around their waists and were doing all they could to prevent men from being washed overboard. It didn't take long to realize that few of their sparse crew had ever been in a blow of this size. Lucas heard the death cries of several of them as the mountains of water pounded across the deck, snapped the ropes around their waists, and dragged them to watery graves.

God rest their souls.

Every barrel and rigging not tied or hammered down washed overboard in the first big thrusts of the storm. Thorpe and Sinbad both yelled at the top of their lungs when the mizzen and then the foremast, with sails strapped tight around them, cracked like pistol shots and washed into the sea.

For many hours, no hint of daylight permeated the thick darkness and the blowing deluge that tossed the ship.

Lucas, his hands melded to the helmsman's, fought to steer the ship slightly upwind and nose the sloop into the massive swells, bracing himself against the shuddering wash of water that followed, then wrestling the ship back a notch. These maneuvers took so much effort that the two men groaned with one voice.

When the mainmast of the ship exploded like a cannon and blew away, Lucas knew the ship would be lost.

God save us!

It might have been an hour later, or it might have been a year—Lucas' exhausted body felt like it was the latter—when a violent lurch of the ship and a cracking sound from the keel alerted him that the ship had struck a coral reef, although he could see nothing for the blanket of darkness that still lay upon them. At the same time, the wheel went slack in their grip, and Lucas knew the rudder had broken.

"Oh, my God!" The helmsman slumped against Lucas.

"Do not give up yet, my man!" Lucas had trouble forming the words with the wind and rain pounding his face.

The ship, with great creaks and shudders, continued to move forward, driven by the sea, until it came to rest on the reef, wedged between coral formations. Lucas held his breath. Would the wanton waves dash what was left of the ship—and them—to pieces on the rocks? In desperation, he cried out to God in his loudest voice the very words that Jesus spoke to a storm. "Peace, be still! In Jesus Christ's name, peace, be still!"

Lucas could scarcely breathe. Had the wind snatched his words away? But in the next few seconds, something happened he would never forget.

The rain, wind, and punishing waves abated. The darkness lifted. The sun came out and glistened across the soaked deck and destroyed mast stumps. The ship's groaning and crunching sounds reduced to a moderate rocking with the sea. Lucas gasped a deep, relieved breath and forced his stiff fingers to untie the ropes holding him and the helmsman to the wheel's pedestal. They staggered apart.

It was a new day. Twenty-four hours had passed since the storm began.

The helmsman turned to Lucas, his eyes wide and wild. "W-what w-we gonna do now, Cap'n?" The man's face gained back a little color as he wiped the streaming hair from his face.

Lucas ached in every part of his body, and thirst burned his throat. He squinted against the bright light and scanned the deck of the destroyed brigantine. Only by a miracle were they not on the ocean floor. He saw Sinbad, Thorpe, and two other crew members—the only ones to survive—untying the ropes that had saved their lives. His heart lifted more when he saw that by some stroke of luck or prayer, one longboat had survived and still hung by a tattered rope. *Thank God.*

"We'll have to abandon ship, Damon. This coral reef must be part of an island. Let's pray it's inhabitable."

Damon stood up straighter and took a long breath. "I'm jist a-thanking the God of my old mother we ain't all scattered down in Davy Jones' locker."

Lucas scanned the waters past the reef. Was that a line of green just on the horizon?

Thorpe and Sinbad stumbled toward the quarterdeck like sleepwalkers, soaked to the skin and bone weary like Lucas and Damon. The four men threw their arms around one another, breathing one word. "Saved."

Lucas added, "Thank God."

Thorpe handed a precious water skin that had survived the storm to Lucas, and he gulped a large quantity. Then his breath fled his lungs.

Travay, Merle. Had they survived the terrible pounding and tossing of the ship in the storm? Was the lower deck flooded? He forced his weary legs to move toward the battened-down hatch to the cabins below.

CHAPTER 17

Lucas bent and tried to loosen the wooden block over the lower deck opening. It wouldn't budge. The crew had battened it down well, and now the wood had swollen with water. Curse words came to Lucas' mind, but he bit them back. The desire to see if Travay and Merle were safe burned through him like thirst had moments before.

Sinbad came to Lucas' aid with a piece of an iron railing he had torn from the battered ship's tackling. In two minutes, he had the hatch pried open.

"Travay! Merle!" Lucas slid down the steps. Tremors traveled up his spine when his boots sank into a foot of water at the bottom of the stairs. Was the ship taking on water this fast?

"We're fine, Lucas. Exhausted and thirsty, but fine," Merle responded just as Lucas reached their cabin door. He heard her struggling to lift the bar.

"It's swollen with water, Lucas. We can't lift it." This time Travay's voice called out, and Lucas' heart sang.

Sinbad, standing just behind his captain, tapped Lucas on the shoulder.

Lucas smiled, pointed to the hinge, and commanded through the door, "You two move away from the door. Sinbad's coming through."

The large black man moved as far away in the narrow passage as he could, then leaning in with his massive shoulder, he bolted toward the cabin entrance.

The door flew from its hinges and skidded to the far wall.

"Oh!" Both women cried out as one. They sank into the water

at their feet, their bouffant skirts bobbing and soaking up moisture.

Lucas strode to Travay, who was trying to control her garment, and lifted her from the storm water. She had a bruise on her forehead and her soaked clothing dragged at her body, but otherwise, she seemed fine. He took a deep breath and helped her gain her footing in the dark seepage. She lifted tired eyes to his, causing his heart to thunder. For a moment, he thought he saw more than gratitude in her face, but then she turned toward Merle.

"Thank God. Thank God." Merle uttered her simple thanks as Sinbad helped her to her feet.

"Where are we, Lucas? We are shipwrecked, aren't we?" Travay's lips quivered. Her glorious hair, now escaped from all its pins, hung down her back. Crumpled, wet, and exhausted, she was still the most beautiful woman he had ever seen.

His voice softened. "Yes. But the ship is wedged between coral reefs for the moment, which should give us time to abandon it before—"

"We'll be cracked up on the rocks." Hysteria crept into Travay's voice.

"Travay, do you think the Lord has preserved us through all this danger to abandon us now?" Merle sloshed through the water to touch her niece's shoulder, her voice strong and unwavering.

Lucas put on his sternest but calmest demeanor. "Ladies, as fast as you can, gather what you must have to take in the longboat. By a true miracle, we have one left intact. And I believe an island may be nearby. Also, there are two water skins left. You're welcome to partake."

"Yes, sir, Captain." Travay's voice was steady enough, but her eyes glistened.

Lucas cast her a quick glance, then he and the other men sloshed through the water and up the steps to the deck.

Travay grabbed items and stuffed them into a pillowcase Merle had pressed into her hand.

"I believe we should dispense with our hoops." Merle lifted her skirt dripping with water and pulled down her hoop. "They'll be a problem in the longboat and of no use on an island."

Travay smiled at her practical aunt and blinked away weary tears. She lifted her skirt, stepped out of her wet hoop, and kicked it across the standing water.

At the door, she turned to scan the cabin. She tossed her hair behind her shoulders and fingered the locket at her throat, her most precious possession.

The two climbed to the deck, clutching their small bags of belongings. Thorpe handed Merle, then Travay, a water skin. They drank deeply and thanked him. Travay watched the men lower the longboat to the turquoise water. Lucas and Sinbad helped them down the side of the ship to the waiting craft, already loaded with the few supplies that had survived the storm.

Travay, with Merle beside her, squeezed next to the canvas sacks foraged from the ship's store, to make room for the three surviving crew members, whose odor had been lessened by the rain that had pounded them. Their eyes ran over her, and she tossed her head and lifted her handkerchief to her nose. Two of the pirates grinned. But the eyes of the younger one Travay had heard Lucas call Damon, held an apology. He frowned and punched the one next to him on the arm. The other man cursed then laughed.

Lucas, Sinbad, and Thorpe, with their swords, cutlasses, and pistols strapped to their waists, boarded last.

The men took up the oars, and the small boat skimmed across the now calmer sea, with a southerly breeze lifting Travay's hair. Even though the sun shone down on them, she shivered as the cool air permeated her wet clothing. Lucas reached down in the supplies and dug out a blanket for her. Though damp, it provided some protection.

"Thank you, Captain." She drew it around her and Merle's

shoulders.

A deafening crack caused all the survivors to turn and look back. They watched as the abandoned ship sank beneath the sea. The rowers fought the wave that rushed toward their small craft. Travay shuddered and fought dizziness as their boat rocked but remained upright.

The slice of green on the horizon that Lucas had pointed out earlier became a beach with coconut palms at its border. The men rowed faster, and soon the longboat was close enough for its occupants to disembark. Lucas, Sinbad, Thorpe, and the other three pirates jumped into the foam and beached the boat on the white sand.

Thorpe assisted Merle out of the boat, and Lucas lifted Travay. She had never known such tiredness. Her bones even seemed to ache. She let her head fall onto Lucas' shoulder. He smelled of sea and salt and perspiration, but somehow his scent was right. He carried her in his thick arms with ease. How could he have so much strength left after the harrowing storm?

When he set her feet down on the warm beach, in the partial shade of a palm tree, she lowered herself to the sand and stretched out. She sighed, enjoying the heat on her face and arms. Her clothes would soon be dry. The scent of tropical flowers and lush greenery seemed more pleasant than she could ever remember. But how were they going to survive on this island until a ship found them? She frowned and closed her eyes.

Lucas dropped down beside her. "Travay, are you sick or injured in any way?"

She opened her eyes and looked up into his troubled ones. "No, I am just tired. I was so afraid during the storm, and it took all my energy to keep from being slammed into the walls." The relief in his face pleased her.

Merle came to sit beside Travay. "What can we do to help, Captain?"

"Stay here for now. Get your strength back. There will be plenty to do when we make camp."

Before sleep claimed her, Travay heard Lucas say, "How about staying near the ladies, Sinbad, while the rest of us look around for a suitable place to make camp?"

Travay awoke, and her eyes widened when she saw a small shelter of palm fronds the men had erected for her and Merle at the edge of the trees. Both of them moved to sit in its open doorway.

A few feet away, Sinbad laid dried branches around a hole dug for a fire. Thorpe lit them with a tinderbox he'd rescued from Low's ship.

Merle reached out and touched the long, tangled ringlets hanging across Travay's shoulder. "Dear, I wish there was something I could do to help you manage these curls." Her own hair had not escaped its customary tight knot at the base of her neck except for a few strands.

Travay tossed her thick locks behind her back. "What does it matter, Aunt Merle? I am more worried about surviving on this island." Her stomach rumbled like an echo of the tide slapping against the beach.

Lucas and Thorpe walked up with fish they had managed to spear as well as several large crabs. The other pirates brought coconuts and palm fruit for the meal. Sinbad wrapped the fish and crabs in palm leaves and laid them on the coals. Soon a savory smell wafted toward Travay and Merle.

Lucas crossed the sandy stretch toward them. "If you ladies will join us, I think you'll find something to your liking in our first island meal."

Travay looked at him, squinting against the sunlight. His ripped shirt revealed hard, tanned muscles on his shoulders and arms, and dark curly hair on his chest. He smiled at her. Heat climbed up her cheeks—he had caught her staring. She stood and faced him.

"I am so hungry, anything will taste good, Lucas." She glanced into his eyes. That was a mistake. Her heartbeat doubled in tempo. She took a deep breath and turned to her aunt. "How about you,

Aunt Merle?"

"Famished. Thank you, Lucas, and we owe you and your crew thanks for a lot more."

They walked to the circle of men and sat down next to Thorpe.

Sinbad looked at Lucas before passing the food he had piled on palm fronds. Lucas cleared his throat. "Let us thank God for this food and for saving our lives."

Travay bowed her head as murmurs of approval came from around the group.

Lucas prayed. She opened her eyes to look at him. His strong voice rolled over them as if he were practiced at addressing God. What made him think God would hear the prayer of a pirate? God never seemed to hear hers.

The hearty island meal refreshed Travay, but it didn't relieve the uneasy thoughts clouding her mind. She sat just beyond the group, staring at but not seeing the colorful rays of the sun beginning its path toward the ocean. The shades of pink, blue, and lavender arching across the sky did not lift her spirits. Surely they were far from help of any kind unless it was the wrong kind of help—pirates of Ned Low's sort. She shuddered and hugged her arms to herself.

"Cold?" Lucas came to sit beside her.

She shook her head.

He brought her a coconut with the eyes pierced so she could drink the sweet milk. A spark moved up her arm as his callused hand touched hers. Though dark shadows circled his eyes, his handsome face still sent a familiar shiver of awareness through her.

"Lucas, where do you think we are?"

"I would guess we're somewhere northwest of Jamaica and Cuba, probably in the archipelago called the Bahamas. We lost our compass in the storm and were blown who knows how far off course."

Lucas regretted being so blunt when he saw Travay stiffen and frown. "But I am not worried. We will be found, and this island seems to have plenty of fish, oysters, and crabs—not to mention coconuts and palm fruit." He smiled down at her brooding face, wishing he could take her into his arms and soothe her. But he knew he must keep his distance. A relationship between them was out of the question. She was above his class, just as she always had been. And she hated pirates—including privateers. Despite this knowledge, she was still a temptation. He turned to see Merle watching them.

Lucas stood and walked toward the sea. Sinbad came after him. When Lucas stopped and sat on a rock to watch the tropical sunset heighten its glory, the boatswain sat down near him. Lucas looked at the half African, half Arab he had rescued a year earlier when on a rare trip to African waters. He went seeking knowledge of his parents along Spanish trade routes, but found Sinbad instead, chained in the bottom of a ship Lucas captured. It was one of his luckiest finds—Sinbad proved to be a loyal friend to Lucas and a skilled crew member. He even spoke some English he had learned from other captives.

The man's red fez he had often worn had not survived their first shipwreck, so his large head looked even bigger with his curly, ebony hair exposed.

"Cap'n, I … wants to ask you about that blow."

The question surprised Lucas. The giant of a man, once a slave warrior of a Moroccan Muslim ruler, had surely seen many storms in his years on the Mediterranean and African seas. Probably a lot more storms than Lucas had seen.

"What do you want to know, Sinbad? I hope I have the answer you are looking for."

"You called on yo God, and he answ'd."

Lucas' heart moved in his chest. He looked into the dark, searching eyes. "His name is Jesus Christ."

"He speak to you, this Jesu' Chris'?"

"Not in words out loud, but I know His voice and His power when it comes."

Sinbad straightened at the word *power*, a warrior coming to full attention. "I would know this God who speaks and gives you command to calm sea."

Lucas smiled, joy bubbling up inside. "And He would know you, Sinbad."

"What is the price required of me?" The man's eyes gleamed in the falling darkness.

"If you mean gold or sacrifice, there is none, my man." Lucas took a deep breath, wishing Ethan Wentworth was here to explain. Instead, it was Lucas here on this deserted island with a man who needed an answer he could understand.

Lord, help me help Sinbad.

"It is required of you to declare that you know your ways have not pleased the true God of the earth. His Son's name is Jesus Christ. He came to earth to save all men and help them live holy lives. And you must believe in Him and ask His forgiveness."

"His name not Allah?"

"No."

Sinbad sat back and thought a moment. "After I join my master in the big mosque, we told must bow and pray every day to Allah and kill all who call themselves Chris'ans."

Lucas winced. "Yes, there has been much bloodshed over religion, Sinbad. But our God is a God of love, and one day He will bring all of us, of every tribe and nation, who love and live for Jesus, home to heaven where He is. And we don't have to kill anyone to get there. Jesus Christ Himself died for us on a cross in the land of Israel, but He also arose from the dead. What we have to do is accept Jesus Christ as God's Son and the only way to the Father. We have to pray and ask Him to forgive our sins and come live in our hearts."

Sinbad sat silent for a time as the sun slipped further into the ocean. "All these years, I never see Allah calm the sea or heard of one who rose from the dead." He stood and strode a distance down the beach. His heavy steps pounded indentations near the lacy edge of the tide. Then he came back to sit again. He fixed his gaze on Lucas. "This act you say we must do, it seem too small."

Lucas leaned toward him. "That's because the main act, the big sacrifice once and for all, already took place when Jesus died on the cross for our sins."

Sinbad bowed his head for several moments. Then he took a deep breath and looked up at Lucas in the twilight. A smile spread across his face, exposing his even white teeth.

❦

The next day, Travay sat beneath a palm tree and wove a mat from grasses. Sinbad had shown her how to do it to pass the time.

Lucas strode up to her. She recognized his manly scent of sea and sun, and she could feel the heat from his body as he stepped into the shade, out of the hot afternoon glare.

"Did you find more water?" She glanced up at him and then turned her eyes back to her work.

"No, but I found something I want to show you."

The eagerness of his voice caused her to seek his face, now tanned deeper from the island sun. He had pulled his braids behind his head and tied them with a strip of red cloth. Her heart slammed against her ribs, and she looked away.

"Will you come?" Lucas held out his hand to help her stand.

Travay glanced around. Merle was having her afternoon siesta, as were most of the others, including Thorpe. Only Sinbad seemed alert. He leaned against a banana tree, squinting toward the ocean with his sword and pistol at his side.

He turned to regard them as Travay took Lucas' hand and stood. When Lucas looked at him and lifted an eyebrow, the African gave a slight nod and returned to his watch. Travay shook her head. It was uncanny the way the two of them communicated without words.

About a half-hour later on their trek around the island, Travay wiped perspiration from her brow. More trickled down her back, dampening her gown. They had seen all kinds of fish in the shallows and a giant sea turtle sunning on a rock. Clouds of birds rose at their approach to a sandbar. She touched Lucas' arm. "How much longer?"

"You need to rest?" He stopped and pulled her under a palm tree. She sank down, pulling her long skirt around her feet. They sat for a few moments, and he made a fan for her from dead fronds scattered about the base. "It's a little bit of a walk, but I promise you, you'll be glad you made it."

She looked at him and his boyish enthusiasm. Was this just a ploy to get her alone? He had made no advances toward her.

The next second, he stood and gave her a hand up. "Come, my surprise is waiting. Are you willing to walk a little farther?"

"I am." They started tramping again on no path Travay could discern, but Lucas led with confidence. It was all she could do to keep her garment free from the small bushes they brushed by.

For a quarter of a mile, walking became difficult thanks to the marshy area they entered. Mangrove roots spread up in twisted forms to hinder their progress. Lucas took her hand. At times, the thick stems seemed larger than the stunted, umbrella-shaped trees themselves. Beyond, Travay could see level ground, and she took heart. Lucas kept her hand cradled in his until they stepped out from the risky path.

She started to make a remark, but he put his finger to his lips.

She lowered her voice to a whisper. "Where are we bound, Lucas Barrett?"

He put his finger to his lips again and inclined his head toward the narrow path ahead.

Travay saw a glimmer of water beyond some fronds. Lucas slowed their pace and led her through the grass at the edge of a lagoon. He drew her down beside him in the green overgrowth

Travay took a deep breath of the fresh scent of the grasses.

Birdsong and clucking sounds filled the air. She looked through the tall blades hiding them. Her eyes widened.

The small body of salt water was a nesting ground, its entire surface covered by a flock of elegant birds. Some of them were snow white, others pink as a morning sky. All the birds were waders, but unlike gangly herons or cranes, their stilt-like legs were part of their beauty, along with their curving necks and black beaks.

Some of the birds were guiding their young in uncertain flights that soared briefly above the trees and circled back to the nesting ground. Others still sat on nests in the grasses and overhanging tree branches. Still others seemed to move in an exquisite dance without music.

❧ ☙

"What are they?" Travay's voice was so low, Lucas almost missed it.

"I don't know," he whispered in her ear. "But isn't it the most beautiful thing you've seen?"

She turned toward him. "Yes. Thank you for showing me."

Her face was so close to him that her breath feathered his chin. He looked at the curls framing her face and hanging down her back in tangled glory. He touched a soft coil. Suddenly, he couldn't breathe. She still looked at him with the eyes that often challenged him in his dreams. He traced his gaze around her face and stopped at her lips. Before he could check himself, he leaned down. His mouth brushed hers in a gentle, undemanding kiss. Her lips parted, and her arms reached around his neck. He drew her closer and deepened the kiss, tremors traveling through his body. He broke away and moved her from him before he lost all control.

She sat very still, and then her hand came up to slap him. He grabbed her wrist.

"Don't tell me you don't feel exactly as I feel, Travay." His voice was hoarse, and he forgot to whisper, causing a huge response on the lagoon. Young and old birds alike rose from the water with a great whirling of wings and raucous honking. With a sentinel bird at the head, they flew in battle formation. Only the solitary nesters stayed at their posts.

They both lifted their heads and watched as the birds winged north. In a matter of moments, the whole flock was lost from view.

The moment ruined, Lucas stood and reached out a hand to Travay.

She refused it and followed him back on the path until they reentered the mangrove trees with their difficult roots poking up in their path. Almost falling over once, she grabbed for his arm and held on until their path became easier.

❧ ☙

Two days later, Travay noticed Lucas, Thorpe, and Sinbad with their heads together just after breakfast. She and Merle sat at the opening of their palm frond home, dreading the heat they knew would soon beat down from the tropical sun. The three pirates whose names she couldn't remember wrestled on the beach and shouted obscenities at each other.

"I'd give anything for a good bath without salt water. How about you?"

"You know I would, Aunt Merle. But right now, the real need is for more drinking water."

"Yes, I know." Merle's voice was edged with concern. She inclined her head toward Lucas' group. "I believe that's probably what that meeting is about."

Lucas soon confirmed her statement. He approached them and gave a slight bow.

"Ladies, as I am sure you've noticed, our fresh water situation is getting critical. Thorpe and I are starting a journey across the island to search for a better source. We may be gone a couple of days."

Travay frowned and shaded her eyes with her hand as she looked up into his face. "What? You can't leave us here with …" She threw her hand toward the three pirates who were horseplaying on the beach.

"Actually, I am taking the smaller one, Damon, with me and Thorpe. He will help us bring the water skins. Do you doubt Sinbad's ability to protect you from the other two?"

Travay looked at the large African stooped beside the morning coals, raking them into a pile. She breathed a little easier—the man struck fear in all three of the crew.

Lucas turned his glance from Travay to her aunt. "Let's all pray we find fresh water soon."

Merle laid her hand on his arm. "Lucas, that will be my daily prayer—and for your safety and ours."

Travay watched Lucas, Thorpe, and Damon pick up their packs and head into the interior of the island. Her throat constricted, and she swallowed, not trusting herself to speak. Whatever was wrong with her? Why should she feel desolate as the three disappeared into the bush?

The second night after they left, sleep evaded Travay in the frond lean-to. Why hadn't Lucas and his group returned? She arose, donned her dress, and moved to the entrance. She almost stumbled over Sinbad who lay blocking the door. He rose up and moved from her path, the whites of his dark eyes shining in the night. She took a deep breath. "Nothing is wrong. I just can't sleep. I thought I'd walk on the beach, just a little way."

He nodded. She walked, and he followed five paces behind her, glancing back often at the lean-to. Soon the magic of the island sounds—the waves lapping at the white sand, the soft cooing of birds in the inland trees—did their work. Travay went back to their little palm frond home and immediately fell asleep.

Just before dawn, she awoke with a start. She turned toward her aunt's pallet. Merle sat there, equally alert.

Sounds of battle ensued from the beach. Both Travay and her aunt bolted upright. Slipping into clothing as fast as possible, they crawled out into the dawn and stared down the beach.

Sinbad fought a mortal conflict with about ten pirates just beyond the camp. There were two still forms lying grotesquely on the beach—the other two pirates Lucas had left.

As they watched, Sinbad slashed deadly blows to three of the attackers, but more came from the bushes.

Travay put her hand over her mouth to stop a scream that rushed up from her throat. Merle clapped a hand over her own mouth, then grabbed Travay's arm.

"Hurry. We must run into the jungle before they see us." Merle's low voice was laced with horror.

The two of them ran toward the shadowy trees and pushed through vines and bushes until they were completely out of breath and their skirts were in tatters. They stopped a moment in a small clearing to look behind them. Travay's breath came out in ragged spurts. Blood oozed from scratches on her face and arms. Merle had her own wounds and could scarcely stand.

"Dear ladies, don't trouble yourselves. I will protect you."

They both whirled around. A blond pirate with a white silk shirt and red sash stuffed with a cutlass, sword and pistol smiled at them. A long scar ridged one side of his face.

Travay's breath strangled in her throat.

The man whipped off his hat and bowed. "Captain Byron Pitt at your service."

CHAPTER 18

Travay grabbed Merle's hand, and they both turned and ran. Their blindly retreating steps, harried by their gowns catching on every bush and limb, eventually brought them out onto a different section of beach.

To an encampment of pirates.

Merle stumbled but recovered her footing.

Travay stopped dead in her tracks and struggled for breath. A swarm of laughing pirates passed around a jug on the beach. A tall ship bobbed in the waters beyond the cove.

Pitt sauntered out of the trees behind them. "Welcome to our little camp, ladies. My men have just finished careening our ship, and they are ready for a party. Please join us."

A group of pirates burst from the trees below them, dragging Sinbad, bound from neck to foot, toward a stake at the water's edge.

Iron bands clamped around Travay's heart. She turned to Byron Pitt. "What are they going to do to Sinbad?"

"From the looks of it, he gave my men quite a fight. Seems they have something special planned for him."

Nausea rose in Travay's throat as the men tied Sinbad to the stake. Blood flowed from cuts on his legs and arms. Something jogged her memory. Her voice raised three notches. "What are they going to do?" Merle touched her arm.

"I doubt if you ladies would be interested in knowing. I invite you to take residence on my ship. We will be loading into the longboats shortly." He leaned in as if to whisper a secret. "In fact, I know if I don't get these men on board before they get much more rum in them, I will have a problem getting them aboard at all." He winked.

Travay stood stiff as a board. She planted her feet firmly in the sand and tossed her unbound curls behind her back. "I will not board your ship. And I demand you tell me what they are doing to Sinbad."

Captain Pitt's lip curled, and all hint of a gentleman's tone left him. He threw out his chest and glared at Travay. "They are tide staking the African, if you must know, and you will board my ship, or be trussed up as he is and carried aboard like a slave.

Tide staking. Now she remembered the sentence of some unlucky pirates in Jamaica. Once she and her mother had driven nearby and heard the screams of men being eaten alive by crabs who came in with the surge.

"No," she choked and broke into a cold sweat. "No." She staggered back and sobbed. Not Sinbad, Lucas' faithful friend who had protected them with his life.

Merle kept her from collapsing onto the sand. "Travay, what is tide staking? Why are you so upset?"

Travay only shook her head and buried her face in her hands.

Pitt cursed. He leaned over and pulled Travay's head up by clutching a handful of her curls. "What is this? What's that African to you, girl?"

His breath in her face made Travay's stomach roil. "He's been our protector. He's one of Captain Bloodstone's most trusted men," she spat at Byron.

"So that's it, is it? Yes, I remember the man now. This is good." He released Travay, and she dropped onto the beach in a heap. "He'll come back to find his African half eaten by crabs and the love of his life gone on my ship. We'll sail with tomorrow's dawn. After my crew loads up with fresh fruit and celebrates tonight." The pirate turned to Merle, who glared daggers at him.

"You see this?" He pointed to the long red scar across his cheek. "Bloodstone did this, and I swore I'd get revenge. This is my long-awaited day." He whipped off his hat and bellowed the most awful roar Travay had ever heard. Then he leaned down and scooped her into his arms like she was a featherweight and headed toward a longboat on the beach.

❦ ❦

Walking back from the other side of the island, Lucas heard the strange sound as it echoed off the rocks behind them. He turned to Thorpe. "Did you hear that?"

"Sounded kind of like a mad bull, but we haven't encountered any kind of cattle on the island." Thorpe looked at the young helmsman who hadn't said two words the whole trip.

Damon cocked his head. "Onliest thing I ever heard close to it was a pirate we run into. I swear, when he got into the rum or got mad, he could let a holler rip that would curl your spine."

Lucas dropped the full water skin from his shoulder. *Byron Pitt.* He dashed up the path they had made earlier. Thorpe and Damon scrambled after him.

When they reached the campsite, all three gasped for breath.

Lucas surveyed the bodies littering the beach. "My God." His two crewmen lay among five other strangers. He ran to the palm frond lean-to.

Empty. He swore, then regretted it. He should be praying instead.

Thorpe looked into Lucas' ashen face. "Sinbad's not here. Reckon he and the ladies escaped?"

Lucas wanted to believe it. But his gut told him something different. He wiped sweat from his upper lip with the back of his hand. "We must hurry and search before night falls."

They found two paths of escape through the jungle growth. Lucas recognized the yellow snips of Travay's dress on the bushes of one, and he went in that direction. *Dear God, save her.* The prayer reverberated through his heart with every footfall.

❦ 171 ❦

Thorpe and Damon took the path where it looked like something—or someone—had been dragged by several men.

All three of them burst out into the clearing, now empty but for a man on a stake at the water's edge. Thorpe and Damon reached Sinbad first. They kicked huge crabs right and left only a few yards from Sinbad's bare feet, and then cut the sweating man free.

Lucas saw a tall ship still anchored at the mouth of the cove. He breathed a prayer. *Thank God*. Maybe there was still a chance of saving Travay and Merle.

Sinbad rubbed salt water into his rope burns and wounds. "It's Pitt, Cap'n. The scar face."

"Yes, I guessed it from that bellow I recognized." Lucas looked closer at his friend, remembering how near the crabs were when they rescued him. "Are you all right, Sinbad?"

"Yes. I knowed yo God, our Jesus Christ, would save me. I were not afraid."

Lucas smiled. "Just in time, huh?"

They all four rested on the sand, out of sight of the ship. As the hot sun sank into the horizon, Lucas looked into each of the three faces before him. "There's only one thing to do. Board the ship after dark and do whatever we have to do to rescue the women. We'll have to take the vessel." He hesitated. They would be greatly outnumbered. "Are you with me?"

"We can do it, Cap'n. They's all full of the kill-devil." Sinbad wiped sweat from beneath his thick black forelock.

Lucas looked at him. He was the one crew member Lucas ever had who showed no liking for rum.

"If the crew are sleeping off their rum, we do have a chance. But there's still a lot of risk. Four against an entire crew." He examined each man's face. They could all end up chained in the ship's hold, under the control of Byron Pitt. And the women? Lucas forced that thought away.

"What other choice do we have on this deserted island?" Thorpe spoke up, sifting white sand between his fingers. He looked at

Lucas. "And the women. Who could leave them at Byron Pitt's mercy?"

Damon cleared his throat. "I heered about a small band of pirates who boarded a ship of rum-blasted sailors and put chains on their feet 'fore they knowed what happened. When they woke up, they give 'em the choice of join' wi' the new captain or stay in chains."

Sinbad and Thorpe turned to stare at the younger man.

Lucas grinned. "That just might be what we need to do, Damon. If you are all in agreement, we can start our planning." He took a deep breath and leaned forward. "But first, would you men join with me as we ask God's wisdom and protection tonight?"

"Yes, sir." Thorpe and Sinbad spoke together.

Damon's eyes grew bright. "I sure will, Captain. I'll never forget your prayers during the storm. Made me think of my grandma back in Wales."

Lucas found the courage to lift his gaze toward the three men. Words of Ethan Wentworth flowed into his spirit, and he spoke them. "'No matter what may befall me this night, I know that come the day I leave this earth, I will enter my eternal home in the heaven of heavens. That glorious door has been opened for me, a sinful man as any I've known, by Jesus Christ—who died for me, that I might live with Him forever.'"

All three men murmured, "Aye."

Then Lucas got on his knees in the sand and lifted his hands toward heaven. He was surprised to hear the clank of the other men's swords as they knelt also. He prayed words he scarcely heard. But a presence enveloped him and the men with him. He knew God was with them on their island somewhere in the Caribbean.

※ ❦ ※

Aboard the *Revenge*, Travay lay on the bunk in the cabin where Pitt had locked her and Merle with instructions to dress for dinner at the captain's table. He had pulled two fancy dresses from a trunk in the corner and thrown them over the table before he left. In the next hour, a pirate brought two buckets of water.

Merle took a deep breath. "My dear, I'm afraid I can't resist a bath and getting out of this ragged, dirty dress." Merle lifted a lovely blue dress and held it up for size. "This one is definitely too small for me, Travay. It's probably just right for you. The maroon one ought to fit me."

Travay pushed up from the cot, her tears all spent for Sinbad. "I refuse to dress for that monster."

"Don't do it for him, dear. Do it for yourself. Think how we've longed for a bath." Merle began her toilette, and Travay soon joined her.

After they had bathed and dressed, Merle rummaged around in the trunk and found a small hairbrush and three pearl combs.

"Good," she exclaimed. "Now I can tackle those tangles and twigs in your hair."

Travay sighed and sat down. Her aunt went to work on the wayward locks.

Soon Travay's gold-flecked hair trailed down her back in shining glory. Merle took two of the combs and deftly brought the sides up, leaving curls to frame Travay's face.

"There, now let me see what I can manage with one pearl comb." In a few minutes, Merle had her long gray-streaked hair twirled up and back and clamped firmly into a twist.

Travay tried to smile, but her face crumpled instead. "Oh, Aunt Merle, will we ever be safe again? Anywhere? I detest Byron Pitt, but there's still Roger Poole to contend with if we should somehow manage to make it back to Charles Town. One thing is sure. I never want to get on another vessel." She hung her head, and a tear escaped down her cheek. What chance was there Lucas could save her and her aunt this time? Or poor Sinbad? By the time Lucas returned to the camp from the search for water, Byron Pitt's ship would be far out to sea. It was to sail on the morning tide.

Merle put her arm around her. "Listen to me, Travay Allston, and listen well. Wipe those tears away. We will survive this, but we must use our wits. You know this Captain Pitt, or at least you've met him before. What can you tell me about him? At first, he sounded like a gentleman."

Travay wiped her wet face with her hand. "He told me once he was the third son of a nobleman and with no inheritance, he had to make his own way. But he is definitely no gentleman, believe me. You see the scar on his face? Lucas gave it to him after he attacked me on the way back from Jamaica."

"So that's what happened." Merle looked thoughtful. "Let's play the part of ladies and appeal to his gentlemanly background—if he told you the truth and he was once a gentleman. And let's pray the Lord will give us favor and protection." Once again, Travay knelt beside her aunt, hoping God heard them.

They had no more than stood from their prayer when they heard the door being unbolted from the outside. Byron Pitt entered wearing a stunning black-and-silver outfit and with his blond hair pulled into a queue. A shining sword jingled at his side. He stared at Travay, surprise on his face, which quickly ignited into lust. Merle moved toward him and held out her hand like she would have done in a Charles Town drawing room. He came to her side with his right arm extended. But he ogled Travay and extended his other arm to her. Travay swallowed her disgust and finally laid her hand on his arm.

At the door, he dropped Merle's hand but held firmly to Travay's in the narrow passage. Travay's satin skirts rustled against the tight walls as he led them to dinner at his table.

Travay stared wordlessly at the well-set table and cloth. But why not? Byron was a pirate who had undoubtedly stolen all the lovely plate and silver from a Spanish galleon.

He seated Travay at his right and Merle at the other end of the table. A middle-aged pirate soon entered and swaggered to a place beside Merle. His dark countenance and pointed black beard suggested he might have Spanish blood. A sword and two muskets clanged on his person when he sat. The smell of rum hung over him like a blanket.

Byron stood and bowed to the ladies. "You will have to excuse my other officers for their absence. Tonight is the crew's celebration of the hard work they've done the past three days restoring the *Revenge* to tip-top sailing condition." He tapped on his goblet with a spoon and a servant entered with bottles of red and white wine and a tray of food. Travay covered her goblet with her hand when he came to pour hers. But Merle nodded and held her goblet for the white wine. The servant poured all around, then placed the bottles on the table with the fare and left.

"I see your aunt has fine taste, Travay. Why don't you try the white wine too?"

"No, thank you, Byron." Travay tried to keep the scorn from her tone, but some must have slipped through. His lips puckered with annoyance. Out of the corner of her eye, Travay saw Merle give a small shake of her head. Then her aunt turned to the pirate next to her. "I am Merle Allston of Charles Town. May I ask your name?"

Red crept up the man's thick neck.

Byron guffawed at the other end of the table. "Sorry, Cortez is not used to polite dinner conversation. But he does have other talents, I can assure you."

Merle would not give up. "Cortez is your name? May I ask where you are from?"

"Vera Cruz, ma'am." The man emptied his wine glass and filled it again.

Pitt proceeded to eat heartily. He washed each bite of chicken and brown bread down with wine. He stopped when he noticed Travay had not taken a bite.

"Eat, milady. You are going to need your strength." He poked her with his elbow.

At the other end of the table, Merle picked up her fork and ate a small piece of chicken, all the while looking at Travay.

Finally, Travay lifted a nibble to her mouth. To her, it tasted like rubber, and she wanted to spit it out, but she continued to chew and finally swallowed it. But it didn't go down well, and she began to cough.

Byron stared at her as she grew red in the face. "Water," he bellowed, and the servant came quickly with a goblet of water.

Travay took it and finally got the offending food down. She didn't attempt to eat anything else, and Captain Pitt didn't seem to care. He had already downed a bottle of wine.

❧ ❧

As soon as darkness fell, Lucas and the three men entered the water and swam toward the ship. Each had a knife in his mouth and a sword tied to his waist. Lucas whispered a prayer of thanksgiving as the quarter moon sailed behind clouds. They had gone over their plan three times. The cool water washed away the sweat and grime of the past two days and refreshed Lucas and his partners.

The name *Revenge* painted on the brig's hull became decipherable. Lucas climbed the longboat ladder still hanging down the side and eased over the ship's rail. The half-asleep pirate on guard duty opened one eye as Lucas loomed over him and put him into a deep slumber before he could utter a word. The other three men slipped aboard. Pirates lay all over the deck, snoring.

The only sound of voices came from the captain's quarters. Lucas stationed Sinbad among the sleepers with a club to make sure they fell back to sleep while Thorpe and Damon rounded up ropes and chains.

Lucas tied a rope to the quarterdeck railing and lowered himself over the side. Braced against the hull, he grappled his way to the captain's quarters on the ship's outer ledge until he reached the row of windows to the cabin. He looked down into Byron Pitt's lair.

Pitt sat at the captain's table next to Travay. Merle sat beside another large pirate with his massive arms propped on the board and a mug cupped in his thick hands like it held a precious brew. Both Pitt and his mate had obviously been imbibing, by the looks of their slouching positions.

Lucas' lips thinned into a tight line as he saw the scratches on Travay's face.

Pitt leaned over and punched the other man on the arm. "I said, Cortez, why don't you escort Miz Merle to her cabin. Now."

The man lifted his bleary eyes from his tankard and looked at his captain. Pitt winked at him. Cortez staggered up and started toward Merle.

"I'm not leaving Travay." Merle stuck out her chin and grasped the arms of her chair.

Pitt took another long swig from his silver challis and sniggered. "You know how to handle an overripe tigress, don't you, old boy?"

"Corse I do." Cortez stopped behind Merle and lifted her still in the chair and staggered toward the door; Merle tried to kick at him. He just laughed at her efforts. At the door, he started to back out with her still in her seat but forgot to stoop. He struck his head on the frame with a loud thump and fell forward. The chair jolted to the floor, and Merle tumbled out. She sat on the floor, stunned for a moment, before pulling her skirts around her legs. The pirate didn't move. She stood shakily to her feet.

Pitt guffawed and yelled at Travay who had run to Merle's aid. "Come here, lassie." His words slurred. "I've waited a long time for you, girl."

Travay tossed her head and eyed him coldly.

"I said come 'ere!" Pitt stood and lunged around the table toward the ladies. He pulled Travay into his thick arms. She tried to push away from him. Every curve of her body spoke defiance.

Lucas kicked in the long window and burst through the opening onto the table, then jumped to the floor. "*You* come here, you dogsbody!" He pulled his sword from his side and stomped across broken glass toward Pitt.

Pitt pushed Travay aside so fast she fell against the wall. Merle rushed to her. They wrapped their arms around each other and huddled in the corner.

Pitt whisked his sword from its sheath and drove at Lucas. Lucas jumped aside. They parried back and forth, swords clanging and shooting sparks. Lucas found that even with a lot of drink in him, Byron was still a deadly foe.

Sweat broke out on both men's faces. Lucas swiped it from his eyes and scrambled away just as Byron made a running drive toward him, bellowing curses. When Lucas bolted aside, Byron's forward thrust propelled him through the wide broken window and into the sea below.

Lucas heard the splash, then silence.

CHAPTER 19

Lucas pushed his sword back into his baldric, swiped the sweat from his brow, and strode over to Travay and Merle. He took a moment to catch his breath. "Are you two all right?"

"Yes. Thank God for your rescue, Lucas. Again." Smiles wreathed Merle's face.

He looked at Travay. Her beauty in the bare lights of the lanterns astounded him. Her thick hair, now broken loose from its pearl combs, tumbled down her back. She had not uttered a word. Fear, stark and vivid, glittered in her eyes. His rasping breath stopped in his throat. If that swine had … had … "Are you well, milady?"

She lowered her face, and he saw a tear escape from under dark lashes. A fire burned up from his gut. He took her by the shoulders and pulled her to him. He lifted her chin with his thumb. "I asked if you are well, Travay. Did that slimy scalawag hurt you?"

"No, no, Lucas. He didn't harm me, and you are hurting my shoulder."

Lucas's breath came easier, and he released her. But she caught his arm.

"Oh, Lucas, they tide staked Sinbad!" Her moist eyes glistened like sapphires.

So Travay was becoming a compassionate woman. A great step forward from the arrogant, self-centered woman he had first rescued. "Sinbad is fine. Or at least he was when I left him on deck. I'd better get back up there and see how he and Thorpe and Damon are progressing with the besotted crew. And throw a rope to Pitt if he lives."

Lucas didn't miss the brightness that filled Travay's face when she heard Sinbad was fine. Nor her whispered, "Thank God."

He walked over to the still unmoving Cortez splayed out on the floor. Lucas took the pistol and sword from the man's side, then pulled a cord from his baldric and tied Cortez's hands behind his back. He strode back to Merle and Travay. "You two go back to your cabin and bolt the door until we secure the ship."

Merle nodded, and the two of them stepped around Cortez and headed back up the corridor.

After one more glance around, Lucas dashed up the passage.

A black servant, with a cook's apron, cowered behind the steps to the deck. He came out and fell down before Lucas. "Capt'n, I'se glad that man's gone. He wuz a bad one. I'se be glad to serve you if you spare me."

Lucas pulled the trembling youth to his feet. "You have nothing to fear if you mean that. Go back to your quarters and plan to serve breakfast to my crew in the morning."

"Yessir. Yessir." The man hurried off.

On deck, Lucas found an amazing sight. Sinbad and Thorpe had several pirates who had roused from their stupor already in chains and hobbles. Damon continued to check other chained members of the crew who groaned as he pushed at them with the toe of his boot.

"Great work, men." Lucas took a deep, relieved breath.

"We'll just leave them in these chains until they decide to sign our articles, huh, Captain Bloodstone." Thorpe wiped the sweat from his upper lip and forehead.

"That's right, Thorpe. Meanwhile, I'm going to drop a rope over the side. Byron Pitt might need it." Lucas hurried to the side of the gently bobbing boat and looked all around in the dark waters. He saw no trace of Pitt. He continued to search around the other sides of the ship in the moonlight, now bright on the island waters.

He turned to his three-man crew. "At first light, we will search ashore."

"Why do you care about the man? He was evil." Damon stared

at Captain Bloodstone.

"Because he's a man made in God's image, that's why." Lucas looked steadily into the young pirate's eyes until the man ducked his head and resumed tying up Pitt's crew.

❧ ❧

At first light the next morning, Travay and Merle heard loud groans and curses coming from above. In their cabin, they hurried their morning ritual and slipped up on deck. The sight staggered them. Pitt's entire crew struggled and cursed against the ropes and chains that held them as they lay or sat scattered about the deck. The smell of rum and unwashed bodies stung Travay's nose.

Thorpe, Sinbad, and Damon stood among them, smiling. Lucas stood on the quarterdeck with an eyeglass, scanning the waters and the cove. He stopped and looked long at the beach.

The chained pirates saw the women and began to whistle and make catcalls until Sinbad and Damon kicked them.

Thorpe spoke to Travay and Merle. "We think most of these pirates will readily agree to sign articles and sail with Captain Bloodstone when their only other choice is to spend their days and nights in irons. And we've just got Captain's articles written out."

One of the pirates, a stocky, deeply tanned middle-aged man, cocked his head at him. "I was forced on this here ship as carpenter, and I swear I'll be glad to join yer crew if you'll just get me back to Jamaica. There's several others got pressed here the same way."

Lucas turned to them from the quarterdeck. "Release the carpenter, Thorpe, and have him sign the articles."

Other pirates called out and held up their chained wrists. One yelled he was the head cook and if released he'd fix up some grub in no time. Another yelled he was the ship's doctor and would gladly assist the cook. Sinbad frowned but released both of them after a nod from Lucas. The two men skittered below deck. Two others said they'd be glad to sign articles and sail with Captain

Bloodstone and that they were good with the cannons.

Lucas snapped his eyeglass shut and motioned for Thorpe to join him aside. "Before we release any more, Thorpe, lower the rowboat so I can go bury Pitt. I believe that's his body on the beach. I'm leaving you, Sinbad, and Damon to handle things until I return."

Travay's heart jolted, and her pulse pounded as Lucas approached them dressed in a billowing green shirt, his dark hair now pulled into a queue. Tight brown breeches disappeared into knee-high boots. The look in his eyes when he met hers sent a tingle to the pit of her stomach. "Ladies, it will be best for you to stay below for the time being. I don't know how many of this crew we'll be able to trust, and I will have to release some more to sail the ship."

"Lucas, what are you going to do? What are *we* going to do?" Travay searched his handsome face and willed her heart to slow.

"First, I am going to bury Pitt."

Travay and Merle both flinched.

"Then we are going to sail the *Revenge* back to the nearest port where I can find passage for you two to Charles Town." Lucas turned on his heel and climbed over the ship's side to the small boat below.

Travay walked to the railing and watched Lucas row toward the white strip of sand. She sighed, her mind a crazy mixture of hope and fear. Would she and Merle make it to Charles Town like Lucas promised? Would she ever feel safe again? She turned and trudged down to the lower deck with Merle behind her.

An hour later, a knock sounded at the cabin door. Travay opened it and Lucas entered, a frown shadowing his face.

Travay's stomach clenched. "What is it, Lucas?"

"It's strange, but when I arrived on the beach, I could not find a body. I walked a half mile up the beach both ways but found nothing."

Her throat suddenly dry, Travay swallowed. The crabs? Or was Byron Pitt alive and well and still planning revenge?

A few days later, Lucas stood on the quarterdeck looking out over the waves sliced by the ship's hull. From the crow's nest, Damon cried, "A sail, a sail!" Thorpe bounded up to the quarterdeck as Lucas snapped open his eyeglass.

After studying the approaching ship, Lucas handed the glass to Thorpe. "What do you think? It's Spanish, all right, but look what's hanging from the masthead."

Thorpe stared through the glass for a full minute. "It appears to be a bell, but it shines so in the sun I can't be sure."

"It is a bell. A wedding bell." Lucas took the glass back and confirmed it.

"A wedding bell. What does it mean?" Thorpe scratched his head.

"It means it's a bride ship, taking a Spanish noblewoman to wed some Spanish viceroy she's probably never seen."

"Will we let her pass peaceably?"

"Of course." Lucas spat across the railing. "But don't mention anything about the bell to the crew. Some of them may know what it means and that usually there is a dowry of gold on board with the bride-to-be."

But ten minutes later, cannon shot splashed close across their bow. Lucas looked up at the masts and swore. One of the crew they had released must have replaced the English flag he had hoisted earlier. Pitt's pirate flag flapped in the wind. The next shot hit the mizzen sail. Lucas ducked and began shouting orders to Thorpe. The choice was out of his hands. He would have to unchain a few more men and deal with the culprit later. With Sinbad's help, he chose the men to be released and then issued orders. "Man the cannon, run up powder cartridges from the magazine, sand the top deck, have the men we can trust arm themselves with pistols, swords, and boarding axes!"

❧ ❧

In the cabin, Travay heard the cannon blasts and thumping feet and shouts on the deck. She trembled and moved close to Merle when someone banged on their door. Merle opened it.

Damon stood there, his eyes wide. "Cap'n says you leddies are to stay b'low deck. We got a battle on our hands, fer sure."

Merle dropped to her knees beside the bed. Travay sat on the bed and wrung her hands. Would she ever want to board another ship? Not if she made it off this one alive.

❧ ❧

Lucas knew the only way to avoid a broadside from the many guns of the galleon was to sail around her and attack across her bow when her crew least expected it. Their smaller brigantine could move faster and with more ease than the larger galleon.

Boom! Boom! Boom! He smiled at the expertise of Pitt's gunman. Every shot hit its mark. But the sound of snapping wood and the weird ripping of canvas told him the enemy's cannon had also reached a mark. He didn't move fast enough. Pain shot through him as a piece of wood sliced into his arm. He jerked the protruding missile out and pressed his palm against the warm flow of blood. Then he tied his bandana around it as tight as he could. He looked back at the Spanish ship.

"Fire all guns!" Lucas shouted, and the gunners went back to work. In moments, the simultaneous shots rocked the brigantine under Lucas' feet from bow to stern. Smoke filled the air and caused him and the pirates below to cough.

Smoldering flames rose from the Spanish galleon, and by the way its crew scurried on deck, Lucas knew some shots must have hit below the waterline. He directed the helmsman to steer near the beleaguered ship, now with a white flag hoisted on its mast.

"Prepare to board!" The crew had been waiting to hear the word. They threw their grappling hooks across to the other ship and followed Lucas as he swung aboard, his injured arm all but forgotten. The Spanish fought bravely but were no match for the motley crew with Lucas. Amid crippling cutlasses, screams of pain, and curses, the pirates overcame the ship's crew in a matter of minutes. Puddles of blood stood on the deck and bodies lay in grotesque death poses.

Lucas and the Spanish captain crashed about the deck in a deadly sword fight. All the pirates and the Spanish prisoners stood and watched. Finally, Lucas clobbered the sword of his opponent so hard it flew from the man's hand. Lucas touched the captain's throat with the tip of his sword. The man backed up to the railing, his rasping breath the only sound. Like a true soldier, he awaited Lucas' thrust, an angry scowl creasing his face rather than fear of imminent death.

The pirates shouted obscenities and yelled, "Kill him! Kill him!"

The Spanish captain crossed himself, and his eyes betrayed him as if he had just realized his next breath might be his last.

Lucas pulled his sword back and pushed it into his scabbard. He readjusted the bandana, now a bright red, on his injured arm. He gulped air into his needy lungs. "We really had no plan to harm you, sir. You fired on us first. Now, this motley crew I have to put up with will want any treasure you have aboard."

He motioned the captain to take his stand with the other prisoners.

A flash of gratitude crossed the man's face, and he moved like a wooden soldier to stand in front of his captured crew. He turned back to Lucas, his bushy brows raised. "What will happen to us, Captain?"

Lucas' nostrils flared. "We practice no Inquisition, sir. You will be carried to an island where you will hopefully be picked up by one of your Spanish ships." He turned away, swallowing bile that had risen in his throat as a face floated into his mind. His sweet mother. What had the Spanish done to her?

Sinbad stood guard over the prisoners. Thorpe came up to Lucas. "We've got to get off this ship as soon as possible. She's listing. And we need to take a look at that arm of yours, Captain."

"It's not deep, just a little bleeding, Thorpe." Lucas turned to acknowledge a grisly old pirate at his elbow.

"Cap'n, when you gonna give us the signal to search out th' hold?" The man swiped sweat from his scarred upper lip.

Lucas shouted to his crew gathered around him, "Search the hold."

The pirates scurried down into the bowels of the ship. Soon they came back with disappointment on their swarthy faces.

"Cap'n thar ain't no treasure in the hold we can find. Just some powder and foodstuffs and chests of women's clothes. But there is a door barricaded down the passage. Do you want us to knock it down?" The large pirate who spoke had a huge scar down one side of his scraggy face. His dark eyes gleamed with greedy anticipation.

Lucas glanced at Thorpe. *The bride's chamber.* "No, let me see to it." Another woman to protect until they landed portside. Just what he needed.

Lucas and Thorpe went to the door. Lucas knocked and spoke in passable Castilian. "My lady, I am an English captain who has overcome your ship. You and your party must come forth. This vessel is sinking. We will not harm you."

A man's confident voice answered. "I am the priest of the capital city of Mexico. I accompany the young daughter of the viceroy of Mexico, Contessa Maria Alvaro. Do you promise not to harm her, her maid, or her duenna?"

Three women. Lucas groaned. "We will not harm any of you. And I assure you, time is of the essence." Lucas stepped back as he heard the bars being raised on the other side.

The door opened, and a gray-headed priest in a black robe faced him. As he took in Lucas' and Thorpe's pirate attire and the obvious signs of battle on them, he inhaled sharply. Then his piercing eyes searched Lucas' face. He turned and beckoned to the women in the room. "Come, Senora Pilar, Contessa. I do not believe these men will harm us."

Two women, dressed in black high-necked bodices and both wearing mantillas, glided toward the door. One of the women was clearly the matron. Older and stouter, her pale face under her dark lace head scarf was as harsh as a blustery winter day. She swished rich silk skirts as she came to stand behind the priest.

The other woman, dressed as a servant, moved to stand behind her, stuffing a jeweled case under her shawl. Lucas smiled. The ladies probably had a fortune of other jewelry stashed under their clothing.

A lovely young woman of no more than fifteen came from behind a screen and joined them. She pushed her white lace head covering back from her flawless oval face. Her startling amber eyes widened in astonishment as they came to rest on Lucas. "Are you a real pirate?" Her lush lips spread into a smile, and she attempted to move closer to him.

Her duenna laid a restraining hand on her arm and hissed, "Contessa Maria, do not approach the man."

Lucas tried not to smile at the young woman's intense gaze. "No, milady. I am not a pirate. I am a privateer."

The elder lady covered a snort, and the priest looked toward heaven.

"And you have been wounded!" The girl's perusal rose from Lucas' blood-soaked bandana to his face. Then she looked away, color staining her cheeks.

Thorpe folded his arms and threw a raised brow toward Lucas.

"Milady, 'tis nothing. But you and your party must hurry. We have to abandon ship." Lucas pointed up the passage, and the priest led the way. The women followed.

The young Contessa kept turning back to glance at Lucas, her thick, dark curls escaping from her mantilla as she pressed up the passage. Her full skirt swished against the walls.

Lucas shook his head at Thorpe when the man tapped him on the shoulder and grinned.

⚜

Two days later, Travay sat in the cabin with Merle, the duenna Senora Pilar, the young Contessa Maria, and her maid Carmen. The Spanish ladies embroidered, their fingers flying. Travay and Merle worked at a more unhurried pace on the intricate squares pressed into their hands by the visitors.

Contessa Maria laid aside her piece and spoke directly to Travay in perfect English. "The Capitan, he is so handsome." The young woman's face glowed pink under its golden hue.

Her maid nodded in agreement and smiled.

The duenna's face stiffened, and she stopped sewing. "You must not say such things, Contessa." She shook her head at her charge. "You must remember you are to be the bride of the Viceroy of Cartagena, and your eyes must see no other man."

The Contessa's full lips protruded in a pout. "But I've *never* seen him. How do I know I will like him?"

Travay looked up from her own stitching. "You mean to say you have never seen the man you are to marry?"

"No. It is the custom. But I don't like it." The young woman sighed, laid down her work, and stood to look out the porthole.

Travay admired the elegant yellow silk gown, which rustled with every move the girl made.

The duenna shook her head and continued with her needlework.

Merle hesitated in her embroidery. "I have heard that noble Spanish families sometimes make these arrangements even in childhood. Is this not true, Senora Pilar?"

The woman grunted and suddenly laid her work aside. "Come Contessa. Let us walk on deck for some fresh air. That will make you happy. No?"

The young woman's eyes brightened. "Oh, yes. That will make me happy, Senora. And Carmen will come too."

Travay frowned. Of course it would make the girl happy. She would get to see Lucas. The girl was taken with the "Capitan."

The older woman searched in their trunk. "Get your cloaks. You know you must hide your faces from this awful pirate crew." The three of them donned dark cloaks with hoods. The younger two chattered as they headed up the passage.

Travay set her needlework aside and stretched back on the bed where she had been sitting in the cramped cabin. If the young Contessa was taken with Captain Bloodstone, why should she care? She turned her face to the wall as Lucas' handsome face invaded her thoughts. She clenched her eyes shut, but the vision only became stronger. She stood.

Merle looked up. "Heading to the deck too?"

"I think so." Travay grabbed a shawl and went into the passage. The sunset should be lovely. That was the reason she would go. At least she told herself it was.

When she stepped up on deck, she saw the Spanish ladies at the railing, their words muffled by the breeze. She moved behind some rigging to watch. The Contessa stared at the quarterdeck. Travay glanced up at Lucas in a flowing white shirt and black britches with a green sash blowing in the wind. His dark hair hung to his shoulders in plaits. He made a striking picture.

At that moment, Lucas' attention turned toward the Spanish ladies. The Contessa, her cheeks pink, gave a slight nod and a smile played on her lovely lips. Lucas bowed and turned back to scan the waves.

Travay's lips compressed into a tight line. Did he have any idea the young lady—a child, really—was besotted with him? She turned and flounced back down the hatch and passage to await the call to dinner.

Later, dressed in a green silk dress from a chest Lucas had found in the hold, Travay sat across from the priest and tried to carry on a conversation. "Do you know how long it will be before you and your party may arrive at a safe port?"

The elder man's pale gray eyes turned to her after he set his wine goblet down. "The captain says we should arrive in Jamaica within a week. From there we will be able to gain passage to Cartagena, I am fairly certain. Perhaps on a Dutch ship."

Of course, Lucas could not risk taking them to a Spanish port. She took another bite of the sea flounder on her plate. "I hope it all works out well for the Contessa."

"I am sure it will, milady." Then he added in a lowered voice, "It was very good of the captain to allow her to keep her dowry intact."

What? Lucas had kept back treasure from his gold-thirsty pirate crew? Travay glanced at him laughing with Thorpe, and with the undivided attention of the Contessa across the table.

※ ⤻

Lucas walked up the steps to the quarterdeck and watched the amber sun sinking below the white-capped waves. A rustling noise behind alerted him. He whipped around, his hand on the hilt of his sword. It was the Contessa's maid. He relaxed and prepared to warn her it was not safe to be about the decks alone at this time of evening.

"It is I, Contessa Maria, not my maid. I borrowed her cloak." The soft, silky voice moved closer. A graceful hand pushed the cloak back from the shining black upsweep of hair held by golden combs.

"Milady, you must not come on deck alone like this." He forced his voice to sound stern but kept it low to avoid being overheard. "Let me escort you back to your cabin. And stop talking, or the whole crew will know you've been foolish." He extended his arm.

She ignored it and leaned toward him, whispering. "Wait. I see your eyes flashing those sparks I've seen when you are angry." Her lovely young face glistened with a glossy sheen in the gathering darkness. "I have only known of one other with eyes the color of jade like yours, dear Capitan. But it was a woman. An English woman captured by one of our Spanish galleons."

Lucas's heart bolted in his chest. He grabbed her by the shoulders.

She winced but then smiled up into his face.

"Tell me what you know of this woman." His voice grated up from his throat. It had been louder than he wanted, and he pulled her into the shadows, hoping none of the crew had heard.

She leaned closer. Her breath came in short gasps. "Do you want to kiss me, Capitan?"

Lucas almost swore. "No, I want to know about this woman with the same eyes." Without realizing it, his hands pressed hard into her small shoulders.

"You're hurting me, dear Capitan. But I don't mind. Kiss me, and I'll tell you about the lady." She stood on her toes and lifted her mouth to him with a pretty pout on her tender lips.

Now Lucas did swear, but under his breath. He drew her to him and touched her lips with his own. Then he moved her back an arm's length.

Her dark lashes fell, a wonderful smile spread over the lips he had just tasted, and she started to sway, her eyes closed.

"Contessa, open your eyes and speak to me. Tell me all you know about this woman. And keep your voice low." Lucas struggled to keep his own voice soft with the blood pounding in his temples at what the girl had revealed.

The young woman expelled a long, deep breath. She opened her heavy lids and gazed at him. "Yes, I did promise, didn't I?"

He turned her and placed her hands on the railing to support her trembling body, but he still held her around her waist to keep her upright.

The girl took a deep breath and leaned into Lucas. She laid her head on his chest and closed her eyes. He dared not push her away for fear she would stop talking.

"The woman has been my best friend's governess for the past many years. I don't remember how many." She turned back to look Lucas in the face. "I often visited, so I saw much of her. Why are you interested, Capitan? Surely she is too old for you." The girl giggled but gasped when Lucas' hands gripped her shoulders once more.

His mind whirled. How much dared he tell her? "This woman is still your friend's governess? She still lives?" His heart beat so fast, he was sure the girl could hear it.

"She was alive when I left St. Augustine a month ago."

Lucas' mind soared. St. Augustine. He would find his mother and bring her home. "What family is she with?" He must know the name.

But the girl was a vixen. She turned and leaned toward him again. "That information deserves another kiss." She lifted her chin and puckered her lips.

He leaned down and kissed her. She reached her arms around his neck and flung herself against him. He pushed her back, gritting his teeth at the heat rising in his body. She was only a child. Again, he had to hold her to keep her from falling.

"Tell me now." *Or I might be tempted to throw you over this railing, my lovely young one.*

"It is the Carlos Santiago family in St. Augustine." The girl breathed deeply and smiled up at him.

Lucas turned her toward the steps with a firm hand. "Come, I will escort you back to your cabin."

"Yes, Capitan." The girl clung to his arm as they moved down the quarterdeck steps toward the lower-level entrance.

Travay had found their cabin stuffy after dinner and decided to take a brief walk on deck. She covered her bright hair with a scarf and decided to keep to the dim areas where the fading sun failed to reach. No need to beg for trouble from the pirates on watch. She held her skirts close to reduce their swishing sound as she passed from shadow to shadow toward a secluded spot in the stern where she could look out over the glassy sea.

She leaned over the railing and took a wonderful deep breath of fresh, moist air. Suddenly she heard sounds from the quarterdeck. She saw two people standing very close. They whispered, then embraced and kissed. She heard the rustle of silk as the woman drew back, her face now clear in the moonlight. The young Contessa. Then she heard a low, commanding voice, one she knew too well.

Travay turned quickly and headed back into the passage before the two coming down the steps could see her. A pain squeezed her heart. Her walk for a little fresh air had been most enlightening. This was the real Lucas. An unscrupulous man who would take advantage of an innocent young woman, another man's fiancée. A cradle robber in addition to being a pirate and thief. Her conclusion left her with an inexplicable feeling of emptiness.

CHAPTER 20

The next morning, Lucas stood on the quarterdeck enjoying the cool morning breeze flapping the sails. His mind churned with the possibilities of how he would rescue his mother. Surely the woman the Contessa described was his precious mother. He leaned over the railing and thanked God for the new hope.

"A sail. A sail!" The lookout's voice rang from the top mast.

Lucas whipped out his eyeglass and scanned the ocean. He saw it too. Coming up fast on their larboard side. Could it be a Spanish treasure ship? Then he saw their colors and lowered the glass. A frown creased his brow.

Thorpe swung up on the quarterdeck, and Lucas handed his first mate the glass.

"A British ship, a large one. In fact, if I'm not mistaken, it's a man-of-war." Thorpe turned to Lucas. "What do you think a British man-of-war would be doing so deep in these Spanish waters? Could we be in open war with Spain?"

"In that case, I think we'd be seeing a fleet, not a lone ship." Lucas kept his eyes on the ship as it overtook them. Instead of passing, the man of war sent a shot over their bow.

"What in tarnation?" Lucas frowned and lifted the eyeglass again. Couldn't they see his English flag flying in the wind? He looked straight into the glass of the captain on the man-of-war. He saw him lower his glass and heard him shout, "Heave to, *Revenge*, you're under arrest by the British Crown. We have all our guns trained on you."

Lucas almost dropped his eyeglass and glanced at Thorpe. The man's face had turned pasty under his deep tan. Surely he had heard wrong.

Every crewman on board, including Sinbad at the ropes, stopped dead still and watched the British ship draw near.

The *HMS Greyhound* lowered a longboat and soon boarded the *Revenge*. The British captain in his impeccable Royal Navy uniform marched up to Lucas with a number of marines trailing him, guns drawn.

The leader stopped before Lucas. "I am Captain James Hawkins of His Majesty's Navy. Sir, are you the captain of this ship?"

Lucas' breath stopped in his throat. The young man who had taken Travay to the Drakes' ball in Charles Town. But the captain would not recognize Lucas who had been in his fastidious merchant's costume at the soiree.

"Yes, sir," Lucas answered. "What's the idea of firing a shot over our bow? Can't you see we're good English citizens? We sail out of Charles Town."

"Are you Captain Bloodstone, alias Lucas Barrett?"

Lucas's eyes narrowed, and his body stiffened. "Yes, sir."

Beside him, Thorpe put his hand on the hilt of his sword, but Lucas stayed it.

"You're under arrest, and this ship and crew are now seized by the Crown." The captain turned to the men with him. "Take both these men. Put them in chains in the hold."

"Aye, aye, sir." The robust soldiers moved toward Lucas and Thorpe almost in step.

Lucas' face flooded with heat. "Wait a minute, sir! Why are you arresting us?" The marines proceeded to tie his hands and Thorpe's behind their backs, and none too gently. They also divested them of their swords and knives.

The captain took a document from inside his coat. "Captain Lucas Bloodstone Barrett, I arrest you for firing upon and plundering Spanish ships against the edict of King George who revoked all letters of marque and who has decreed the death sentence for all pirates who did not sign pardon papers by the twenty-first."

Lucas dug his heels into the deck as the soldiers tried to pull him forward. "I've been at sea these five weeks. I did not hear about the new edict."

"Too bad." The captain motioned to the marines. They pulled Lucas and Thorpe to the side of the ship and forced them into the longboat. Sinbad's murderous growls from the deck and curses from the marines trying to subdue him filled the air. Lucas grimaced. It took six marines to knock the African out and get a chain on him.

※ ﾞ

Travay continued to peer out the porthole after the boom of a cannon blast, but whatever was going on, it was happening on the other side of the ship. Were they under attack again? A strange silence reigned for a time before a loud knock sounded on their door of their cabin followed by a command. "Open in the name of His Majesty, King George."

Her eyes flew to her aunt, who dropped the embroidery from her hands.

Merle opened the door and stood aside, cocking her head, as a British captain entered, his gold-trimmed officer's hat under his arm.

Travay gasped. Captain James Hawkins, the solicitor's nephew and pirate hunter.

His eyes brightened as he recognized her. He gave a deep bow. "Miss Allston, it is my distinct pleasure to see you again, although I regret the circumstances. May I ask after your health and that of your aunt?" He turned toward Merle and bowed.

Travay's heart pounded, and her mouth went dry. What had happened to Lucas? "Captain Hawkins, what is the meaning of this?"

"Milady, we have taken this ship and arrested its captain and all the crew. I am here to rescue you and your aunt."

Lucas taken. "But who will sail this ship home?"

"I have appointed a British squad to sail the *Revenge* to Charles Town. I request that you and your aunt pack your belongings and board my ship as soon as possible. And do I understand there are other passengers?" He directed his question to Merle.

She cleared her throat and replied, "Yes, just down the corridor. There is a priest, and two Spanish ladies and their maid."

He bowed, turned on his heel, and proceeded down the passage.

A marine waited at the door as Travay and Merle bundled the new clothing Lucas had given them into a trunk in the corner.

✸ ✸

Lucas sat in the dark, stinking hold of the British man-of-war in a cell with Thorpe and five others of their crewmen. One of them turned to Lucas. "Wonder where they are taking us?"

Sinbad, in his own special cell down the row, growled, "Charles Town, I done heard. To them hanging gibbets at low tide. But they'll never hang me is what I say."

Ayes erupted from the other prisoners, followed by curses.

His stomach rebelling with hunger pangs, Lucas picked the weevils from the hardtack they had been served and stuffed the bread into his mouth. How were Travay, Merle, and the Contessa faring on a British man-of-war? And would the young captain pursue Travay at every opportunity? What did she think of him? He had escorted her to the Drakes' Ball.

Lucas pushed away familiar jealous feelings. He had no claim and never would have a claim regarding Travay Allston. He forced his mind back to the information the young Contessa Maria had given him about a woman who sounded much like his mother, and his heart lifted. Why would God give him this new information and then let him be hanged before he could rescue her? He knew God better than that. He took a deep breath and leaned back on the straw and soon fell fast asleep.

On the third day at sea, Travay sat at the captain's table, dressed in a frothy rose gown found in her cabin. She suspected the giver might have been Captain Hawkins but had no way of knowing. She and the other women had been brought aboard the man-of-war when the marines assigned to sail Lucas' ship to Charles Town took command. They had been treated with respect. The captain, formal in his British uniform and responsibility, kept his distance. But when she met his eyes across the table, she saw the bright interest he wanted to conceal from his men. He must never learn of her friendship with Captain Bloodstone, or it might go even worse for Lucas.

Her heart rolling in turmoil, she pushed the food around on her plate. What were the prisoners in the hold being fed, if anything? But why should she care? Disgust rose in her throat as she remembered Lucas kissing young Maria in the shadows on the deck of the *Revenge*. He had seemed to avoid the Contessa afterward, but what did that signify? Had they met again secretly? Why did that idea bring a pain to her heart? Travay forced such thoughts from her mind and looked around the table.

Merle and Senora Pilar seemed to be enjoying the British ship's fare and the captain's conversation.

The Contessa, shining like an angel in her white silk and lace, leaned toward Travay and whispered, "I hate this capitan. I detest what he is doing to Capitan Bloodstone. He may be beaten and hurt. How can you sit here and act like nothing is wrong?"

Travay looked at the younger woman and sighed. "What else can we do?"

"We can ask to visit the prisoners." The Contessa sat up tall in her chair and pushed the white lace mantilla from one ivory shoulder with a graceful movement of her wrist. "I will see to it."

The eye of every male present turned toward her when she

cleared her throat.

"Sir Capitan, I have a great favor to ask." She gave him a beguiling smile and cocked her chin.

Travay could well imagine Maria twisting almost any man around her dainty finger. Lucas had proven no problem.

Captain Hawkins' face turned pink as he looked at her. "And what is that, Contessa?"

"I want to visit the prisoners."

He blotted his lips with his napkin and laid it on the table beside his plate. "Why would a lovely young woman like you want to visit the brig? It is no place for women."

"But I demand to see if they are being treated kindly. I am well aware of what goes on in the holds of ships. My father has ten ships." Her dark eyes narrowed, and she banged her small fist on the table.

The captain exchanged glances with his first lieutenant. The air around the table grew tense.

The captain cleared his throat and surprised Travay with his next words. "Very well then, milady, you shall indeed see the brig and the prisoners." He turned to his second mate, a young man of no more than twenty. "Mr. Braswell, escort Contessa Maria and her duenna to the brig first thing in the morning. After breakfast, of course."

Senora Pilar rapped her silver spoon on the table. Every head turned in her direction. "No. I cannot allow it, and I will not go." She sat back as if the matter were settled.

Captain Hawkins lifted a brow as he looked from Maria to her duenna.

Travay took a deep breath. So this had been his plan to start with. He had known the elder woman would never agree. Travay's voice cut the thick silence. "I will go with her."

The captain turned to look at her. His face and voice softened. "You, milady? Surely you do not wish to do this. Do you have any idea what the prison on a ship is like? The smell is terrible. The hold of a ship is often infested with—"

"I will go." Travay did not hesitate to reply.

The man loosened his collar, frowned, and looked straight ahead. "Very well. I suggest both you ladies take handkerchiefs. You will surely need them." With that, the captain stood, signifying the dinner was over. He turned on his heel and left without another glance at either Travay or the Contessa.

Walking down the passageway, Travay couldn't help smiling when she thought of the boldness of the young Contessa.

Maria touched her arm. "I will bring a handkerchief, but it will be filled with good things." She pulled pieces of bread from her sleeve. "And tomorrow I will get boiled eggs and cheese, too."

The next morning, Travay awoke at the sound of the five-thirty bells. By the seven-thirty bells, she and the Contessa, Merle, and the duenna sat at the captain's table, although he was not present. Travay found herself stuffing everything she could into her pockets when no one was looking. She knew Maria did the same. They would have enough to bless several prisoners.

Finally, Second Mate Braswell stood and bowed before them. "Ladies, if you are ready, we will descend."

Merle leaned over and slipped a sausage into Travay's already stuffed pocket.

Senora Pilar sniffed and glared at the Contessa.

Carmen came up from the servants' quarter and slipped another egg to Maria.

The walk down into the bowels of the ship made Travay's breathing difficult as fresh sea air grew scarce and the smell grew putrid.

Mr. Braswell lit a lamp from the wall and carried it in his hand when they reached the bottom level where no sunlight could invade.

"Watch your steps, ladies, and the puddles of ... water."

Travay saw the bars as the lantern lit the way.

"Is this it? Where is Capitan Bloodstone, sir?" The Contessa's young feminine voice echoed down the dark passageway, and all sorts of voices rose in catcalls.

"Hey, fellows, we got us a leddy visito—or maybe she's just a 'hore."

"Hey, my pretty, why don't you sidle over here and gi'me a lit'l kiss?"

The second mate rattled his sword against the wall. "Shut your foul mouths, men, or it will be twenty lashes for each of you." He stopped beside a cell.

Lucas came to the bars. Travay gasped. He looked pale and shaggy with three days' beard on his face, but his eyes caught hers, and he smiled.

"Oh, Lucas." Tears sprang to Travay's eyes, but the Contessa pushed in front of her and reached her hand through the bars to Lucas.

"Look, we have brought you good food." She began to empty the contents of her pockets into Lucas' hands, then Thorpe's and the other hands that quickly stretched out in the light of the lantern held by Braswell.

Travay blinked back the tears threatening to spill down her cheeks, and she filled the hands reaching from the cells.

Thanks erupted from the prisoners before the sounds of eating made words impossible for several minutes.

Then Lucas' deep voice rose from within the cell. "Travay, Contessa, we appreciate what you have done, but this is no place for you to come again. Do you hear me?" His words carried the strong authority they always did. He came to stand as near as the bars allowed, close to Travay. His eyes searched her face as if making a memory. "You must go. Now, Travay, and don't come back."

The Contessa leaned against the iron rails toward him. "I will get my father to have you released."

Travay backed away and tried pulling the Contessa with her. Something scampered across Travay's foot, and Maria's satin-encased foot stepped on whatever it was. It squeaked, a piteous sound.

The Contessa screamed and jumped back toward Second Mate Braswell who managed to catch her around the waist with his free arm. The lantern in his other hand swung ominously.

The young woman turned and looked up admiringly into the mate's face, which was a scant inch from hers. He promptly turned a deep red. She giggled.

He struggled back into his British officer composure. "Ladies, let's go." He helped Maria regain her footing and removed his arm from her waist.

"Certainly, Mr. Braswell." The girl's full lips spread into a deep smile as she moved away from him and adjusted her skirts.

"Goodbye, Lucas." Travay's voice broke. Would she ever see him again?

"Goodbye, Travay."

Lucas's voice, calm and assured, did not give her any relief from the clamps around her heart. How could he be so at peace in such a horrible place?

The Contessa stayed close to the second mate as they ascended from the hold. At the cabin door, she lingered behind Travay and awarded Mr. Braswell a warm gaze. He promptly turned two shades of scarlet, bowed, and departed.

So, the little fox had another bird in mind to charm. Sorry, Lucas.

CHAPTER 21

In Charles Town, His Majesty's soldiers escorted Lucas, along with Thorpe and Sinbad and the rest of the crew of the *Revenge*, down the moldy steps of the Court of Guard dungeon. As they reached the lowest level, the smell of sweat, unwashed bodies, and decay hit Lucas' nose like a portentous cloud. Who knew how long they'd be held here before the trial.

He tromped between the guards through the labyrinth of corridors. Their boots echoed on the uneven stone, and his captors' swords clanged at their sides. Lucas surveyed the brick walls, floors, ceilings, and the small slits that passed for windows emitting little light. What hope of escape was there from such a place?

As they passed the cells, catcalls, curses, and petitions for help from prisoners packed six or more to a space followed them. Sobs rose from a corner filled with dirty straw. Lucas frowned to see a woman in the same cell with men. As he passed more cells, another woman reached out a thin, pale arm and touched his shoulder. He turned to glance at her.

"Hello, there, handsome. Wish they'd put you in my cell."

He looked into the smiling, dirty face of a middle-aged woman dressed in rags, with rotten teeth and empty spaces souring her smile. What had she done to deserve this hole?

Up the corridor, the guards stopped and herded Lucas' crew into two cells, but they held him back. Sinbad and Thorpe looked at him through the bars, their faces impassive. A guard jabbed Lucas, and he made his way forward down the passage.

One of the guards snickered as he pushed Lucas into a smaller cell with another prod between his shoulder blades. "You get your own little corner of hell, being the captain and all. Big pirate man." He slammed the heavy iron-barred door shut with a rusty clang. His raucous, mocking laughter, joined by the other guards, spread through the dungeon as they stamped back up the passageway and the steps.

A hopeless silence descended in the thick shadows. It was worse than the catcalls. Lucas sat down on the corn husk mattress and inspected his new home. Fairly clean straw littered the hard floor. A water bucket sat near the door and another bucket for personal matters sat in a corner. All in all, he'd been in far worse places— in the hold of Ned Low's ship, for example. With that memory, Travay came back into his mind. How desperate the straits she and her aunt must have found themselves in to attempt returning to England. Thank God, they had all escaped the insane pirate Low.

I delivered you because I delighted in you.

Lucas almost fell off the cot. Had God spoken to him? And how could God delight in a man who had done all he had done and who still held revenge in his heart?

A man like David. Or Paul.

Lucas listened for several minutes. Would the voice come again? Finally, he leaned back on the meager bed, even though it was probably full of lice. What he wouldn't give for his Bible, now seized, along with his ship, by His Majesty's Royal Navy.

Lord, if that was you, then you know I am in need of deliverance again. And my men.

He listened for a time and then fell asleep.

On the third day, Lucas looked up from his solitary cell to see a visitor coming down the corridor escorted by the guard.

Sir Roger Poole.

The pompously dressed council member strolled up to the cell door and looked at Lucas, now dirty and smelling like all the rest of his crew, none of whom had had baths since their arrest in the Caribbean.

"Well, Lucas, imagine your ending up here, like this." Sir Roger lifted a perfumed handkerchief to his nose. "Pirating doesn't pay well, does it?"

Lucas disdained to give any kind of retort. He sat on what passed for a bed and glared at the man.

"You know, you might say your life is really in my hands. Let's see. You will stand trial, and you'll most surely be convicted with the witnesses we have lined up. Then you'll be hanged at low tide. I wonder if I can get Travay to watch."

Lucas jumped up and reached through the bars for Roger Poole's throat, but the man stepped back just in time. He smirked and walked away. He turned back in the corridor, his form outlined by the dim light streaming down the steps. "You know Travay *will* marry me, eventually. I always get what I want."

Lucas shook the bars and then paced back and forth in the small cell. Disgust flowed out of every pore. He knew he should pray, but he couldn't get the fire out of the back of his throat. How he would love to get his hands around the man's neck.

"Lucas, what are you thinking?"

The voice of Reverend Wentworth stirred Lucas from his dark thoughts. The man had slipped down the corridor while Lucas was too furious to notice.

A guard opened the door to admit the minister into the cell. Ethan sat on the corn husk mattress holding a covered dish in his hand. He motioned Lucas to come sit beside him.

Lucas plunked down, stiff as a board. "I wouldn't want to tell you what I'm thinking, Ethan. And even after I believe I heard God's voice when I first came here."

"That's great news, Lucas. Hannah and I have been praying hard for you. What did the Lord say to you?"

Lucas looked at the gentle face of his friend and tried to feel once more something of the closeness he had felt with God just three days earlier. "I was thinking about the time we were captives on Ned Low's ship. Travay and Merle became captives also, but God delivered us all from that insane menace. As I was thinking about that, I heard the voice of God say that he delivered me because he delights in me."

"That's wonderful, Lucas. Of course God delights in you and how you've given your heart to Him. I believe He's going to deliver you again. And I'm going to pay the guard to let me bring you water to bathe, as well as some fresh clothes." Ethan uncovered the bowl in his hands. "But here's the first thing we need to take care of." He uncovered a container of warm soup and pulled a thick chunk of bread from inside his coat. "Hannah sent this."

Lucas' stomach quivered in anticipation. He made short work of the succulent beef stew and crusty bread. After the last swallow, he turned to Ethan. "What can you tell me about Travay?"

"Travay and her aunt are fine right now. Sir Roger Poole is still pressing his suit, of course, and so far Travay has refused him."

Lucas shook his head. How could he be of any help to her now?

Ethan continued. "Hannah and I have done, and will continue to do, everything in our power to help them. But Hannah, my precious Hannah, is due almost any time now."

Lucas looked up. Guilt assailed him for not even asking about Ethan's pregnant wife.

"How is Hannah doing?" A dark sadness seized Lucas, and his shoulders sagged. The hangman's noose swayed like a specter before his eyes. Would he live to father a child?

Ethan's face lit up with a strange light. "Hannah is doing fine. And I want to tell you I believe the Lord just confirmed to me you will one day have a wife as loving as Hannah and have children around your knees."

Lucas' head jerked up. The man seemed to have an uncanny ability to read a person's thoughts. Or did God relay them to Ethan?

The minister laid his hand on Lucas' arm and prayed for him. Warmth ran up Lucas' arm and touched his besieged mind. Ethan's prayers always seemed to help.

The guard's heavy tread descending the steps echoed through the dim cubicle.

Lucas took the minister's hand. "Ethan, thank you for coming. Thank you for that good word. I receive it. I choose to believe it."

Ethan leaned close before leaving the cell. "Tomorrow, the water and fresh clothes, and as much bread as I can carry for you and those of your crew." At the cell door, he turned and whispered, "After that, I plan to bring Travay to see you."

Lucas' heart jumped into his throat. How he longed to see her. But did she want to see him? He sniffed and grimaced. Not until after the bath. Definitely not.

Lucas called after the minister. "And I have some good news to tell you when you come back, my friend."

The minister turned and smiled, and then disappeared up the stone steps.

❧ ❧

Two days later, Travay sat in the carriage beside Reverend Ethan Wentworth and tried to concentrate on what he was saying. Her heart kept singing. *Lucas, Lucas, I'm going to see Lucas.* Bird song, plenteous in the trees over Bay Street, seemed to echo her melody, as did the clip-clop of the horse's hooves on the cobblestone streets of Charles Town. The silence of the reverend caused her to turn and face him.

"I'm sorry, did you ask me something?"

The minister smiled. "I said you need to prepare yourself, milady."

Travay turned cold. Was something wrong with Lucas? Was he injured? Would he be in heavy chains? She couldn't imagine Captain Lucas Bloodstone Barrett in any form but fierce. "Prepare for what, Reverend Wentworth?"

"Charles Town's Court of Guard dungeon. It's not a pretty place, Travay. I doubt you've ever seen what you will see today."

"But is Lucas well? He's not injured or sick?"

"Lucas is fine. He's not injured, at least not physically."

Travay sighed in relief.

He turned to look at her. "This is a real test for Lucas in many ways. He has lost almost everything, except the most important thing."

She looked at the man. Would he start preaching to her? Yet she had to ask the question. "And what is that, Reverend Wentworth?"

"His faith in God."

Inwardly, Travay wanted to scoff, but she had too much respect for the minister whom she had come to know over the past week of Lucas' imprisonment. He and his wife Hannah had befriended her and her aunt when they needed friends in the Carolina colony. Especially now that they were almost penniless, and with no funds left to sail to England. Solicitor Hawkins saw to it that they had food. Captain James Hawkins had wanted to help but was back out to sea.

Her arch enemy was very much still in the city. Bile rose in Travay's throat at the thought of Sir Roger Poole and his constant attentions. He had allowed them to move back into Merle's former home. They had no other choice.

Travay clutched the minister's arm as they descended the steps into the dungeon behind the guard. A terrible stench of unwashed bodies, urine, and decay arose from its shadowy depths. She held a handkerchief to her nose. The cold dampness increased with every step down, and curses echoed from its stone walls. They were leaving sunlight and everything good behind them. Tears sprang to her eyes as she thought of Lucas held in such a place.

At the bottom of the steps, Reverend Wentworth guided her down the corridor. She could hardly see as they left the shaft of sunlight behind. Something crawled onto Travay's satin shoe, and she kicked it away. She side-stepped and lifted her skirt to see in the dim light. On the damp stones, next to her foot, a giant cockroach lay on its back, its long legs flailing in the air. Travay screamed.

A cacophony of growls and grunts responded down the corridor.

"That were a woman's scream," a guttural voice announced.

Hopeless, dirty faces gathered and shook the bars of the cells. Prisoners called out vile invitations.

The guard yelled, "Shut up, ye slimy rats, or ye'll get what for."

Reverend Wentworth pulled Travay close to his side and whispered hoarsely, "Sweet Jesus, have mercy on these souls."

The brief prayer calmed her.

Soon the guard stopped before a cell and left them. As her eyes adjusted, Travay saw a movement in the shadows near the back stone wall. Lucas stepped forward, kicking aside straw and looking every bit the Captain Bloodstone of her dreams with his dark braided hair and worn black boots. He wore a simple white shirt and black breeches. Tears pooled in her eyes. She pushed her hands between the bars. He took them into his callused ones and raised them to his cheek. He opened a palm and kissed it.

"Lucas, didn't I try to warn you about piracy? How can you stand such a place?" Her voice cracked.

His flashing eyes caressed her face with such tenderness, a tear plopped down her cheek. He reached between the bars and wiped it away. "I've been in worse."

He released Travay's hands and turned toward the minister. "Greetings, my friend. I was in a quandary about your bringing her here, Ethan, but seeing Travay makes me want to live."

Icy fingers slivered up Travay's spine. "Live? Oh, Lucas. What will happen at your trial?" How could she live without him? That startling thought reverberated through her being and warmth spread to her cheeks. How had she fallen in love with a pirate? Maybe she had loved him since childhood when he took that terrible beating for her over the horse accident. All her disgust at his becoming a pirate dissipated with the force of this new comprehension. Her knees turned to water, and she grasped the bars.

Then she remembered the Contessa and Lucas' kisses she had witnessed that night on the quarterdeck. She stiffened. "Would you rather see Contessa Maria, Lucas?"

"The Contessa? That vixen? I have to tell you, Travay, the

information I finally wrestled out of her."

"Information?"

"Yes, I believe the Contessa has seen my mother alive. And I must somehow get to St. Augustine and rescue her." He turned to the minister. "Ethan, that's the good news I mentioned."

Ethan's eyes grew warm. "Praise God."

Travay raised a brow. "Wrestled out of her? Was that what you were doing? I happened to be on deck one night when you and the Contessa were thick as thieves. It didn't look like you were getting information, Lucas. You took her in your arms."

"Travay, she would not give me the details unless I kissed her. Can you believe the guile of one so young?"

Travay smiled. Yes, she could believe it after the way she saw the Contessa go after the second mate until they docked in Charles Town. The duenna had taken the girl in hand and rushed her aboard a Dutch ship headed toward Spanish waters.

"Lucas, what about ..." Travay couldn't voice her fear of the trial and verdict.

His voice held hope. "I believe things are going to work out for me, Travay. False charges have been brought, but the good Lord will deliver me. Like He has many times. Why else would He give me this great hope about my mother?" He looked at the minister.

"It is my and Hannah's fervent prayer, Lucas. Is there anything you can tell us to do that will help?"

"Yes, what can we do, Lucas?" Travay's voice, hoarse with emotion, surprised her.

"Ethan, you know I've never fired on a British ship. In fact, I've helped deliver at least two from Spanish attacks. You might see if you can get in touch with those captains.

"I'm already working on that, my friend."

Lucas' warm gaze brushed Travay's face again. "And surely the judge will see that I could not know my letter of marque had been revoked when I was on the high seas with no way to hear the news."

Ethan cocked his chin. "I certainly hope that's true, Lucas.

But in case it's not, will you give me permission to write to your mother's brother in England? Surely he has better contacts."

Fire flashed in the startling eyes Travay knew so well, and Lucas' features hardened.

"Lucas, please let Reverend Wentworth write to him." Travay reached between the bars again and touched his tight cheek. "You must know how much this means to me."

❧ ☙

Lucas' heart threatened to hammer out of his chest. He gazed at Travay's face, followed each plane and dimple. Was she saying that she loved him? He saw it in her clear blue eyes and the way her lips trembled when his eyes paused there. Could he break his parents' twenty-year silence enforced by his mother's noble family—the same proud family that had been the cause of their leaving England to become indentured servants? He was only a child of nine at the time, but he understood more than his parents realized. Bile rose in his throat. He'd rather hang than ask her family for help now.

"No. I do not want you to contact him, Ethan."

CHAPTER 22

In the carriage, Travay stamped her foot. "I can't believe he can be so stubborn when his very life might depend on it. Why won't he let you write to his uncle?"

Ethan Wentworth appeared unruffled. "There's still a lot of bitterness in Lucas, I'm afraid. For one, the way he and his parents were treated by her aristocratic family after his mother married a common tutor."

"I don't care what happened back then. I just ..." Tears began to course down Travay's cheeks. She brushed them away. "Reverend Wentworth, I just care what happens to Lucas now, and I want to find any help we can."

The minister patted her hand. "Absolutely. So do I. So do I." He smiled at her, his eyes bright with a special light. "Don't worry. I learned long ago that I must listen for the voice of God and do whatever He says as final authority."

What did that mean? Would he write the letter anyway? Had he *already* written it? She wanted to ask him, but the carriage stopped at her aunt's door.

❧ ❧

The day of Lucas' trial dawned dark and stormy for early November in Charles Town. Reverend Wentworth advised Travay not to go but she couldn't stay away. She had worked it out with their old friend John Hawkins, Merle's solicitor, to come by for her in his carriage.

He helped her into the coach at quarter of nine. The heavy clouds burst, and rain pelted the carriage all the way to the colonial building that served as His Majesty's courthouse.

When they walked into the crowded, noisy room, moldy dampness, human sweat, and uncleanness assailed Travay's nose. Male and female voices in English, French, and an occasional Scottish burr fell on her ears as they searched for a vacant seat. She kept the hood of her cloak pulled close over her head until they found a place in a shadowed corner in the back. Only then did she push the cloak back and shake clinging raindrops free.

The command rang out for all to rise, and silence fell louder on Travay's ears than all the earlier voices in unison.

Sir Roger Poole appeared from a side door and strutted into a high, privileged box with the other council members. Travay sank back into her cloak.

The attorney for His Majesty marched in with his powdered wig touching the shoulders of his black robe. He held a lace handkerchief to the tip of his long, crooked nose as he walked to his table. The judge followed him, also capped with a curled white wig, and he took his place in the high seat. He rapped sharply on the desk before him three times. The sound reverberated throughout the chamber.

A door at the back opened, and the prisoners trooped in. Guards with large clubs in their hands and swords strapped to their hips marched beside them. The prisoners' chains clanged as they jostled and shuffled to their bench. All of them looked soaked to the bone. Had they made them march from the dungeon in the downpour?

Travay looked closely at each as he turned to sit and face the bench. Thorpe and Sinbad lumbered in with their chains and sat. A tall, broad-shouldered figure followed them.

Lucas.

His wet face, steaming shirt, and disorderly braids could not hide his look of contempt or his proud stance. He scanned the courtroom just before he sat. Travay shrank back in her seat.

Moisture gathered in her eyes.

A movement beside her drew her attention.

"Travay, I wish you had not come." Reverend Wentworth slid onto the bench beside her. He acknowledged the solicitor with a nod of his head, then leaned to whisper to her. "Unfortunately, I cannot stay but a few minutes. Hannah's time has come, and I must get back to her and Seema."

The minister's face was drawn and tired, like Travay had never seen it. Was it because of Hannah's birthing or Lucas' trial? She flicked the tears from her cheek and bestirred herself to act with some kind of courtesy. "Reverend Wentworth, I hope all goes well with your wife. Thank you for all you have done to help Lucas."

"I've not done all I hoped to do." He looked toward the row of prisoners.

Travay knew when his eyes fell on Lucas. A muscle in the minister's face tightened, and his brow knit together.

"But surely you have done all you could, sir." Travay managed a tentative smile.

He looked into her face. "My letter either never arrived, or the uncle chose not to respond."

"You did write to Lucas' uncle?" Her heart jumped against her ribs.

"Yes, but you see us here at the trial without a single word." He frowned, and then his face brightened. "However, the Lord can still surprise us. He does not always answer in the way we expect." He pulled a small gold watch from his vest. "I have to get back now. John, will you let me know the outcome of the trial?"

"Most certainly, sir." John Hawkins smiled and nodded to the minister.

Travay sat riveted to the bench when Lucas' turn came. The prosecutor for the Crown in his dark robe and heavy wig read out all the charges against Lucas. The officer looked around the room as if daring anyone to deny the crimes he rolled off his tongue in a loud, sonorous voice.

Lucas spoke on his own behalf. Every eye in the courtroom stayed on him through his brief but clear defense. Travay couldn't help but be proud of the way he stood and spoke with sincerity and calmness, denying the charges and telling how he was at sea when the letters of marque were canceled. But the supposed crimes blasted against him remained in the stale air of the courtroom like cannon fodder set ablaze.

In the end, however, nothing Lucas said or the mumbled denials of the other men arrested as pirates made any difference.

When Lucas stood to receive sentence, Travay, already convulsed into a knot, jumped when the judge's gavel came down hard. His booming voice rolled over her like ice water. "Guilty on all charges. Lucas Barrett, I sentence you to be hanged at low tide on Friday next."

A cry escaped her lips. She stood and ran to the door, then into the street, oblivious to the cold rain and John Hawkins calling her name. She ran and ran until her breath came out in gasps, and her hair and clothing streamed with water.

Finally, she fell against a brick wall, barely able to catch her breath. Her knees buckled, and she gave in to great sobs as she sank down onto cold, wet cobblestones.

A carriage stopped in the street, and a person stepped out of it and came toward her. "Well, well, what do we have here?"

Polished boots appeared before her, and someone reached down and fingered a wet curl that had escaped her cloak. A sickening fragrance assailed her, causing her stomach to roil.

Sir Roger Poole. She pushed the hand away and glared at him.

"I saw you run out of the courtroom, and it's a good thing I followed. You know this is not a safe part of town. Let me help you into my carriage, Travay."

"Never." Travay struggled to her feet, not an easy task with her drenched skirts and petticoats.

"Don't be ridiculous, my girl. I can't leave you here alone. It is several blocks to your aunt's house. Besides, do you want to catch your death of cold?" He reached out for her, and she drew away. Too fast. Her head began to spin. She fell back against the wall.

Another carriage stopped behind Poole's, and John Hawkins stepped down and came hurrying toward her. "Hullo there, Travay, are you all right?"

"I'm trying to help her listen to wisdom, John. I've offered to take her home. She certainly can't stay here." Sir Roger's voice wove in and out of Travay's consciousness.

"Never mind, Sir Roger. I brought her, and I'll take her home. Come, Travay."

Travay reached out for him. He caught her just before she passed out. Without another word to Roger Poole, John carried her to his coach.

❧ ☙

The following day, Lucas sat on his shuck mattress in the Court of Guard watching mice nibble sparse crumbs from his morning fare. All night and even now, he was trying to grasp the verdict rendered the day before. In all his life he had never dreamed he would come to such a turn. Part of him cried out in faith, believing he would never hang. Another part looked more realistically at the situation. And Travay filled his thoughts. Had she heard about the verdict? Thank God, she wasn't in the courtroom. Or was she? He still remembered a brief cry from a back corner when his guilty verdict and sentence was hammered out by His Majesty's judge. He had glanced back but had only seen someone in a dark cloak hurrying out into the storm.

When Ethan came today, Lucas would tell him about the provision he'd made for Travay and her aunt, in case … He blocked that next thought from his mind and studied the small window slit where light filtered down across the straw on the floor.

Within the hour, Ethan did come, his gentle face pale and lined as if he, too, had not slept well.

"Hello, Lucas." His voice was cheerful. He carried a covered dish and wore a waterskin hanging from a strap on his shoulder.

Knowing the man well and how hard hopefulness might be for him, Lucas came right to the point. There was no use keeping the minister away from his wife long. "Ethan, I'm glad you came. I want to talk to you." Lucas made space for him to sit.

"Sure, my man. Didn't you know I'd come? And I am not giving up hope. Hannah and I are still praying. And, by the way, we have a beautiful baby boy. Joshua. Born last night." He handed Lucas the water and food. "Seema prepared this while Hannah is recovering."

"Oh, Ethan, how are Hannah and your little one?" Lucas devoured the thick brown bread and chunk of cheese interspersed with long, cool drinks of water.

"Our little Joshua and his mother are fine. And Seema is a great help with both. Thank you, Lucas, for bringing her to us. I think the Lord has a plan for her life when she decides to yield her heart to Him."

"Of course she will, Ethan, with both you and Hannah to help lead her." Lucas wiped his mouth with his sleeve and sat up straight. "I want to ask your help, Ethan, on something important. A request. You're the only one I would trust with this." He turned to look into the face of his dear friend and minister. His voice came strong and clear. "I have some money put away. If I do end up in that noose, I want you to get it to Travay."

Ethan looked at him levelly. "Lucas, I truly believe the Lord is going to intervene. But we don't know exactly what He may do. I will most certainly carry out any of your wishes to the best of my ability."

Lucas lowered his voice. "In the floor of my mercantile office just under the left back leg of the desk, you will be able to pry up a loose board. You will find a leather bag I managed to deposit there on my last trip in. Give half the contents to Travay. It was actually always meant to be hers one day. Even half is quite a fortune in gold. She and her aunt should be fine for many years."

"Lucas, I will most certainly carry this out, if the Lord does not see fit to rescue you. But somehow, I believe He will."

"Don't wait, Ethan, I want you to write this up in a note for me and deliver it now to Travay and Merle. Just tell them someone has made provision for their future." He looked away, then back. "Promise them they need not fear. They will be taken care of. No need to give them the details for now." Lucas smiled his old smile. "And you're welcome to go check out this buried treasure of an old pirate and put it in a safer place, my dear friend."

Ethan grinned. "I'll write the note right away. And check out your treasure. But what about the other half?"

"One more request. You know I always planned to find and rescue my mother from Spanish hands if she still lived. The Contessa Maria told me of a captive English woman with my same green eyes working as governess with a family in St. Augustine.

Ethan sat up, interest spreading across his face. "Yes, you mentioned that earlier, Lucas. But how can I help?"

Lucas glanced around the cell and took a deep breath before meeting the minister's eyes. When he spoke, his voice did not falter. "If I am ... unable to go after her, Ethan, would you pray about trying to find her? I know you once sailed the seas yourself. I ask you to take the other half of the money, buy and outfit a ship, hire a good crew, and see if you can find and rescue her ... if the woman is my mother."

Ethan groaned and lowered his head. When he looked up, his fists were clenched. "Lucas, you've blasted my mind with sea longing again when I thought I had it conquered."

"What do you say, my friend?"

Ethan closed his eyes for a long moment. When he opened them to look at Lucas' face, he spoke with the conviction that was part of his character. "I believe one day you and I both will go after your mother together. But if for any reason you can't go with me, I will attempt to do it alone."

"That's my man. Thank you, Ethan. I'll never forget this."

After the minister left, Lucas lay back on the mattress, satisfied, and slept soundly.

❧ ☙

For days, Travay did not know when the sun rose or set. Feverish, sick in more ways than one, and confined to her bed, she tried to make sense of her disjointed thoughts when wakefulness played against her eyelids. Nightmares plagued her when weariness finally dragged her into unconsciousness. At times, hands touched her hot brow with a cool cloth and someone held a spoon to her lips until she opened her mouth. Then broth made its way to the back of her throat and caused her to swallow.

The third evening, she sat up in bed, pushing through the darkness that weighed her down. What day was it? *Lucas! Sentenced to be hanged!*

Shadows moved from the corners of the room and gathered around her. They clung to her, choking out breath. She dropped her head into her hands and sobbed. "Oh, God, oh, God." Would He answer her desperate cry?

She became aware of her aunt's voice in the next room, laced with tears and crying out indistinct words. Was her aunt praying for her?

She heard a sound just outside her door and knew Mama Penn had taken her post in her rocking chair, which she called her seat of prayer. Travay heard humming so soft it sounded like angel song. Then the black woman's voice flowed under the door. "Lord, I knows you are working with the heart of Miss Travay even in all this sickness. In Jesus' name, I bind every demonic thing that would keep her from turning her heart to you." The voice faded, and the humming resumed.

Inside the room, the darkness lifted. The soft glow of sunset lit the windows. A golden-pink sunbeam flowed through the window nearest her bed. Travay wiped the tears from her face and looked at it, wondering if she were dreaming. Silver sparkles danced within the beam. Like a heavenly staircase, it rose from the foot of her bed to the window. She reached down and put her hand into its radiance. When she did, warmth traveled up her arm and enveloped her. Suddenly, she had a glimpse, a taste, of the most wonderful peace. Peace like she used to know when in her mother's presence as a small child.

I have loved you with an everlasting love.

The voice filled Travay's heart. She recognized the supernatural tugging of it throughout her being. "My Lord and Savior!" Words poured out of Travay's mouth unbidden. New strength flowed to her weak limbs. She rose and knelt beside her bed. "Please forgive me for all my pride, my hate, my doubt. I need You in my life so much, Lord Jesus. Now I know you are real." Tears streamed down Travay's face. "And Lucas, will you help him, Lord?"

Call unto me and I will answer you.

"Lord, please help Lucas. Save his life."

Peace blossomed like a rose in her heart and mind. She basked in its fragrance, its healing balm, as time stood still. Finally, she crept back under her blankets and slept without dreams.

The next morning, Travay sat up in bed. "Aunt Merle! Mama Penn!" When the women entered the room, Travay pushed the covers away and stood. For a moment, she swayed.

Mama Penn steadied her. "You be careful, young lady. You been abed too long to jump up so fast."

Travay took hold of the bedpost before the woman reached her. She smiled at her aunt and Mama Penn. "The most wonderful thing has happened. I believe the Lord visited me last night."

Merle and Mama Penn's faces broke out in wide smiles.

"Praise the Lord, chile," Mama Penn said. She dabbed at her eyes with the edge of her apron.

Merle hugged Travay. "Thank God, thank God. Now tell me, Travay, do you feel any heaviness in your chest or throat?"

"No, none at all."

Mama Penn patted Travay's shoulder. "The Lord done did a work on you. What with you getting soaked and cold and shocked like you wuz, you could've died."

"What day is it, Aunt Merle? How long has Lucas …" Travay's brow creased.

Merle sat down on the bed and patted a spot for Travay beside her. "It is one week until the sentence is to be carried out, Travay." Her face held nothing but sadness.

One week.

Travay refused the tremble that started up from the pit of her stomach. She took a deep breath. The Lord would work something out. Wasn't that why He visited her last night? Again, she felt peace. When Mama Penn came in with a breakfast tray, Travay allowed herself to be treated like a queen. She sat back on fluffed pillows, placed the tray on her lap, and ate with appetite.

That afternoon as she was heading from her room to the top of the stairs—her first trip down in four days—Roger Poole came to visit.

He had dropped by almost every day, and the flowers he had brought stood in vases all over the house, but Merle and Mama Penn had refused to invite him in.

Travay sank back in the shadows of the hall as Merle answered the door.

Poole stepped over the threshold and looked into her aunt's face. He lifted his brows and tapped his silver cane.

"Travay is better." It was not a question.

Merle sighed. "Yes, she is better. How did you know?"

"My dear, your countenance looks as if a ten-pound weight has been lifted from your shoulders, and I must say I am glad." Pulling off his white-plumed tricorn hat, he bent in an exaggerated bow, and then eased another step into the hall. "I must see her, Merle. If you don't let me, I promise you she will never forgive you."

"What do you mean?" Travay's aunt frowned and studied

Poole's face. Travay wondered what the man had up his sleeve now. His black eyes flew around the hall, up the stairs, and then toward the parlor.

He turned back to smile at Merle. "Just let me see her. She'll be very glad to hear what I have to tell her." He pushed past her aunt to hand his hat to Mama Penn, who stood at the entrance to the sitting room. She took his hat, but a thundercloud darkened her brow.

CHAPTER 23

Travay entered the parlor, her back erect and her face relaxed. The proper demeanor taught to all young women of quality rescued her as she walked toward her nemesis. But what did she have to fear from Roger Poole anymore? Her heart had a new refrain. The Lord was going to work out something for Lucas. Wasn't that the assurance she had received last night?

Sir Roger stood from the king's chair he always claimed, one of her aunt's few treasured pieces of furniture she still owned. He bowed toward Travay and indicated the worn queen's chair beside him with a sweep of his hand.

Travay took another seat as far away from him as possible and adjusted her yellow silk skirts to make sure Sir Roger would not catch a glimpse of even an ankle. Merle sat near the door, observing.

Roger moved to the faded floral settee near Travay. He adjusted his coattails and settled back on the sofa, his hands folded over the handle of his polished cane. "Travay, I can't tell you how happy I am to see you recovered."

She knew she should say "thank you," but she had long ago given up being civil to Roger Poole. She turned her head away instead.

"You will look at me, Travay. And you'll listen to me this time."

His voice sounded so assured, she cast a glance his way. His dress coat of mauve silk, his white cravat, and his carefully curled wig were pretentious for afternoon.

Roger leaned toward her. "Do you want to save our childhood friend from hanging?"

Travay stiffened. "Roger, do not talk to me about Lucas. I will not listen to any of your lies."

Sir Roger sat back with a satisfied look. He tapped his cane on the wool rug. Then he smiled and patted the front of his coat. "Oh, my dear, dear, girl. If you only knew what I hold here in my breast pocket."

Pricks traveled up Travay's spine. Her eyes widened. Was this something the Lord was working out for Lucas? Could she believe anything from the lips of Sir Roger?

"I have right here in my pocket, *a pardon* for our dear childhood friend, one I need only to enact."

"Roger, don't lie to me, or I will hate you forever."

"Hate? Hate?" He sat back, breathing hard. "I only want your love, Travay, and your forgiveness for the past. I am sincere." He pulled a document from inside his coat. "Let your aunt read this and see if I am telling you the truth. She will recognize this for the legal document it is." He looked at Merle who had remained silent until now.

Travay stood, blood rising in her face, making her dizzy. How dare he play this wicked little game with her? "How horrible you really are, Roger Poole. I will never love you. Never. Do you understand? And I don't believe your lies." Travay sank back down onto her chair, trying to breathe.

Merle stood, lifted her skirts, and marched toward Sir Roger. "Let me see the document." Her voice was flat and her eyes hard. She held out her hand.

Roger unfolded the document and handed it to her.

Merle scanned the paper with its bold Charles Town Royal Colony heading even Travay glimpsed. Her aunt walked back to her chair and sat down so fast it tilted. "Travay, this looks authentic. It only requires the signature of a council member of Carolina colony." She turned blazing eyes on Sir Roger. "Why did you withhold this, Roger? It is dated three days ago."

"Well, I might never have brought it forth, actually. And, as you see, I still have to sign it." Roger stood and walked to the mantel and leaned his shoulder upon it. He pulled a gold box from his pocket and sniffed a pinch of snuff. He took his time pulling a lace handkerchief from his sleeve. He waved it at them both. "I will sign it, Travay, the day we wed."

Travay's body became as stiff as a statue. Even her blood seemed to stop in her veins. *Lord, is this what You have worked out?* She studied Roger as an icy gust enveloped her mind, her will, and her body as the truth sank in. The only way to save Lucas would be to marry Roger Poole? Her soul shriveled.

Merle dropped the pardon and walked to stand behind Travay's chair. She laid a hand on Travay's shoulder. Her own face mirrored the same despair choking Travay.

Sir Roger stood, picked up the pardon, and came to stand before the two of them. "Travay, I give you my word. I will sign this pardon the moment we are wed. But we have so little time."

Tears filled Travay's eyes and ran down her cheeks in spite of all her efforts to check them. Roger Poole would see them as sure evidence he had won.

He smiled and licked his lips. "We must hurry our wedding plans, my girl, if we are to save Lucas. I will be back first thing in the morning." Sir Roger strutted to the door where Mama Penn stood with his hat. She all but threw it at him. He ignored her and sailed across the threshold. She slammed the door after him.

Travay stood, and Mama Penn came to her. "Chile, don't you worry none. It ain't over yet." The black woman pulled an envelope from her pocket. "I forgot. This was delivered yesterday by the Reverend Wentworth's man. We wuz so busy looking after you, I plain forgot." She waited expectantly.

Travay opened and read the brief letter from the minister. Treasure to rescue her. But only she could rescue Lucas from hanging. She stifled a sob, handed the note to Merle, and left the room.

❦

Lucas sat on his prison bed and stared up at the tiny window slit at ground level, his only source of light. Hooves and carriage wheels clattered down the street above him, muffled by the November rain drenching the cobblestones. A steady stream of foul-smelling dirty water poured down the wall from the opening. A sizeable puddle now lay just beyond him. He shivered more from his thoughts than from the cold, damp air hovering about him like a dark cloud.

He stood, angry lines creasing his brow, his fists clenching and unclenching. *God, are You still with me?* Silence. He walked to the cell door and shook the bars. Then he paced back and forth, avoiding the fetid puddle. On his third round, his heart smote him. He was acting like the rest of the prisoners down the corridor. He could hear their curses and banging on cell doors with the wooden bowls that were filled with a weak broth twice a day.

Two more days until the hanging. At least he thought it had been seven days since the travesty of a trial.

He forced himself back on the corn husks and spent the next hour recalling every verse of scripture he could until fitful sleep finally came.

Lucas awakened when Ethan showed up at the cell door early the next morning.

"Good morning, Lucas. Thank God the rain has ceased, but the sun still fights through clouds that don't want to give up." A smile spread across the minister's face. But Lucas had not missed the frown that had wrinkled his friend's brow as he came down the corridor.

The guard unlocked the door and clanged it shut behind Ethan.

"I am fighting through clouds, too, my friend, and I will not give up." Lucas shook the minister's warm, outstretched hand, then sat and ate the wonderful crusty bread and piece of dried meat he had brought. "This is good, where did you get the beef?"

"The Lord provided."

Lucas wiped his mouth on his sleeve that had been used often as indicated by the stains marking it. "When are you going to tell me whatever it is you are trying not to tell me?" He studied the minister's face. Lucas had not sailed the Caribbean for years as captain over men of every cut and color without gaining some discerning of bad news.

"Travay is preparing to wed Sir Roger at noon tomorrow." Ethan almost groaned the words out.

Lucas' face felt as if it had turned to stone. He threw the remainder of the food across the cell and stood. "I don't believe you."

Ethan folded his arms across his chest and sighed deeply. "It's true." He ducked his head as if to avert a coming tempest.

"So she never loved me? Is that what you are trying to tell me?"

"No. No, Lucas. It's not that way at all."

"Then what way is it? It can't be for her and Merle's survival, not after what I told you last time. You did send them the note?"

"Yes, of course."

Lucas kicked the mattress and yanked a braid of his dark hair. "Then why in the name of … is she doing this?"

"It's actually because she loves you. More than you know."

"How can she love me and marry that lying cur?" Lucas stormed across the cell and shook the bars of the door so hard a yell came down the corridor from the guard desk.

"Any more of that, you pirate dogs, and you'll get the whip across your shoulders."

Ethan took a deep breath, his eyes full of compassion. "My friend, she begged me not to tell you, but I see I must. Roger Poole has a pardon for you that lacks only his signature. He promises it the day she marries him."

Lucas roared and drove his fist against the stone wall. Blood darkened his knuckles.

Ethan shuddered as if feeling the pain Lucas did not feel.

When Lucas drew back as if to clobber the wall again, Ethan stood and gripped his wrist. "We are still praying, my friend. I believe God has a plan."

The fire died out of Lucas' eyes, and he sank down on the corn shucks. "Is that the kind of God we serve? One who would save me but not her? Even if there were any truth in the promise, which I am sure there is not. Truth is not in Roger Poole's vocabulary."

"Then shouldn't you be praying that Truth will come to this man, Lucas? Aren't we to pray even for—especially for—our enemies?" Ethan's soft voice penetrated Lucas' ears but not his heart.

The minister laid his hand on Lucas' shoulder. "Keep faith. Let go of all bitterness. Forgive everyone. Give up control and look to God for His plan. That's what releases God's help."

"How do I do all that?"

Ethan sat beside him and took a deep breath. His voice broke. "Do you remember, we talked about this before, when you first decided to become a Christian? And it's the same answer. You have to forgive, Lucas. Extend the same grace to Roger Poole and his father for all the wrong they've done to you and your family that the Lord extends to you. And, I might add, forgiveness to Seema."

"Seema?" Lucas stiffened.

"Yes, Seema. Yesterday, she confessed to me and Hannah with tears that she had told Byron Pitt about your alias, and Byron apparently planted the two pirates on the *Blue Heron* who sabotaged your ship. God is doing a work in Seema."

Lucas dropped his head into his hands and groaned. "Forgive and forget? Ethan, what you're asking—what God is asking—is impossible."

"I didn't say forget, Lucas. Real forgiveness is not forgetting what happened. There's something far better than forgetting. It's remembering and realizing the sovereign grace of God is at work as in His promise that all things will work together for good."

"Do you really believe any good has been or will be worked in all this?"

Ethan moistened his lips and leaned back against the brick wall. "Would you say meeting Travay again after all these years worked for your good in any way?"

Lucas closed his eyes and envisioned Travay's face, her lips, her hair, the way she'd looked at him during her last visit, love pouring like liquid gold from her lingering glance on him. Yes, thank God she had fled from Roger Poole, and Lucas had found her again.

"Yes, yes. But there's no way Travay walking down an aisle in marriage to that lying swine could work any good thing. Surely you agree. Why should Roger win in the end?"

"One thing people don't understand about forgiveness is that it does not remove the consequences of sin. Roger Poole, like all sinners, faces some severe consequences unless he avails himself of the grace of God with true repentance, as Seema is doing."

"And what about Travay? How can she even think of marriage to the man, even to supposedly save me?" Lucas glared at Ethan.

"Would you believe that she intimated to me that this would be one way she would be able to repay her debt to you for the several times you saved her, Lucas?"

Lucas stood. "Begad! She owes me nothing. I only did what was the good and right thing to do at the time." He paced the cell and then stopped in front of the minister, his face tight and frowning. "You must tell her not to go through with it. I don't want to be rescued by her marrying Roger Poole, even if there were any truth about the pardon. Will you tell her that for me?"

"Yes, I will. But I can't promise you I can change her mind."

"You must, Ethan. You must. I am trying to hold onto the last shred of my faith that you or God will stop this joke of a marriage."

Lucas heard the guard's steps.

Ethan laid his hand on Lucas' arm and prayed a fervent prayer for him.

His last words seemed to hang like a cloud in the cell. "Lucas, I will attend the wedding tomorrow, and then I'll come here with the pardon if there's any truth to it."

After Ethan left, Lucas closed his eyes and ground his teeth. Forgive? How could he do it? How could he erase from his heart all the evil Roger Poole and his father had done to his parents, to him, and Roger was now attempting to do to Travay? He stood and paced the cell like a wounded tiger. Fury singed his mind and body. If he could just get his hands around Roger Poole's neck.

That murderous thought brought others, and Lucas fell into a hellish, demonic wrestling that lasted hours. He lost track of how many times the cell walls receded, and he found himself back with his parents, indentured servants of the Pooles. Every unhappy confrontation until the day he stole away and boarded a Royal Navy vessel as ship's boy played out again in his unwilling mind. At other times, he found himself aboard the *Blue Heron,* the sun shedding golden rays over him, the captain, and the sea air filling his lungs and heart with joy. Then a storm of mammoth proportions arose with black waves sweeping against the ship, and his every effort to keep the ship afloat was to no avail.

Finally, exhausted and weary with the visions and the damp darkness about him, Lucas fell to his knees and cried out to God for deliverance from his anger and his unforgiveness. The response came swiftly, peacefully, like a gentle hand on his head. He looked up and saw a ray of sunlight filter down from the small window, announcing morning.

His last day. Travay's wedding day.

CHAPTER 24

Travay tried to keep tears from splotching the lovely sapphire wedding gown Sir Roger had sent by carriage the day before. It had taken both Mama Penn and Merle to help her dress in such finery with its many petticoats and wide hoop. And all three of them were shocked to find Merle's pearl and diamond necklace included in the dress box. So Roger Poole had been the purchaser. Travay wanted to give the necklace back to Merle, but she insisted Travay wear it.

Travay looked at herself in the mirror. The lovely necklace twinkled and glowed, but it brought no cheer to her heart. Could she do it? Could she walk down an aisle with Roger Poole and say "I do"?

A sob tore from her lips. The sound of it in her quiet room ignited white-hot fury in her breast against the man who had tormented her for years. It scorched its way through her brain and birthed a fluttering idea. *There must be a way to outwit Roger and still save Lucas.*

Steel traveled down her spine. She walked over and threw open her closet door. Searching in a corner, she pulled out the old boots she had worn during her escape from Jamaica. She had never worn them again, but now she would draw them back into service.

She sat on the edge of the bed and slipped out of her pale blue satin slippers. She reached for the boots and then hesitated. Was her marriage to Roger Poole the way the Lord had made to save Lucas? And for her to repay her debt to a pirate?

How many times had Lucas saved her? First, he had rescued her from the deep waters of the Caribbean bay after her jump from the cliff, and then from the attack of the obnoxious pirate they called Knox. She closed her eyes. The terrible sword fights with Byron Pitt and the horrid battle with the evil Captain Ned Low flooded her mind. For a moment, she could smell again the smoke of the burning ship and the blood spilled across its deck. She shook that memory away.

But Lucas' rescues went further back. Many times he had saved her as a child from snakes, from unruly horses, and then that last time he had taken a terrible beating for her when the elder Sir Roger Poole's prize horse she'd insisted on riding had to be put down. His stiff face as a boy of sixteen came back to her then, every strong line already imprinted on his jaw, his green eyes flashing with fire as Sir Roger swung his whip against the braced young shoulders. Travay's father had pulled her away. All she heard were her own sobs, for no sound came from Lucas. Could she ever forget that day? But Travay had never seen Lucas again. Until the day he rescued her from the bay.

Yes, she owed him her life, and more.

She sat in silence for several minutes, hoping she would hear God's voice again as she'd heard it once before. Some confirmation of what she should do. But the only sounds that came to her ears were horses' hooves trotting down the street below and birds singing in the trees outside her window as if it were a wonderful day. It was not a wonderful day. It was a horrid day. The worst of her life.

All things work together for the good.

The words that seemed to come from just above her head shocked her from her reverie. It was something she'd often heard her mother say when things were not going well for one or both of them. Could this forced marriage to Roger Poole today turn into anything good? It seemed too impossible.

She took a deep breath, and a strange peace flooded her heart. She pulled on the boots. Turning before the mirror, she saw that her billowing satin skirt would hide them completely. A small, tremulous smile touched her lips. The boots would be much better for running. Once she got her hands on the pardon.

❧ ❧

The guard opened the small food door of Lucas' cell and pushed in a foul-smelling bowl. "Last meal, huh, Captain Bloodstone." His voice oozed with mockery. "This time tomorrow, you won't be needing no bowls in this here cell." He laughed. "It'll be empty, and you'll be hanging in that gibbet cage at low tide for all to see."

When he caught sight of Lucas' thunderous visage, he started back from the cell door as if he thought Lucas would burst through.

Lucas kicked the bowl against the wall.

The guard, now two feet from the door, drew up to his full height and gave a derisive salute. "That's your right, milord. Eat or don't eat. Ain't no concern of mine." He swaggered back down the corridor, whistling.

Lucas paced the cell until he heard the town clock strike the eleventh hour. One hour until Travay's wedding. *Lord, I'm trying to trust you. I'm trying. Don't let her marry him.*

A commotion at the top of the dungeon stairs and a powerful, annoyed voice flowed down the corridor and interrupted Lucas' desperate prayer.

❧ ❧

At eleven thirty, Sir Roger's carriage came for Travay. Footmen on white horses rode in front of and behind the gold-draped carriage. Merle got in first, and then a footman helped Travay.

Mama Penn helped press Travay's wedding dress into the carriage. She patted her arm. "This ain't right. This ain't right, milady. And I'm not giving up. I'm gonna go right back to my praying. You'll see. God will show up."

Merle wiped a tear from her eye with her lace handkerchief.

❧ 239 ❧

Travay looked straight ahead.

Going up the high steps to the church, Merle saw the boots. "Why, my goodness Travay, whatever in the world are you doing wearing boots?" She whispered because Sir Roger's servant was right behind them, holding the train of the gown.

Travay shook her head and continued up the steps, holding the front of her blue skirt aloft just enough to keep from treading on its lace hem.

At the top, the servant hurried in front of them and swung the wide doors open. The church's interior reeked of lemon oil, but it didn't cover the stronger odor of unwashed bodies from overnight visitors who often sought a place to sleep. Down the aisle they walked together, Merle's face stony and pale, Travay's molded in marble. Merle took a seat in the first box.

A Church of England priest stood at the front of the church in his long white robes. Sir Roger stood by him dressed in a most ostentatious blue velvet suit with silver braid and buttons adorning the front and sleeves. Ivory lace flowed from his cuffs and cravat. Travay's gown, when she stepped in place beside him, swished against his gray hose and shiny black shoes with large silver buckles adorning them. His wolfish face was wreathed in smiles as he gazed at Travay. He leaned toward her. "My dear, you are a vision of loveliness. How I've dreamed of this moment. And see how I planned our wedding garments to match in color?" He took her hand and squeezed it. The smell of his strong perfume failed to mask sweat and tobacco.

Disgust boiled up in Travay's stomach, and she withdrew her hand. "Where is the pardon, Roger?"

"Why, right here in my breast pocket, of course, my dear." He patted his coat.

"I want to see it in your hand."

The minister hesitated and looked from one to the other. Sir Roger shrugged and pulled a folded document from his pocket. He nodded at the minister. "Let the nuptials begin."

The priest opened the small book he held. "Dearly beloved, we are gathered together here in the sight of God and in the face of …" he glanced up at the empty church until his eyes lit on Merle. "This congregation, to join together this man and this woman in holy matrimony, which is an honorable estate, instituted by God, signifying unto us the mystical union betwixt Christ and the Church." The priest turned the page.

Travay made her move. She grabbed the pardon and twisted around to run. But the thick arm of Sir Roger caught her about the waist. He pulled her back into place tightly against him. Disappointment and the overpowering sick smell of his cologne made her want to gag.

The priest frowned.

Sir Roger addressed Travay. "You want the pardon, my dear? 'Tis fine, you may hold it." But he kept her molded firmly to his side. He smiled at the priest and nodded.

The words droned on and on, but Travay hardly heard them. She felt as if she were falling into a pit. Even the light dimmed from the windows. Her knees would have buckled except for Sir Roger's hard arm holding her in place. Her chin lowered until it almost rested on her chest. Finally, the words of a question blared in her ears, causing her skin to crawl with loathing and dread.

"Sir Roger Poole, wilt thou have this woman to be thy wedded wife, to live together after God's ordinance in the holy estate of—"

The priest's words were lost by the enormous noise of the sanctuary doors crashing open behind them.

"No, he will not have her."

Travay's head shot up. She knew that voice echoing through the church. That commanding voice could be heard by an entire ship's crew in a hurricane. Sir Roger slackened his grip on her to turn and see who had interrupted the ceremony.

A wonderful fresh breeze blew down the aisle from the open entrance, and blazing sunlight streamed through the windows as if the sun had moved from behind a cloud.

Travay twisted around. Her heart pounded against her ribs, and her breath stopped. *Lucas.*

He strode down the aisle, his eyes for her only. They were brimming with love and joy. He was dressed in fine new clothes of royal blue, scarlet, and linen. A sword hung at his side.

Lucas ripped Sir Roger's arm from around Travay's waist and flung him aside. He took Travay's hand in his. A deep smile creased his face. His eyes glowed like emeralds.

Someone came up beside Lucas. Sir Roger gasped and stumbled backward.

Without taking his eyes from Travay, Lucas inclined his head to the man who stood with them. The gentleman dressed in London finery exuded a presence that would not be trifled with, not even by Sir Roger Poole.

"Travay, I would like to introduce Lord Graylyn Cooper. My uncle."

Travay took her eyes from Lucas' for the briefest of moments and smiled at Lord Cooper.

Lord Cooper bowed to Travay and moved to confront Sir Roger. "Sir, I have papers in my possession that accuse you of piracy in the Caribbean. You must stand trial."

Sir Roger's face turned chalk white. He sputtered, "But, but what—how? It's a lie. I never ..."

"You can tell it all in court, sir. Right now, I place you under arrest in the name of His Majesty, King George."

Three loud ayes came from the rear of the church. Dwayne Thorpe, Sinbad, and Damon, with glad grins spread over their faces, stood at the back.

Soldiers stood in the church entrance. They came forward and marched Sir Roger down the aisle and out to the street.

Lord Graylyn turned to Travay. "I also have the real pardon of my nephew, Lucas Barrett, here in my breast pocket, milady, with a commendation and land grant from His Majesty for despoiling his enemies and also rescuing one of His Majesty's ships."

The priest cleared his throat.

Lord Graylyn winked at Lucas. "But, of course, we can talk about this later."

Lucas glanced at the priest, then back to Travay. He lifted her chin and looked deep into her eyes. "Travay, will you marry me?"

Her heart felt as though it would burst from joy. If Lucas hadn't put his arm around her waist, she would have swooned. She managed to whisper, "Yes."

CHAPTER 25

Travay awoke groaning from her old nightmare of the cliff jump. At first, she didn't know where she was and then realized she was in her old room on her parents' former plantation. Lucas stirred beside her. Her beloved husband. Joy flowed through her as she remembered their marriage the afternoon before. Thank God, she had not awakened him with the nightmare. He might have taken it entirely wrong.

She looked at him, his dark plaits spread across the pillow, his gentle breathing so different from the evening before. She blushed remembering the passion that had rocked them both the night before as if on the *Blue Heron* in a tropical storm. She trailed a finger over his bicep and down his arm. He opened his eyes, smiled, and clasped her close. He planted a kiss on her forehead, then her eyelids, and trailed down to her lips. Heat emanated from him and reignited sparks of the night before.

"Wait, Lucas. I still don't know how we came to be here. Last night, you never explained how your uncle managed to come and free you from prison just in time."

"Last night was a time for action, my darling wife. Not words." He leaned to kiss her again, but she pushed back.

"But I want to know how we are now here, in my old home place. In my very own room I grew up in." Consternation creased her brow.

He kissed her earlobe, her cheek, and once again, claimed her lips. He lifted his mouth from hers to whisper, "At breakfast, my dear. At breakfast, I'll answer all your questions."

Then she was lost in his embrace and his ardent kisses matched by her own.

Breakfast proved an interesting affair once Lucas settled down to eating. It did Travay's heart good to see how he put away Mama Penn's biscuits, eggs, bacon, and fruit. Her own appetite surprised her. Finally, she pushed back from the table and looked at him.

"Now, tell me, Lucas. Tell me how all these things happened."

He wiped his mouth with his napkin, stood, and came to her. He bent down and kissed her soundly on the lips. "Only if you come sit on my lap, my sweet."

"Lucas!" Travay decided it best not to resist when he picked her up in his arms and headed to a sofa in the parlor.

She insisted on moving off his lap to sit beside him, hoping Mama Penn had not seen them at breakfast.

Lucas took her hand and trailed kisses up to her elbow. "Ethan wrote my uncle in England before the trial. But it seems Lord Cooper was ready to sail to Charles Town, having investigated my whereabouts after hearing of my rescue of an English ship. The ship turned out to be one of his. That's the story."

"That is not the story. How did we come to be here in my old home place?"

"Lloyd Graylyn brought me the title. After your stepfather moved you and your mother to the sugar plantation in Jamaica, he ran into financial problems and let the taxes lapse on this place, and it reverted to the Crown. King George saw fit to award me this original land grant of seven hundred acres and the house."

"Oh, Lucas, nothing could make me happier than to have this place back." Tears gathered in her eyes.

He drew her into his arms. "We'll have nothing of tears on our wedding morn, my dear wife. Actually, there's more to tell if you can stand it."

"What else could there be? This has made me so happy. You have made me blissful."

He kissed her long and deeply. "No, you've made *me* so happy. I've loved you since I was a boy, and you didn't know I was alive."

"I certainly knew you were alive, and I hated the way the Pooles treated you and your family."

Lucas released her and stood up. He pushed the braids of his hair behind his shoulders, stretched, and turned to look at her. His voice lowered, and a shadow crossed his face.

"Travay, that part of the story is not over until I know about my mother. I will be outfitting a new ship and going to search for her very soon."

Then his voice lightened, and he took her hand and drew her up into his arms again. "But I have more good news. If Sir Roger is convicted of piracy, and I believe he will be, the Jamaica sugar plantation will revert to the Crown. And I plan to buy it back for you, my darling. After all, it once belonged to your family."

"Oh, Lucas, is that possible?"

"Of course it is. Lord Graylyn has assured me he'll be right on it on our behalf, my dearest wife." Once again, he kissed her forehead, her earlobe, and trailed down her neck.

Something very much like a chuckle escaped from Travay as she met Lucas' lips with her own. He didn't know it yet, but if he sailed the seas again, he would have an extra crew member sailing with him.

AUTHOR'S NOTE

Dear Reader,

As an author, I took a little liberty with dates for this novel. For example, the story is set in 1720 and an historical character, the notoriously wicked pirate Edward "Ned" Low, battles my hero, Captain Bloodstone, in a sword fight. According to my research, Ned Lowe did operate as a pirate in the Caribbean in the early 1700's, but he may not have been so notorious quite as early as 1720.

On another note, you might wonder about the difference between privateers and pirates. What set a privateer apart from a pirate was a piece of paper known as a Letter of Marque, according to Cindy Vallar in her *History of Maritime Piracy*. "Governments bestowed these commissions on privately owned ships during times of war as an inexpensive way to weaken the enemy. Privateers—a term that refers to a ship, a captain, or a crew—preyed on the merchant ships of a specific country's enemy. In exchange for providing the privateer with a safe haven and license to attack, the issuer shared in the profits. Sometimes, privateers turned to piracy during times of peace. While Henry III of England was the first to employ privateers, they fought in European and North American wars into the 19th century. Since the United States Navy owned few ships, privateers played a key role in the War of 1812."

Many British naval seamen eventually became privateers to get away from the harsh treatment of seamen on British ships. When Britain was not at war, these men had few opportunities to find work on the sea unless they signed onto a merchant ship, a privateer, or pirate ship. History does record that privateers often turned to piracy. Blackbeard is an example. Supposedly born in Bristol, England, he served first on a privateer ship. When peace finally came to Europe, he embraced piracy and became the charismatic legend history records.

Manufactured by Amazon.ca
Bolton, ON

13339675R00150